"I see nobody on the road," said Alice.

"I only wish *I* had such eyes," the King remarked in a fretful tone. "To be able to see nobody. And at that distance, too! Why, it's as much as *I* can do to see real people, by this light."

LEWIS CARROLL
Through the Looking-Glass

CONTENTS

A VERY LONG
ENGAGEMENT

Saturday Evening

Once upon a time, there were five French soldiers who had gone off to war, because that's the way of the world.

The first soldier, who in his youth had been a cheerful, adventurous lad, wore around his neck an identification tag marked 2124, the number assigned to him at a recruiting office in the department of the Seine. On his feet were boots taken from a dead German, boots that sank into the mud of trench after trench as he plodded through the godforsaken maze leading to the front lines.

All five of the soldiers were bound for the front. They went single file, labouring at each step, their arms tied behind their backs. The German army boots made loud sucking noises as men with guns led the prisoners from trench to trench, towards the dying light of the cold evening sky glimmering faintly beyond the dead horse and the lost cases of supplies and everything else that lay buried beneath the snow.

There was a great deal of snow. It was early January, and the year was 1917.

Number 2124 staggered along the narrow trenches, hauling himself through the mud, helped now and then by one of the guards, who would shift his gun to the other shoulder without a word and grab the prisoner's coat sleeve, tugging at the stiff cloth, helping him wrench one leg after the other from the mud.

And then the faces.

Dozens and dozens of faces, all lined up along the same side of the cramped passageways, and the eyes in these muddy faces watched as the five exhausted soldiers made their way ever closer to the front, straining forward, their bodies bent almost double with the effort. Beneath the helmets, in the evening light filtering through the mutilated trees, along the sinister earthen walls, mud-ringed eyes stared silently for a moment, all down the line, at the five passing soldiers whose arms were bound with rope.

Number 2124 – nicknamed the Eskimo, also known as Bastoche – had been a carpenter, in the good old days. He dressed boards, he planed them, and in between kitchen cabinets he wet his whistle at Little Louis's bar on the Rue Amelot in Paris. Each morning he wrapped a long strip of flannel about his waist, for support. Around and around and around. His window opened on to slate roofs and flights of pigeons. There was a woman with black hair in his room, in his bed, who said . . . What did she say?

Watch out for the wire.

They advanced, bareheaded, towards the front-line trenches, these five French soldiers who had gone off to war, their arms tied with rope as sodden and stiff as their overcoats, and every once in a while, as they passed by, a voice was heard, a different one each time, a toneless, impassive voice telling them to watch out for the wire.

He was a carpenter, court-martialled for self-mutilation because they'd found powder burns on his wounded left hand. They'd condemned him to death for something he hadn't done. He'd been trying to pull a white hair from his head. The gun, which wasn't even his, had gone off all by itself, because for a long time now, from the sea in the north to the mountains in the east, these man-made labyrinths had been the playground of the devil. He never did manage to pull out the white hair.

In 1915, he'd been awarded some money and mentioned in dispatches for taking a few prisoners. Three. In the Champagne region. The first one had raised his empty hands overhead, he had a lock of blond hair falling over one eye, he was twenty years old and spoke French. He said . . . What did he say?

Watch out for the wire.

The other two had stayed with a dying comrade just breathing his last, his belly ripped open by who knows what. Flashes of artillery fire, flashes of sunlight, flashes. Beneath a half-burned cart, crawling along on their elbows, still wearing their grey forage caps edged with red, a sunny day, a good day to surrender. Where was that? Somewhere or other, at the tail end of the summer of '15. One time he'd got off a train in a village and there'd been a dog barking on the platform, barking at the soldiers.

Number 2124 was hale, robust, with the strong shoulders of an active man who'd gaily set off in his youth for adventure in America. The shoulders of a logger, a carter, a prospector, shoulders so broad they made the rest of him seem smaller. He was now thirty-seven years old, almost to the day. He believed everything they'd told him to justify this madness, all those reasons lying shrouded in the snow. He'd taken the boots from an enemy soldier who no longer needed them, he'd taken them to wear on those cold nights on sentry duty, to replace his old shoes stuffed with straw or newspaper. They'd tried him in a schoolhouse, convicted him of self-mutilation, and he'd been in trouble once before, unfortunately, because he'd been drinking and had done something stupid with a few pals, but that business about the mutilation, it wasn't true. He'd received a commendation, he'd been doing his best like everyone else, he simply couldn't figure out what was happening to him any more. Since he was the oldest, he was the first prisoner in line, slogging through the flooded trenches, his broad shoulders bent forward, watched by those mud-ringed eyes.

The second man's number was 4077, issued at a different recruiting office in the department of the Seine. He still wore the tag bearing this number beneath his shirt, but everything else, all badges and insignia, even the pockets of his jacket and overcoat, had been torn off, as they had been from his companions' clothing. He had slipped while entering the trenches and been soaked through, chilled to the bone, but perhaps this was a blessing in disguise, for the cold had numbed the pain in his left arm, pain that had kept him from sleeping for several days. The cold had also dulled his mind, which had grown sluggish with fear; he could not even imagine what their destination might be, and longed only for an end to this bad dream.

Before the nightmare he'd been a corporal, because they'd needed one and the fellows in his platoon had chosen him, but he hated military ranks. He was certain that one day all men, including welders, would be free and equal among themselves. He was a welder in Bagneux, near Paris, with a wife, two daughters, and marvellous phrases in his head, phrases learned by heart, that spoke of the working man throughout the world, that said . . . For more than thirty years he'd known perfectly well what they said, and his father, who'd so often told him about the Paris Commune, had known this, too.

It was in their blood. His father had had it from his father, and had passed it on to his son, who had always known that the poor manufacture the engines of their own destruction, but it's the rich who sell them. He'd tried to talk about this in the billets, in the barns, in the village cafés, when the proprietress lights the kerosene lamps and the policeman pleads with you to go home, you're all good folk, so let's be reasonable now, it's time to go home. He wasn't a good speaker, he didn't explain things well. And they lived in such destitution, these poor people, and the light in their eyes was so dimmed by alcohol, the boon companion of poverty, that he'd felt even more helpless to reach them.

A few days before Christmas, as he was going up the line, he'd heard a rumour about what some soldiers had done. So he'd loaded his gun and shot himself in the left hand, quickly, without looking, without giving himself time to think about it, simply to be with them. In that classroom where they'd sentenced him, there had been twenty-eight men who'd all done the same thing. He was glad, yes, glad and almost proud that there had been twenty-eight of them. Even if he would never live to see it, since the sun was setting for the last time, he knew that a day would come when the French, the Germans, the Russians – "and even the clergy" – would refuse to fight, ever again, for anything. Well, that's what he believed. He had those very pale blue eyes flecked with tiny red dots that welders sometimes have.

The third man was from the Dordogne and his number was 1818. When they'd assigned it to him, he'd nodded slowly while a strange feeling had come over him, because he'd been a ward of the Child Welfare Bureau, and in every centre to which he'd been sent as a boy, his cubbyhole in the refectory or dormitory had always been number 18. Ever since he had learned how to walk, he had done so with a heavy step, now made even heavier by the mud of war. Everything about him was heavy and patient and obstinate. He'd done it, too, he'd loaded his gun and shot himself in the hand – the right one, as he was left-handed – but without closing his eyes. On the contrary, his outlook on the whole affair had been circumspect, withdrawn, unfathomable, for his vantage point was that of solitude, and number 1818 had been waging his own war for a long time now, all alone.

Watch out for the wire.

Number 1818 was without doubt the bravest and most dangerous of the five soldiers. During his thirty months in the army, he'd given no one cause to speak of him, he'd told no one anything at all about himself. They had come out to his farm to get him one August morning, they had put him on a train, and as far as he knew, it was up to him to stay alive if he ever wanted to go home again. Once, he'd strangled an officer in his company. It was by the Woëvre, during an offensive. No one had seen him. He'd pinned the man down with a knee to the chest and strangled him. He'd grabbed his gun and run off, bent low beneath the fireworks overhead, and that had been the end of it.

His wife had been a foundling, too, and now that he was far from her side, he remembered the softness of her skin. It was like a tear in the fabric of his sleep. And he often recalled the perspiration pearling on her skin, after she had worked all day long with him, and her poor hands. His wife's hands were as cracked and hard as those of any man. They'd hired up to three day labourers at the same time, and there was more than enough work for the lot of them on the farm, but all the men, everywhere, had been sent away to the war, and his wife had been left to carry on alone. She was twenty-one, nine years younger than he was.

He also had a little boy, who'd been conceived during his first visit home on leave, and then he'd got his second leave because of the baby, who was already walking from one chair to another, a strong little fellow like his father, with his mother's soft skin. They'd named him Baptistin. In thirty months, he'd been home twice on leave, and once he'd simply hooked off on his own, without getting any farther than the Gare de l'Est in Paris, because it just hadn't been in the cards, but even though she was a thousand kilometres away from him and could barely read or write, his wife had understood what to do, and for the first time in his life, he had wept. Ever since his earliest memory – of a plane tree, its scent, its peeling bark – he could not recall ever shedding a single tear, and with any luck, he would never cry again.

The third soldier was the only one of the five condemned men who still believed there was a chance they would not end up before a firing squad. He reasoned that the army would hardly be going to the trouble of dragging them all the way to the front lines of a different combat zone simply to shoot them. The prisoners had been tried in a village in the Somme. There had been no attenuating circumstances for the fifteen men who had set out on this journey. Twice they had halted, so that a few of their party could be taken off God knows where, reducing their number to ten, then five. They had travelled all night in one train, all day in a second one, been loaded on to first one lorry, then another. They'd headed south, then towards the sunset, then to the north. The last five had walked along a road (escorted by some dragoons who were not at all pleased to be there), they'd been given some dry bread and water, and had the dressings on their wounds changed in a village in ruins. Number 1818 no longer had the faintest idea where he was.

The sky was white, blank, empty; the artillery had fallen silent. It was very cold, and except for the miry road, deeply rutted by the war, that ran through this nameless village, everything was covered with snow, as in the Vosges. But there were no mountains, as there were in the Vosges. No gullies, no ridges to wear out poor soldiers, as there were in the Argonne. And the dirt this farmer had crumbled in his fingers wasn't the soil of Champagne or the Meuse. It was something else, something that seemed to fly in the face of all common sense, and it was only after the man now following him through the narrow trenches had kicked over to him an old button from a uniform that he'd been convinced of the truth: they had returned to their original point of departure somewhere in the Artois and Picardy, an area that had become a slaughterhouse for soldiers from Newfoundland. During those seventy-two hours when they'd been carted around all over Creation, snow had fallen, heavy, silent, patient, like himself, and this snowfall had blanketed everything – the savagely wounded fields, the burned-out farms, the trunks of the dead apple trees, the lost cases of supplies and ammunition.

Watch out for the wire.

The man behind him in line – the fourth of the five soldiers who had been stripped of their helmets, regimental badges, insignia, jacket and overcoat pockets, who carried not a single family photo, Christian cross, star of David, crescent of Islam, or anything that would amount to damn-all – had been born in Marseille, in a neighbourhood of Italian immigrants called Belle de Mai. He had been assigned number 7328 at a recruiting office in Bouches-du-Rhône. His name was Angel. In the opinion of all those who had known him, at one point or another during the twenty-six years he'd spent on this earth, never had a man been more ill-named.

He was almost as beautiful as an angel, however, and attractive to women, even virtuous ones. He was slender, sinewy, with eyes darker and more mysterious than the night, two dimples flanking his smile and another gracing his chin, a nose just Neapolitan enough to earn him the proud distinction of a barracks tag ("Big conk, big cock"), thick hair, a princely moustache, an accent softer than a song, and, above all, the general air of someone to whom love is due as a matter of course. But whosoever had fallen victim to his honeyed glances only to be chilled by his stony egotism could vouch for the fact that he was sly, deceitful, quarrelsome, thieving, back-stabbing, stingy beyond belief, willing to swear to the most outrageous lie on the grave of his sainted mother, prone to hysterics at the slightest little explosion, raring to go whenever a neighbouring regiment was sent up the line, adept at trafficking in tobacco and the addresses of pen-pals, a snitch afraid of his own shadow, by trade a good-for-nothing, and by his own admission the most pathetic example of all the Poor Bastards at the Front. Except that he hadn't had time to meet all that many of them, so he wasn't one-hundred-per-cent sure about that last item.

All in all, number 7328 had been at the front for three months, the last three of the year just ended. Before that, he'd been in a training camp in Joigny. He'd learned to recognize a few good burgundies, at least by their labels, and to shift the ill humour of the NCOs on to the next man. And before that, he'd been in Saint-Pierre Prison, in Marseille, where ever since July 31, 1914, when everyone had gone crazy, he'd been serving a five-year sentence for what he always referred to as "an affair of honour", or "an affair of the heart", depending on whether his listener was a man or a woman, when in fact it had been an argument between two neighbourhood pimps that had ended badly.

That summer, his third one behind bars, they'd been scrounging around even for old-timers and common criminals to beef up the depleted regiments, so they'd let him choose. He had chosen to wager, along with some other imbeciles, that the war would be over in a matter of weeks, that either the French or the Germans would inevitably give way somewhere along the line and that he'd be out before Christmas. As a result, after spending two weeks in the Aisne diving into foxholes dodging heavy shells, he'd suffered through fifty days worse than five thousand years in prison, at Fleury, Chauffour Wood, Pepper Hill, fifty eternities of terror, second by second, horror by horror, to retake that rat-trap stinking of the piss, shit, and death of all those on both sides who'd jerked one another around without quite managing to finish it off, Douaumont before Verdun.

Thanks be to Our Lady (who also looks after the criminal element): he hadn't been among the first batch tossed into that meat grinder, thereby risking evisceration at the hands of a previous occupant, and he'd come out of it with at least this consolation – that nothing else, in either this world or the next, could ever be worse. But he had to have fallen fairly low indeed to imagine that there was a limit to human wickedness, which on the contrary delights in proving endlessly inventive.

In December, after six short days of what was laughingly referred to as rest, when he'd been unable to hear a fork drop without cracking his skull on the ceiling, days devoted to bucking up the troops' morale by pestering them relentlessly with petty rules and regulations, they'd sent him, Angel, with all his kit and a regiment reduced to recruiting kids still wet behind the ears, to the banks of the Somme, to a sector where there was a temporary lull in the carnage but where everyone was talking, between shellings of monstrous calibre, about an imminent do-or-die offensive, an all-out definitive assault at any cost. The cannon fodder had learned of this madness from a field-kitchen cook rumoured to be in the know, who'd had it from a fellow completely on the up-and-up, the messenger of an aide-de-camp not given to idle talk, who'd heard it firsthand from his colonel, who'd been invited to the ball given by the general and his wife to celebrate their anniversary.

He, Angel, the poor pimp from Marseille, the street urchin of the Rue Loubon, even though he might be the most miserable flea on the mangiest of dogs, had plainly seen that the only thing an offensive could possibly mean was a counter-offensive, just to stick it to everyone involved, and he'd finally had to admit, like all and sundry, that this war would never end, simply because no one was capable of winning any more, unless they dumped all their guns and ammunition on the nearest rubbish heap and settled the whole thing with toothpicks. Or better yet, by tossing a coin. One of the unfortunate souls walking ahead of him, the second in that sad line, a corporal called Six-Sous, had spoken awfully well, at their lost cause of a trial, about the uselessness of offensives and counteroffensives and the distressing proliferation of cemeteries, and he'd even pointed out to the presiding officers that during the more than two years that the armies of both sides had been burying each other all along the battlefront, if everyone had gone quietly home, leaving the trenches empty, it wouldn't have made any difference – "You hear me, no difference at all!" – and they'd still be in exactly the same position as they were in now, after wholesale slaughter on every ordnance survey map. Perhaps he wasn't as smart as he looked, this Corporal Six-Sous, since he was headed for the firing squad, but what could you say in reply to him? In Angel's opinion, nothing.

After petitioning his major in vain for permission to return to his nice old cell in Saint-Pierre, and after sending the same request, including the same spelling mistakes, to his deputy in the Bouches-du-Rhône district (writing both letters in indelible pencil moistened in a mug of dirty water, since he hated staining his lips violet and had run out of tears a long time ago), he'd begun considering all sorts of ingenious and cruel schemes in the one hope of going on the sick-list, growing even paler than he'd already become over the last few months, livid, ashen, cadaverous.

Ten days before a Christmas he had thought to celebrate in freedom, in the disquieting hour of dusk, after a great deal of wine and considerable shillyshallying, he'd convinced an even greater idiot than himself – a notary's clerk from Anjou who only wanted to return home so that he might surprise his wife *in flagrante delicto* – that they should shoot each other in the hand, and to cap it all, in the right hand, since they both agreed that the incredible would be the more believable.

And so, in a stable where the horses could smell trouble ahead and had already worked themselves into a lather, several kilometres from a front as quiet as the grave, the two of them had done it, awkwardly, hesitantly, swearing blood-brotherhood the way children in the dark seek to reassure themselves while taking fright at their own cries. At the last moment, because his entire being felt revulsion at the prospect of keeping his word, Angel had snatched his hand away from the mouth of the other man's gun and had closed his eyes. He'd pulled the trigger on his own gun, however. Now he was missing two joints from a ring finger and the tip of a middle finger, but the cootie-counting days of the other poor clod were over for good, as he'd taken Angel's blast full in the face, and the horses, desperate to escape this mess of human lunacy, had trampled the rest of him to a pulp.

Yes, he was slogging through the mud because that was his place, fourth in the line of five condemned men dragged there, through that labyrinth in the snow, to stare misfortune straight in the eye, but he had walked too far, he was too tired to defend himself any more, he longed only to sleep. He was sure he'd nod off as soon as they tied him to the stake and blindfolded him, he would never know what had happened at the very end of his life: unsteady, maim, fire – fire, air, water, earth, mud, trenches of mud, through which he tramped, head down, lurching from side to side, labouring towards the reflections in the evening sky, tired to death.

Watch out for the wire.

The fifth and last of those soldiers with their arms tied behind their backs was a "Cornflower", the nickname of the military class of 1917, and though he was five months shy of the official conscription age of twenty, yet he'd already spent more time at the front than the pitiful buffoon staggering along ahead of him, and, given his fevered imagination, he was even more tortured by fear than his companion.

He was afraid of the war and of death, like almost everyone, but he was also afraid of the wind, that harbinger of gas attacks, afraid of a flare tearing through the night, afraid of himself, for he never knew what he might do when he was afraid, afraid of his own side's artillery, afraid of his own gun, afraid of the whine of aerial torpedoes, afraid of mines that explode and engulf a whole section of infantry, afraid of the flooding that drowns you in the dugout, afraid of the earth that buries you alive, afraid of the stray blackbird that casts a sudden shadow before your eyes, afraid of the nightmares in which you always wind up gutted at the bottom of a shell hole, afraid of the sergeant who dreams of blowing your brains out because he's fed up with carping at you, afraid of the rats that come for a little foretaste, sniffing you as you sleep, afraid of the lice and the crotch-crabs and the memories that suck your blood, afraid of everything.

Before all the butchery began, he hadn't been like that at all, he'd been precisely the opposite, climbing trees, clambering up the church steeple, braving the ocean on his father's boat, fighting forest fires, bringing sailboats scattered in a storm safely into port, so intrepid, so generous with his youth that his friends and family all thought him a daredevil. Even at the front, in the beginning, he'd behaved fearlessly. And then there had been an aerial torpedo, one too many, on a summer morning in front of Buscourt, only a few short kilometres from the trench where he was now plodding through the mire. The explosion hadn't touched him, merely blown him off his feet, but when he'd got up again, he'd been drenched in another man's blood, completely covered in gore and unrecognizable bits of flesh, he'd even had some in his mouth, he'd spat out the horror and shrieked his head off. Yes, he had stood there screaming on the battlefield before Buscourt, in Picardy, weeping and tearing off his clothes. They had brought him in naked. The next day, he had seemed his old self again. Every once in a while he would shake uncontrollably, but that was all.

His first name was Jean, although his mother and everyone else back home always called him Manech. In the army, he was known simply as Cornflower. The number he wore on the bracelet around his good wrist was 9692, from a recruiting office in the Landes. He was born in Cap-Breton, within sight of Biarritz, but since geography wasn't the strong point of the Army of the Republic, the men in his section thought he was from Brittany. He'd given up trying to set them straight from day one. He wasn't a nuisance, he avoided useless arguments, and he knew how to get along, in the end: whenever he was in a muddle with his kit or the disassembled pieces of his gun, there was always some Good Samaritan around to help him out, and in the trenches, except for that one sergeant who'd taken a dislike to him, all anyone asked of him was that he keep his head down and watch out for the wire.

But then there was the fear that had taken complete possession of him, the presentiment that he would never go home again, and a leave of absence he'd been promised but no longer expected to receive. And there was Mathilde.

In September, to see Mathilde once more, he'd taken the advice of a "Marie-Louise" (the nickname of the class of 1916) almost a year older than he was: he'd swallowed a pellet of meat soaked in picric acid. He'd become so sick he'd almost turned himself inside out with vomiting, but by that time any medico could spot a phoney case of jaundice without even trying, so he'd wound up facing his first court-martial, within his battalion. They'd taken his age into consideration and given him a suspended sentence of two months, but he'd had to kiss any leave of absence good-bye, unless he could think of a way to take Fritz prisoner all by himself.

Then in November, outside Péronne, after ten days of relentless insults from that damned sergeant, and the rain, the rain, the rain, he'd cracked, he'd listened to another Marie-Louise even more hare-brained than the first.

One stormy night when he was on lookout in the trench, with the only gunfire way off in the distance, this boy who didn't smoke had lit an English cigarette, because they didn't go out as quickly as the cheaper kind, and he'd held his right hand up over the parapet, protecting the little red glow with his fingers, and he'd waited a long time like that, his arm up in the air, his face against the sodden earth, praying God, if He still existed, to invalid him home. The downpour had snuffed out the tiny red gleam and he'd lit another cigarette and still another, until the Kraut across the way, peering through his binoculars, had finally figured out what was expected of him. The Jerry had been a good shot, or else the Germans – who were just as under-standing as the French in these cases – had gone off to find one, because it had taken only one bullet, which had torn away half his hand, and then the surgeon had lopped off the rest.

To crown everything, when the shot came, without dis-turbing those on fatigue duty or waking the others, the ser-geant hadn't been asleep. The sergeant never slept. In the pre-dawn drizzle, all the soldiers, all of them, even the corporals, even the stretcher-bearers who'd come running for nothing since the wounded man could still walk, everyone had begged the sergeant to look the other way, but he'd turned a deaf ear.

"Shut up!" he'd shouted, with that stubborn Aveyron accent, and tears of rage in his eyes. "Damn, just shut up! What does that make me, if I let things like this get by? Who'll be left to defend our position if everyone starts acting like this little bugger? Who'll defend our position?"

As for Cornflower (up before the corps this time, at his second court-martial), they'd defended him as best they could. He was even lucky, they kept telling him, that they hadn't shot him then and there. To defend him and three others his age, the presiding officer had appointed an artillery captain, a lawyer from Levallois, a fine man who had already lost a son at Eparges and was outspoken in his belief that that was enough. They'd heard him out for three, but not four. Not for a repeat offender, a hardened coward, an example so rotten he might contaminate every young recruit in a division. Not one of the judges had been willing to sign the petition for reprieve.

When suffering becomes simply too great to bear, it sometimes precedes its victims to the grave. After the staggering blow of his conviction, something inside Cornflower had quietly broken, like a monstrous abscess, as he lay in the darkness of the cattle truck bearing him and fourteen others to their unknown destination. From that moment on he was unconscious, save for brief spells of bewilderment, of what he had just lived through, the war, his missing hand, the silence of the mudmen lined up as he passed by and who averted their gaze from his, for the look in his eyes was docile, trusting, unbearable, and his fixed smile was the grimace of a demented child.

He walked along smiling so strangely, the last of these five soldiers who had to be punished; he had blue eyes and black hair, his cheeks were dirty but almost beardless, and now at last his youth gave him an advantage, for he had an easier time of it than his companions in the flooded trenches. In fact, he felt an animal sense of well-being at ploughing through the mud, with the cold wind in his face, listening to the shouts and laughter of evenings gone by: he was coming home from school, along the path through the dunes, between the ocean and the lake, and it was that curious winter when there was snow everywhere, he knew his dog Kiki was coming to meet him in the gleaming sunset, he was hungry, he longed for some bread and honey and a great mug of hot chocolate.

Someone, somewhere, said to watch out for the wire.

Mathilde doesn't know if Manech heard this, through all the commotion of his childhood memories, through the crash of the great waves that broke over them as she clung to him at the age of twelve, fifteen . . . She was sixteen when they first made love, one April afternoon, and swore to marry as soon as he came back from the war. She was seventeen when they told her he was lost. She cried a great deal, because women take these things hard, but she did not overdo it, because women don't give up easily, either.

There was still that wire, mended whenever it broke with whatever came to hand, a wire that snaked its way through all the trenches, through all the winters, now up at the top, now down at the bottom, across all the lines, until it reached the obscure bunker of an obscure captain to whom to deliver criminal orders. Mathilde has seized hold of it. She holds it still. It guides her into the labyrinth from which Manech has not returned. When it breaks, she ties the frayed ends together. She never loses heart. The more time passes, the greater her confidence grows, and her determination as well.

And Mathilde has a cheerful disposition, too. She tells herself that if this wire doesn't lead her back to her lover, that's all right, she can always use it to hang herself.

Bingo Crépuscule

One day, Mathilde receives a letter from a nun: a man dying in a hospital near Dax wishes to see her. His name is Daniel Esperanza, formerly a sergeant in the territorial army. He met Manech in January of 1917, at the front on the Somme.

Mathilde spends the greater part of the year, as she did before the war, in Cap-Breton, at her parents' holiday home. She is looked after by a middle-aged couple, Sylvain and Bénédicte, who have known her since she was a child. They retreat into formality with her only when she starts giving them a hard time.

After breakfast, Sylvain drives Mathilde to the hospital. She sits in the front seat of the car, while what she calls her "scooter" rides in the back. Hospitals don't appeal much to Sylvain, still less to Mathilde, but this one is almost reassuring, a charming pink-and-white house shaded by pines.

Daniel Esperanza is seated on a bench at the end of the garden. He is forty-three years old and looks sixty. He has taken off his dressing-gown. He's sweating in his grey-and-beige-striped pyjamas. He still has all his wits about him but he no longer pays attention to anything. His fly is open, allowing a glimpse of white hair. Several times Mathilde gestures for him to close it, and each time he tells her, with peremptory distress, "Never mind, it's not important."

In civilian life, he'd been an exporter of Bordeaux wines. The quays along the Garonne, the sails swelling in the wind, the enormous oaken casks – he has known all these things and he misses them, along with two or three girls in the port of La Lune who would turn out (although he hadn't realized it at the time, when he was young) to be the only loves of his life. The mobilization in August 1914 hadn't taken him away from any family, since his mother and father were long gone and he'd never had any brothers or sisters, and as for women, he was confident of finding some wherever the army went.

He says all this in a toneless voice made ragged by what is killing him. Not in those same words, of course, for Mathilde is a young lady, but it's easy to get the gist of what he means: he has always been an unlucky man.

He glances proudly at Mathilde, to add that she shouldn't get the wrong idea – he'd been tall, strong, and even attractive before his illness. He'll show her a photograph. He'd been a good-looking fellow.

And then two tears trickle down his cheeks.

Without wiping them away, he says, "Please forgive me. I wasn't aware of your situation until just recently. Cornflower never mentioned it to me. And yet, God knows he talked about you all the time."

Mathilde thinks it advisable to interrupt useless commiserations with a small sigh. She breathes a small sigh.

He adds, "You probably understand unhappiness better than anyone."

Her arms aren't long enough for her to reach over and give him a little shake, she's more than three feet away from him, and she also decides against shouting in exasperation, for if she startles him, he'll take even longer to get to the point. She leans forward, encouraging him gently.

"Please tell me, where did you see him? Tell me all about it. What happened to him?"

He sits there in silence, weeping softly, his skin worn down to the bones, in the dappled sunlight drifting through the branches, a scene Mathilde feels she will never forget. Finally, he passes his hand over his face, a hand utterly exhausted from growing old, and decides to get on with it.

On Saturday the sixth of January 1917, when his regiment was paving roads with pebbles near Belloy-en-Santerre, he had been assigned by the military police at Amiens to conduct five infantrymen condemned to death by a court-martial up to a trench on the front line, in the Bouchavesnes sector.

He'd received his orders from his commanding officer, a rather cold and unfeeling man who had seemed surprisingly upset at the time, even remarking to his sergeant, before he dismissed him, "Do what you're told, Esperanza, but nothing more. If you want my opinion, a good half of the high command should be sent off to the nut-house."

Mathilde holds her tongue; perhaps she has already lost her voice.

Daniel Esperanza, as ordered, chose from his company ten experienced soldiers who seemed to him particularly robust and resilient in mind as well as body. They took their guns, some cartridges, and some food. All of them, including their sergeant, slipped on to their overcoat sleeves the sky-blue armbands supplied to them, emblazoned with a black P. Esperanza told them that the letter stood for Provost or Police. At that, a corporal who respected his sergeant but often shared a friendly glass with him had piped up, "Go on, it means patsy, sure enough." They all realized, at that moment, that they'd been assigned to escort men condemned to death.

"And to shoot them?" Mathilde wants to know. And was her Manech one of the five? She's shouting now, she can hear herself shout, but she has no voice.

Daniel Esperanza shakes his head, shakes his old head with its hair the colour of fog.

"Be quiet," he begs her, "be quiet, they didn't shoot them! I'm trying to tell you that I saw your fiancé alive, and that I was the one who copied down the last letter you received from him, I was the one who sent it to you!"

It's true that Manech's last letter, dated Saturday the sixth of January 1917, is not in his handwriting. It begins with these words: "I'm not able to write today, so a fellow-Landais is writing this for me."

Mathilde does not want to cry.

"Are you from the Landes?" she asks.

"From Soustons," he replies.

She asks, in a voice that is barely a whisper, although it comes from deep, deep inside her, "Manech was one of the five, is that it?"

He hangs his head.

"But why? What had he done?"

"The same as the rest of them. They were all condemned for self-mutilation."

He raises a brown, weathered hand, ropy with veins.

Mathilde gasps, stares at his hand, speechless.

31

She does not want to cry.

Daniel Esperanza tells her his story, sitting in that powdery light sifting down through the pines.

A truck came to fetch us, and dropped us off twenty kilometres further north, in what was left of a village called Dancourt, or Nancourt, I don't remember any more. It was thirty months ago, but so much has happened since then, it seems more like thirty years, I can't remember now. That's where those poor prisoners were supposed to be handed over to us.

It was four in the afternoon. The entire countryside was covered with snow. It was cold. The sky was white. You could just make out the horizon, but as far as the eye could see there wasn't a single shell exploding, or a single balloon in the air, or any sign at all of the war, except the desolation all around us in that village whose name I've forgotten, where there wasn't one wall left standing.

We waited. A battalion of Africans being pulled back from the front filed past us, all bundled up in their goatskins and mufflers, stunned little groups of them staggering along in exhausted disorder. Then a motor ambulance arrived, with a medical officer and an orderly. They waited with us.

Corporal Boffi – I mentioned him already, people called him Puffy, but at their own risk – anyway, he was the first man to see someone coming along the road the Senegalese had taken, and he missed another chance to keep his mouth shut. "Christ," he said, "they're not in any hurry to die, are they!" The orderly pointed out to him that it wasn't exactly lucky to say such things, and he was right. I liked Boffi a lot, I used to play cards with him. Well, he died five months later, not in the Aisne, where people croaked right and left, but at a construction site back on the home front, the victim of an avenging crane, while he was sitting beneath it leafing through an old *Vermot*, a farmer's almanac. When he heard about this, our captain delivered a funeral oration to the effect that one should always be careful what one says – and even more careful what one reads.

You're probably shocked, mademoiselle...

It's been a long time since anything whatsoever to do with this war could shock Mathilde,

...that I could bear to joke about something while I'm speaking of that terrible afternoon...

knowing as she does that war breeds only infamy, futility, and excrement,

...but we saw so many horrors, so much suffering, that we ran out of pity...

and that nothing grows on desolate battlefields but the weed of hypocrisy or the pathetic flower of derision,

...and if we hadn't found a way to laugh at our unhappiness, we couldn't have survived...

because derision is the ultimate defiance, the only way to laugh in the teeth of every misfortune.

...so I apologize, please don't misunderstand me.

She understands.

But let him get on, for heaven's sake!

After a fit of coughing, a series of hacking wheezes as sharp as razor strokes, the former sergeant picks up his story again.

The five condemned men were on foot, their arms tied behind their backs. They were flanked by mounted dragoons, wearing sky blue like the rest of us. The officer in charge of the troop, a short little man, was in no mood to wait around. He'd encountered the Senegalese, who hadn't been too pleased at having to move off the road on either side to let his party through. The officer and his men had felt very uneasy, passing between those two rows of rather hostile stares. "Those niggers must have figured we were the police," he said. "Good thing they didn't try to rough us up."

We compared our lists of prisoners. He insisted that I verify each one's identity and that everything be in order. Then he told me to write the date, the time (to within the quarter-hour), and my name on the bottom of his list, as a kind of receipt. The war taught me to be wary of everything, particularly of signing papers when you've no idea whose desk they'll wind up on, but he outranked me, and the medical officer – a lieutenant – had told me straight off he was there simply to look after the wounded and nothing else, so I obeyed. As soon as he got my signature, the officer remounted, wished me good luck, and the dragoons all moved off in a great cloud of frosty breath.

I ordered the prisoners untied. They sat down here and there among the ruins, on a section of collapsed wall or an old wooden beam. We gave them something to drink and some biscuits. They were withdrawn, dirty, cold.

That typed list my commanding officer gave me, I still have it, it's over there, in my dressing-gown pocket, with other things I'm going to give you. You'll find their first and last names on it, but old habits die hard, and it's still easier for me to call them by their army nicknames.

The oldest of the five, thirty-seven years of age, was a carpenter from Paris, from the Bastille district, so he was known as Bastoche, but they usually called him the Eskimo, because he'd once gone adventuring up in the frozen North. I didn't speak much with him then, in that village of rubble, but I saw that his boots were German, and I was amazed that he still had them on. "I was wearing them when I was arrested," he told me. "I asked for regular army shoes, but they wouldn't give them to me." I was also surprised he hadn't been assigned to the territorial army. He told me he'd been three years late for his military service when he came back from America. In any case, by that time they were plugging holes in the ranks with fellows a lot older than he was. I said to him, "So, it wasn't very clever after all, what you did." He told me he'd done absolutely nothing, it had been an accident, and it was a filthy thing to do to him, condemning him like that. He looked me right in the eye.

A second man, about thirty-one years old, was a corporal who'd been reduced to the ranks. They called him Six-Sous, I don't know why. Now him, he came right out and admitted shooting himself on purpose and claimed that if he had it to do all over again, he'd do the same thing. He called me – with all due respect – a lackey for a gang of assassins. He was a welder from a Parisian suburb and a radical trade unionist. He had a fever, and the pain had kept him awake several nights running. I followed the medical officer as he saw to each man in turn, cleaning the wounds and changing the dressings. Of them all, Six-Sous had the nastiest wound. After he treated him, the lieutenant said to me, "This snow is a stroke of luck for him, because if it were summertime, gangrene would get him first."

Another prisoner was called Common Law, twenty-six years old, dredged up out of a prison in Marseille. He was pale and exhausted. Since it wasn't on my list, I asked him what his profession had been back home. He said, "I haven't any. I'm a poor foreigner's son, it's written down in black and white on my service record. So if I'm not really French, why am I getting killed?" He took the cigarette I offered him, saying, "You, it's easy to see you're a good sort. You must wait as long as possible before shooting us. President Poincaré

35

will surely sign our reprieve." I could see from his eyes – very black, they were, and teary – that he didn't believe anymore himself that they'd be pardoned. I told him I wasn't there to shoot anyone and that he had nothing to fear as long as he was with my men, which seemed to reassure him.

Common Law instinctively stayed close to a big fellow from the Dordogne, thirty years old, a peasant who didn't say much but didn't miss much, either. That one didn't have a real nickname. A bit later, the Eskimo and Six-Sous told me they'd seen him now and again around the billets and with relieving troops, he was considered something of a loner, sharing his packages like everyone else but keeping his hopes and troubles to himself. On several occasions, he'd proved himself a good soldier, but one who did only what was necessary to survive, no more. People referred to him as "That Man", and nobody had ever heard him called anything else.

I tried to talk to That Man. He listened without looking at me. I told him my home wasn't far from the Dordogne, I offered him a cigarette. He wasn't interested in either me or my cigarette. As I walked away, I noticed Common Law had been waiting for me to do just that, so he could discreetly kick something over to his companion. That Man picked up whatever it was with his left hand, his good one, looked at it, let it fall. Before we left the village a few minutes later, I went back to where they'd been sitting to find out what had so interested them. It was a button from a British uniform, decorated with a caribou's head, with letters engraved all around the edge: *Newfoundland, Terre-Neuve*. Even though it may seem silly to you, I was pleased to have guessed on my own, simply from observing how smoothly That Man had handled the button, that he was a left-hander, but I'm still puzzled by the pensive, almost surprised look on his face when he picked up that dirty old button. Perhaps he'd figured out for himself, without my telling him, something he was too proud or too mistrustful to ask.

Cornflower, your fiancé, was off on one side and preferred to remain standing. He paced back and forth, talking to himself in a low voice. At some point, he gathered up snow in his good hand, shaping it into a ball that he tossed clumsily at me. Ex-Corporal Six-Sous said to me, "Don't pay him any mind, Sergeant. Sometimes he's not right in the head."

We made Cornflower sit down. While the doctor was taking care of him, he turned his head aside to avoid seeing his wound, but he was smiling. He told me, "I'm so happy to be going home again."

Mathilde asks what Manech didn't want to see and she holds back her tears; she wants to hear about his wound.

So Daniel Esperanza tells her Manech's right hand had been amputated, but that it had happened several weeks before and he was no longer suffering.

And Mathilde closes her eyes, squeezes her eyelids tightly together, gripping the arms of her chair, and she shakes her head to drive away an image or to defy fate. Then she is silent for a long time, her head bowed, staring at the ground: gravel, with some of those tiny yellow flowers that spring up even through cracks in cement, flowers that grow between the flagstones on the terrace at the villa in Cap-Breton.

Mathilde signals Esperanza that she's feeling better, she's ready to hear the rest.

The medical officer and the orderly left as soon as they had finished their work. As he was getting back into the ambulance, I asked the doctor if he thought Cornflower was shamming. "I have no idea," he told me, adding, "What for? What could we possibly do?" I saw that he had dark circles under his eyes, that he was discouraged at having to practise his profession in wartime and, even worse, at having to treat patients awaiting execution. He was a Corsican named Santini, not yet thirty years old. I later found out he was killed as well, two days afterwards, during a bombardment at Combles.

I had the prisoners' arms tied behind their backs again, because those were the orders I'd received. I didn't see the point of it, they were too tired and there were too many of us for one of them to attempt an escape, but after all, it was better that way, since we wouldn't have to shoot in the event that anyone tried something foolish.

We tramped on towards Bouchavesnes, the prisoners in single file, each one flanked by two soldiers. The front-line trench where I'd been ordered to take them had a number, but in war, it's the same with trenches as with men, it's easier to remember nicknames. That one was called – don't ask me why – Bingo Crépuscule. I suppose the Brits called it Bingo Twilight. At the entrance to the trenches, after two kilometres of a road blown to pieces by shells, in a landscape where there was no longer a single house or tree to be seen, only snow, a soldier was waiting to guide us, chatting away with some gunners.

We thought the network of trenches would never end. We floundered along forever in the mire, and the prisoners had all sorts of trouble walking, so we had to help them constantly. Corporal Six-Sous fell into a mud puddle. When we got him on his feet again, he didn't utter a word of complaint. Like the officer in charge of the dragoons, the one who'd spoken to me in the village, I was ashamed to be dragging those wretched men, five of our own, past the eyes of soldiers on the way to or from the front line; they pressed up against the parapets to let us go by. The sun was a big red ball in the winter sky, shedding a chilly light over our positions, the snowy plain, and the winding black ditch of the German lines. All quiet, everywhere, the strangest silence I remember from the entire war. Only a whisper, now and then, always the same anywhere along the front, men asking you to watch out for the telephone wire, because where we were going, this wire was the only link to the world of the living.

A good half kilometre from Bingo, we arrived at an intersection of communication tunnels and second-line trenches that had been baptized Place de l'Opéra, where some soldiers were hard at work. Waiting for us in their midst stood a captain, wearing a balaclava helmet under his kepi and enveloped from the tip of his chin to the tip of his boots in a motorist's fur coat. All you could see of him were a sharp nose, a bitter mouth, and angry eyes. Like me, he'd received his orders from the military police, passed along by a major who had no desire to become involved in such a sorry business, and this captain was fit to be tied.

In the dugout housing the telephone, he took me aside, indicating to the corporal who happened to be there that he should go out for a breath of air. Then he lashed out at me: "God damn it, Esperanza, you couldn't manage to lose these poor sods somewhere along the line?" I tried not to understand what he meant. "Look the other way so they could bugger off? Give them a swift kick in the pants for a good start, whatever?" So I answered, "Then I'd have landed in the soup, and head first! You don't want any trouble, fine, but neither does my commanding officer! Me, my orders are to bring you five men sentenced by a court-martial. What you do with them is none of my business, otherwise they would have told me about it."

That made him even more furious. "Oh, so they didn't tell you about it? Well, I'm not the kind of person to keep a secret like this one under wraps. In fact, I insist on sharing it with you! During the night, they're going to be dumped over the top with their arms tied, in front of the barbed wire at Bingo, where they'll be left to rot or made into Swiss cheese by our neighbours across the way! Those are my orders, Sergeant! Or should I say Provost Marshal? Those are my stinking orders! Have you ever heard of anything so fucking awful in your life?"

He slammed his fist down on the bench where the telephone apparatus was all laid out, tipping over a mug left there by the telephone operator, which sent a stream of wine across the plank to dribble on to the ground. There I was, watching the wine spilling into the dirt, drop by drop, and I simply didn't know what to say. I'd heard about this punishment meted out to poor souls condemned to death, but that had been much earlier, back in 1915, in the Artois, and so many wild stories were told during the war that I'd never really believed it was true.

After his outburst, the captain suddenly grew calm. He sat down on the edge of a cot. He explained to me that his regiment had lost a great many men during the difficult push forward that summer, but that for several weeks now, the entire sector had been practically knocked unconscious. There was a tacit agreement with the Boches that both sides would lie low. "We don't fraternize, we ignore each other, we're conserving our strength," he told me. "Whole days go by without a shot being fired. The artillery's keeping quiet, the trenches are too close together. In October, they were killing their own soldiers, and we were killing ours." He gazed at me sadly. "The men are due to be relieved the day after tomorrow." He sighed. "And now you show up to put us back in the shit."

When we went outside, he questioned the prisoners briefly. Actually, he didn't want to know them, and he didn't want his soldiers getting to know them, either. "It's even worse than I feared," he told me later. "One's a sonofabitch provocateur, another's lost his mind, a third one spends all his time crying and pleading. If those jokers sitting around headquarters in their comfy armchairs wanted to make an example of these fellows, they've had outstanding success. My men are throwing up while the Krauts are splitting their sides laughing."

He wasn't a bad sort, after all, this captain, whose real name was Favourier but who was called Fancy Mouth because of his colourful language. He advised me to take the prisoners to his own dugout, where they'd be out of sight. He ordered the prisoners untied and said that those who needed to go should be accompanied to the latrines.

A short while later, he sent for the lieutenant in charge of Bingo and informed him, out of earshot, of the measures to be taken. Lieutenant Estrangin, who was twenty-six or twenty-seven years old, didn't seem any more thrilled about this business than his captain was. He was particularly upset by Cornflower's condition and insisted on speaking with him, to see for himself. Afterwards, he kept repeating, "It's not possible, it's just not bloody possible." No, I'm telling you, mademoiselle, I didn't meet a single person that day who thought that God, if He exists, was anywhere within hailing distance of that sector.

We waited for nightfall in the shelter, where there was a small stove burning, proof that no one was worried about being spotted by the enemy. On the other side as well, I could see peaceful plumes of grey smoke. Boffi and I had stayed with the prisoners, while the rest of my territorials were outside guarding the door. Six-Sous sat close to the fire so his clothes would dry. Common Law had fallen asleep. Cornflower talked to me about you for at least half an hour. His ravings were a mixture of rapturous emotions, repetitions, disorganized thoughts, but this torrent of jumbled words carried nuggets of truth along with it, like lumps of native gold. I could just imagine you, bright-eyed, in the bloom of youth, and I could guess how you must have loved him. He was happy, he was convinced that he would see you again, that the two of you were going to be married. He wrote you that, even if the letter wasn't in his handwriting. It was there, in the light of the candles and the carbide lamps, that he wrote it to you.

I must admit that it was Lieutenant Estrangin, not I, who thought of allowing the condemned men to send a last message to their loved ones. At some point he returned to the hut, followed by a soldier bringing the evening meal. He asked Cornflower why he hadn't touched his mess tin. With a smile, the boy calmly replied, "I'd like bread and honey and some hot chocolate." The lieutenant didn't know what to say to that, but the soldier with him, a Marie-Louise not much older than your fiancé, said, "Don't you worry, Lieutenant. I'd kill my own father and mother to get him what he wants, and maybe I won't have to go that far." The young man was already out of the door when the lieutenant remarked, as though it were self-evident, "That's Célestin Poux, the Terror of the Armies." It was then that he asked the prisoners if they might like to write to their families.

We collected pencils and paper. Célestin Poux returned

almost immediately with a mug of cocoa and some honey. Of the five condemned men, three were wounded in the right hand, but as I mentioned before, That Man was left-handed, which meant only Common Law and Cornflower were unable to write. Common Law sat down in a corner to dictate his letter to the Terror of the Armies. Me, I spread a piece of paper across one knee to write your fiancé's letter. The other three arranged themselves as best they could.

Before going back out to his post in the trench, the lieutenant warned them all that their messages would be destroyed if they contained the slightest allusion to the terrible situation in which they'd managed to land themselves. Everyone except That Man asked me more than once whether they might say a certain thing or not. It was a strange moment, very peaceful, and very sad. I don't quite know how to explain it to you, but I watched them concentrating like schoolboys, chewing the ends of their pencils. Common Law was speaking so softly you could barely hear him. Cornflower was saying how much he loved you, between mouthfuls of his bread and honey, and I felt as though I were trapped somewhere outside my life and the war, in some other place where nothing really existed, from which I would never escape.

In the end, except for the spelling, I saw no need to change anything in what they had written. None of them wanted to cause any needless pain to their families. I folded the sheets of paper over twice and put them in one of my jacket pockets. I promised to place them in envelopes and send them on their way as soon as I'd rejoined my regiment. Six-Sous told me, "I'd like to believe you, Sergeant Esperanza, but you can't speak for your superiors. They'll make you burn our letters. The reason they've been dragging us around these last three days is so that they can kill us in the dark."

There. What I still have to tell you, mademoiselle, is the hardest for me to say. For a long while now you've been staring down at the ground, you've listened without interrupting me. Would you rather, perhaps, that I spare you the rest, that I tell you what happened – or at least what I saw of it – in one sentence, in a few words, so that it hurts very quickly but once for all?

Mathilde gazes stubbornly down at the little yellow flowers in the gravel. Without raising her voice, she tells Esperanza to close his revolting pyjama fly. Next, she informs him that she is not deaf and has already grasped what happened: five soldiers with their arms tied were tossed, at night, into that area between two enemy trenches called no-man's-land. What she wants to know is, precisely how did it happen? Whatever pain this causes her is her private affair. She's not crying. So he should get on with his story. And when he still remains silent, she encourages him to speak with an abrupt gesture, without looking up.

Esperanza continues in his frail, rasping voice.

It had been dark for some time. We heard the rumble of gunfire, but it was way off to the north. I talked to the Eskimo. Now there was a man who didn't deserve his bad luck. He asked me what was going to happen to them. He'd begun to suspect, by this time, that they were in for something other than a firing squad. I couldn't tell him. He didn't ask again. He thought a while and said, "If it's what I think it is, it's sickening. Especially for the boy and the Marseillais. It would be better to finish them off right away."

At that moment, Captain Fancy Mouth came back. Nine o'clock was the time he'd fixed for taking the prisoners to Bingo. Meanwhile, the soldiers in the trench were supposed to cut a hole in their own barbed wire. One by one, the wretched men were led out of the dugout, because there wasn't enough room in there to tie them up again. That was done outside, with as few words as possible, in the dim light of a few closely shuttered lamps.

The sky was overcast. It was a dark night, but not much colder than the day had been. I was glad, for their sakes, as far as one could be. It was only then – with those faint beams of light casting disturbing shadows over us all, making everything even more unreal, and more brutal, too – that the captain told them what the higher-ups had decided on in place of the firing squad. Just two of them showed any reaction: Six-Sous spat on the generals, while Common Law cried out for help, and so loudly that he had to be quieted. Your fiancé didn't understand what he'd been told, I'm sure of it. That sleepwalker's serenity he'd displayed ever since mid-afternoon didn't change one whit. At the most, he was startled by his companion's cries and the ensuing scuffle. As for the Eskimo and That Man, I'm certain of this as well, they took the news the way I would have in their place: they'd been granted a stay of execution, no matter how temporary, something they'd never have received from the firing squad.

The captain didn't mince words with the Marseillais. "Do we have to gag you?" he said through gritted teeth. "You silly bastard, don't you understand that you've all got only one chance of staying alive until tomorrow morning, and that's to keep your trap shut?" Grabbing him by the coat collar, he drew him right up to his own face: "Try anything like that again and I swear on my balls, I'll blow out whatever it is you use for brains!"

With that, he took me back into the hut to tell me that my mission was completed, that I and my charming territorials could now disappear. I didn't like having to argue with him, but I replied that my mission was to take the prisoners to Bingo and nowhere else.

The captain pointed out to me that shoving people over the top might upset the Boches, in which case things could take a very nasty turn, in which same case my men would be somewhat in the way, given that the trench was already overcrowded. If all hell were to break loose, I'd regret all my life having exposed them to such danger for no good reason.

How could I argue with that?

I told him I would send my men out of harm's way, but that I wanted to stay with my poor prisoners until the end. That's what we did. Boffi set out with the others. They were to wait for me at the entrance to the trenches. Naturally, they'd had a bellyful of this filthy business and were anxious to leave.

Two corporals and six soldiers arrived from Bingo to lead the condemned men away. The corporals were about thirty years old. One, who was named Gordes, had circles of dirt around his eyes that made him look like an owl. The other was a man named Chardolot, from Tours, and I had the feeling I'd already run into him somewhere during the war. With Célestin Poux and the captain and me, that made an escort of eleven once again.

We set out on that wintry night, preceded by a single lantern. In the trenches, the captain told me he'd managed to reach his commanding officer twice on the phone, that he'd complained about how barbarous it was to treat five of our own this way, one of them a boy who wasn't even right in the head any more, but to no avail. The duckboards were slippery, awash with muck, and up ahead I could hear the squelching noises made by the Eskimo's German boots.

"When the Boches see what that fellow's wearing on his feet, it's going to be all over for him," I told the captain, who answered, "Why do you think those lousy sons of bitches left him that way after the sentence? We'll find someone who wears his size to switch with him. At least I'll have something to write up for tonight: Nothing to report except that someone pinched a crummy pair of shoes."

Bingo – like Place de l'Opéra, by the way – was a reversed trench, which means that we'd taken it from the Germans that autumn and had hastily thrown up parapets facing them. All our footsloggers will admit that the Krauts built better trenches than we did. This one was a zigzag trench with beautifully straight sections, and good solid shelters, unfortunately open on the wrong side. I don't know how many men lived there, perhaps a hundred, perhaps twice as many. I could see tarps in two dugouts covering what I took to be machine guns. Beyond a snowy depression, cratered by bombs, were the pale lights of the enemy line, which was so close we could hear muffled noises, snatches of harmonica music. I asked exactly how far away it was. I think Lieutenant Estrangin was the one who replied. One hundred and twenty metres at the closest point, one hundred and fifty at the farthest.

I never saw Bingo by day, but I can imagine it. I saw trenches even closer together, little hells on earth not forty metres away from each other. A hundred and twenty, that's too far for hand grenades, too close for artillery. Gas attacks spare no one, it all depends on the wind. The Boches weren't any keener than we were on revealing the placement of their machine guns, except if they were overrun by an attack. I thought I understood why they'd brought the prisoners to this sector: to shake it up a bit, because they weren't pleased by the truce that had settled in there, for better or worse. I told the captain what I thought. "You think too much for a sergeant," he replied. "If they've shoved this crap down our throats, it's because no one would touch it anywhere else. They tried peddling it around all the battalions without finding a commanding officer asinine enough to buy it, until they found mine."

It was getting on towards ten o'clock. We were up at an observation point, peering into the darkness, trying to see no-man's-land. Lieutenant Estrangin approached us and told the captain, "Ready when you are." From the depths of his fur coat, the captain muttered, "Shit, what a life!" He straightened up, and off we went to rejoin the prisoners farther along the trench. They were sitting in a line on a firing step. Above them, a breach had been cut in the barbed wire, and a ladder stood ready. I noticed that the Eskimo was now wearing regulation army shoes and puttees.

Six-Sous went over first. Two men jumped up on to the embankment reinforced with earthbags. Two others supported the former corporal from behind as he went up the ladder. Before being sent out into the darkness, he turned back to the captain and thanked him for the food. To me, he said, "You shouldn't be watching this, Sergeant Esperanza. They'll make trouble for you. You might tell someone else about it."

The next one to go over was the Eskimo. Before climbing the ladder, pushed by those below and grabbed at the shoulders by the two on top, he said to the captain, "Let me go with Cornflower. I'll protect him as much as possible." And the two of them went off together, disappearing through the barbed wire. The only sound was the crunch of snow underfoot. I thought of fieldmice searching for their burrows. Luckily, there were plenty of holes and shell craters in front of

Bingo. I hoped their bonds hadn't been tied too tightly and that, between the two of them, it wouldn't take them long to work themselves free.

Tears are running down my cheeks, mademoiselle, but they're tears of fatigue, of illness. Don't look at them, they're left over from a long time ago, they don't mean anything any more.

You'd like me to tell you how your fiancé was when they hoisted him on to the embankment, when they shoved him through two inextricable masses of wire entanglements and chevaux-de-frise, but I don't know. I had the impression – I repeat, it was only an impression – that just before he was grasped by the shoulders, at the top of the ladder, he started, and looked searchingly around him, trying to comprehend where he was, what he was doing there. A moment of astonishment – two moments, at the most. After that, I don't know. All I can tell you is that he set out determinedly into the darkness, bending forward as he'd been told to do, obediently following the Eskimo.

Common Law behaved badly again. The soldiers had to wrestle with him. He was thrashing around, he tried to shout, the captain got out his revolver. Just that once, during all the time these things I'm telling you about were going on, I heard That Man's voice. Suddenly he said, "No, don't. Let me handle it." And he kicked unerringly through the arms and legs of the men struggling to control the Marseillais, his foot landing a blow to the other man's head that knocked him for a loop. They dragged an inert mass, barely able to groan faintly, through the barbed wire.

The captain said to That Man, "How did somebody like you end up here?" No answer. "You're the strongest and steadiest of the lot," continued the captain. "Tell me why you shot yourself." That Man looked at him in the dim light. There was no contempt in him, no arrogance. He replied simply, "Because I had to."

They helped him clamber up the embankment, they accompanied him through the barbed wire, and he melted away into the night. As soon as the two soldiers had climbed back down the ladder, some self-deploying networks of iron spikes were tossed over the parapet to plug the gap. We took a short breather. There wasn't a single sound from the opposite trench. They were listening. They suspected something unusual was going on.

This silence didn't last a minute. Flares suddenly lit up the sky over Bingo, and the Boches started bustling around, just as we'd feared. We heard them tramping around over there, we could even hear the clacking of their gun breeches. The "Was ist dass?" of those startled awake carried as clearly through the night as if they'd been sleeping over on our side. I had just enough time to see the Marseillais crawling desperately after Six-Sous, as both of them searched for a shell hole. I didn't see your fiancé, or the Eskimo, or That Man. Afterwards, when other flares went up, machine-gun fire swept no-man's-land, which was all lit up like the surface of the moon, a hopeless sight. Three shattered tree trunks and a pile of bricks that had once been I don't know what were all you could see out in that white desert.

When the firing stopped and darkness returned, Lieutenant Estrangin, who was near me, said shit, he said it wasn't fucking possible. The captain told him to shut up. We waited. No sign of life now over on the Boche side, or out in no-man's-land.

The darkness seemed to have grown even blacker. The men were silent in the trench, and silent across the way. They were listening. We were listening. The lieutenant said shit again. The captain told him again to shut up.

After a good fifteen minutes had gone by, and nothing further had happened, I decided it was time for me to get back to my men. I asked the lieutenant to sign my list of prisoners, just as the dragoon officer had asked me. The captain intervened to say that on no account were any officers to sign any paper concerning this affair. At most, if that would suit me and if they would agree to it, I might have the autographs of the corporals in charge of the escort. What I wanted with these signatures, he couldn't imagine, but that was my lookout, and he, personally, did not give a damn. Seeing the look on my face, he clapped me on the shoulder, saying, "Come on, I'm only joking. You're a good sort, Sergeant. I'm going to accompany you back to Place de l'Opéra because I haven't had any sleep for a long time and I'd like to grab a bit of shut-eye. I trust you'll be gracious enough, before leaving us, to join me in a drop of excellent cognac."

Gordes and Chardolot signed my list, and off we went. The captain took me back to his dugout. Without his fur coat and balaclava, he seemed younger, perhaps about thirty-two, but his face was drawn and his eyes sunken with fatigue. We drank two or three glasses, sitting on opposite sides of his table. He told me that he was a history teacher, on civvy street, and that he didn't like it any more than he did being an officer, that he would have liked to have seen the world, islands in the sun, that he had never married because it was asking for trouble, but that didn't mean one didn't have feelings and so forth. At one point, the telephone operator came to tell him his commanding officer was on the line to find out how everything had gone. He answered, "Tell that gentleman you couldn't find me. That way he'll worry himself sick all night."

Then he talked to me about his childhood, in Meudon, I think, and about postage stamps. I was tired, too, so I wasn't listening closely any more. Sitting there in the hut, that same ghastly feeling came over me, the impression of being outside time, outside my own life. I tried to pull myself together. Across the table from me, the captain was talking about how ashamed he felt for having betrayed the innocent child he'd once been. His eyes glittered with unshed tears. What he missed most of all were the long hours he'd once spent studying his stamp album, fascinated by the face of the young Queen Victoria in the vignettes of Barbados, New Zealand, and Jamaica. He closed his eyes, and was silent for a moment. Then he murmured, "Victoria Anna Penoe. That's it." He put his head down on the table and fell asleep.

I trudged through the mud and the darkness, occasionally losing my way, asking for directions from the men on fatigue duty in the trenches. I found Boffi and the others waiting at the appointed place. They woke up those who'd been sleeping when I arrived, and they all obviously wanted to learn what had happened after they'd left me. I told them it would be better for all of us to forget that day, and never speak of it again.

We marched on and on, through Cléry and Flaucourt, to Belloy-en-Santerre. My head was clear, the effects of the alcohol I'd drunk had worn off. I was cold. I thought about those five men lying in the snow. At the last moment, pieces of cloth or burlap had been found for them so that they might cover their ears, and one of them, I'm not sure who it was, had no glove for his good hand, so Célestin Poux, the Terror of the Army, had given him one of his own.

We reached our quarters at around five in the morning. I slept. At nine o'clock, I went to see my commanding officer to give him my report. He and his orderlies were busy packing up his dossiers in cases. "Have you carried out your orders?" he asked. "Fine. I'll see you later." When I insisted on giving him my list signed by Gordes and Chardolot, he told me exactly what I could do with it, even though I'd never known him to use vulgar language before. He explained that we were moving in two days, that the British were replacing us along a section of the front, and that we were shifting further south. "I'll see you later," he repeated.

Everyone in my company was packing up as well. No one knew where we were going, but the latest rumour circulating in the canteens was that something really big was in the offing to the south, in the Oise or Aisne region, and that even doddering old men were going to be sent to the front lines.

At seven that evening, when I was in the middle of supper, the CO summoned me to his quarters in the house of the local priest. His office was already practically empty, and lit by only one lamp. "I couldn't speak to you in front of the others this morning," he told me. "That's why I was so short with you." He waved me to a chair. He offered me a cigarette, which I accepted, and gave me a light. Then he told me just what I'd said to my men the previous evening, "Forget everything about this business, Esperanza, forget you've ever even heard of Bingo Crépuscule." He took one of the papers that were still on his desk and informed me that I'd been transferred to another regiment, which at that time was stationed in the Vosges, transferred with the rank of quartermaster-sergeant and the promise that if my conduct continued to be exemplary, I could count on being made sergeant-major before the fruit trees were in bloom again.

He stood up, went over to a window. He was a heavy man

with grey hair, sagging shoulders. He told me that he was being transferred as well, but without promotion, along with our captain and the ten men who had accompanied me. That's how I learned that Boffi was being sent to the construction site at the rear, where he wound up crushed by a crane, and that we were being cleverly dispersed, except that I was later reunited with my captain for a few months in the Vosges.

There was something I wanted very much to ask him, but I didn't know how to frame my question. The CO guessed what was troubling me. "We've been at each other's throats for hours," he told me. "They say a lieutenant's been killed, along with at least ten others. I've heard incredible stories. A snowman sitting out in no-man's-land, someone ranting about universal peace and singing songs from the Paris Commune, a plane brought down by a grenade, what do I know! Sheer madness."

I had a bad taste in my mouth when I left the priest's house. I spat out my disgust, but then I realized that I was right in front of the cemetery. We'd buried many of our soldiers there in the autumn, under rough wooden crosses turned out by a company nearby. I thought, Don't worry, they won't hold it against you, you were spitting on the war.

The nun who wrote to Mathilde comes out to them in the garden. She's dressed in grey. She speaks angrily to Daniel Esperanza.

"Will you put that dressing-gown back on this minute! Sometimes I almost think you're actually trying to make your condition worse!"

She helps him slip on the faded blue dressing-gown that

has been washed so many times it's now almost the same colour as her grey nun's habit. From his right pocket he pulls a small package that he gives to Mathilde, telling her, "Look at these things when you get home – I couldn't bear to have you do it in front of me."

More tears are streaming down his cheeks. The nun, Sister Marie of the Passion of Christ, exclaims, "Now what! Why are you crying again?"

Without looking at either her or Mathilde, he replies, "What I did that day was a terrible sin. I only believe in God when it suits me, but I know it was a sin. I never should have obeyed those orders."

Sister Marie shrugs. "Poor man, what else could you have done? When you told me your story, the only sin I could see in it was the hypocrisy of the high and mighty of this world."

He has been with Mathilde for more than an hour. The nun feels that's enough. "I haven't finished," he protests, "leave us alone."

She complains that he'll be tired that evening, he'll be making a fuss and disturbing everyone else all night long. Finally she sighs, "All right," she says, "but not more than ten minutes. In precisely ten minutes I shall return with the gentleman who came with mademoiselle. He's beginning to worry as well."

She leaves, lifting the hem of her habit up around her ankles like a coquette, so that it won't be dragged along the gravel.

The old man of forty-three resumes his story. The breath from his ruined lungs grates shrilly, like chalk on a blackboard.

*

There's not much left to tell you, but it's important. First of all, the next day I learned that the men in Bingo had taken the facing trench and even the Germans' second position. That gave me a reassuring little feeling of triumph and took some of the edge off that other, shameful episode. It's not very pretty, but that's the way it is.

I copied the condemned men's letters, put them in envelopes, and gave them to the first post orderly I saw. Since you received the one from your fiancé, I suppose the other four reached their destinations. The copies I made of them are in the packet there on your lap.

Weeks later, I received a letter, too. It had been written by Captain Favourier, barely a few hours after I'd left him asleep in his hut. The letter finally caught up with me, after its long journey, out in summer pastures: I was laying railway tracks, far from the horrors of the front. You'll love this letter just as I did, I'm sure of it. I'm giving it to you because I know it by heart.

There's also a photograph in the packet I made up for you. It was taken by one of my territorials, when my back was turned. Everywhere he went, he carried along with him, hanging on his belt, one of those little cameras – I don't know whether they were the saving grace or the disgrace of our wretched years in the trenches. So many pictures of self-glorification for having captured a gun or an exhausted enemy soldier, so many pictures of self-satisfaction at the funeral of a fallen comrade ... My man's name was Prussien, which didn't please him any more than you might think. He was killed in April of 1917, in the carnage of Chemin des Dames. I saw his widow in Paris a year later, a sickly woman who seemed determined to rejoin him. She's the one who gave me the photograph.

I'm no better than anyone else. As soon as I was off in the Vosges, in with a new company in a new regiment, I forgot about Bingo Crépuscule. The memory would come back to me only in glancing blows, certain evenings when I'd had too much to drink. Then I was like all drunks everywhere, desperate to escape from my remorse, ready to fight my way out. Bingo Crépuscule. Why that name? I wondered about it for a long time, but I never found the answer.

Last year, when we'd started to push the Germans back along the Marne for the second time, I was wounded in the legs, in the forest of Villers-Cotterêts. They cleaned as much shrapnel out of me as they could, piece by piece. At the station from which I was evacuated, with my medical identification slip pinned to my jacket, I saw Chardolot, one of the two corporals who'd come to take charge of the prisoners at Place de l'Opéra. He was lying on one of the dozens of stretchers lined up along the platform. I was lucky enough to be already up on crutches. His wound – in the belly – was a lot more serious than mine.

I'm telling you, he looked like a corpse, so thin I almost didn't recognize him, but when he saw me leaning over him, he smiled, murmuring, "Well, if it isn't Sergeant Esperanza!" I said to him, "My friend, if I'd known, I'd have let all of them scamper off into the bushes." He tried to laugh when I said that, because of the way I'd put it, but it hurt him to laugh, the way it does me today.

Of course I asked him what had happened after I'd left the trench. He shook his head a little and muttered, "Sheer madness," just what my CO had said a good year and a half earlier. Then he struggled almost up onto his elbows and whispered, "They all died, the five in no-man's-land, the lieutenant, my comrades. The captain, too, when we took the

German trenches." He wanted me to lean closer; I bent my knees so that I could hear him. "We really went for them. We sailed into the first and second positions without losing a single soul, and when we hit the third trench, they clobbered us."

He lay with his eyes closed for a long moment, sucking in great gulps of air, but all he was getting was smoke from the engine. The wounded French, British, and American soldiers – at least those who were strong enough – were fighting to get on the train. "You're sure all five of them died?" I asked him. He gave me an amused, disdainful look. "You're still backing them, Provost Marshal? Which one are you so anxious about?" "Whichever," I replied, "and don't call me that."

He closed his eyes again. I sensed that he had too much to tell, that it was beyond him. I'm only giving you the truth, mademoiselle, even if you find it disappointing. I'd be ashamed to lie to you, feeding you false hopes. They were calling me to get on the train, the stretcher-bearers were telling me to stop badgering the wounded man, and the last words I heard from Chardolot, who had his face turned towards me and a faraway smile on his lips, were "I'd gladly bet two louis with you on Cornflower, if I had them. With his one good hand he built a snowman, out in the middle of nowhere. But I'm broke – the girls cleaned me out."

Later, when we were rolling along, far from the fighting, I went through the cars on my crutches looking for Chardolot, bumping into people. I must have fallen ten times. I never saw him again. Perhaps he died before they ever got him on the train. Death has such a strange sense of humour. Myself, I was demobbed in October, a month before the armistice. I'd come out all right. I might have enjoyed my luck and an honest pension, but no ... It's not the war that's killing me. In Angers, in the hospital where I was a convalescent, I got hit by that damned Spanish flu. They told me I was cured, that the after-effects wouldn't be serious. And here I am, wondering if I'll wake up again tomorrow morning.

The White Widow

Returning to Cap-Breton in the car, Mathilde can easily tell that Sylvain is worried about her and wishes she wouldn't keep her pain bottled up inside. She doesn't feel like talking, or snivelling – she'd like to be back in her room, alone. Luckily, the noise of the engine makes conversation difficult.

When she is alone in her room, at her table, surrounded by photographs of her fiancé, she opens the small packet from Daniel Esperanza.

The first thing she sees is another photo, postcard format, tinted the familiar sepia, taken in a trench like dozens of others she has seen in *Le Miroir* or *L'Illustration*. There are seven men in the picture: five seated, bareheaded, their arms behind their backs; one standing, wearing his helmet and looking rather proud of himself; and a last man almost in silhouette, smoking his pipe in the foreground.

She spots Manech immediately. He's a little off to the left, looking vaguely into the distance. He's smiling, but it's not a smile she has ever seen before. His features, the way he's sitting – she recognizes these things, even though he has grown very thin. He's filthy. They're all filthy, their clothes are shapeless and covered with dirt, but their eyes are shining.

Above each head, written in an ink now faded to grey, is a number that corresponds to a name on the back of the card, except that the man with the pipe has only a question mark between two thick parentheses. The one standing next to the prisoners with an armband on his sleeve is Corporal Boffi.

Next, Mathilde unfolds a paper with worn edges. It's the famous typed list Esperanza says he received from his commanding officer.

KLEBER BOUQUET, carpenter, Paris, military class 1900.

FRANCIS GAIGNARD, welder, Seine, 1905.

BENOIT NOTRE-DAME, farmer, Dordogne, 1906.

ANGE BASSIGNANO, Bouches-du-Rhône, 1910.

JEAN ETCHEVERY, fisherman-sailor, Landes, 1917.

At the bottom of this paper without a heading or official stamp of any kind can be read, in nice, round letters:

Saturday, January 6, 1917, 22:30, Urbain Chardolot, corporal

And more to the right, in a childish handwriting, another signature:

Benjamin Gordes, corporal

Mathilde picks up the photo again and has no trouble identifying the Eskimo, Six-Sous, That Man, and Common Law.

They are as she had imagined them while Esperanza was telling his story, except that all four of them are wearing moustaches and are so drawn with fatigue that they seem older than they really are. Next to them, Manech is like a stray child.

Then Mathilde reads the letters copied on mauve paper by Esperanza, in the same ink now faded to grey. She reads them in the order in which she finds them. She doesn't look for Manech's letter first. Why should she? She received, during the seven months he was at war, sixty-three letters and post-cards from him. She has reread them so many times she could recite them all perfectly, word for word.

The large window of her room is splashed purple with the sun setting on the ocean, gleaming through the pines.

Kléber Bouquet to Louis Teyssier
Little Louis's Bar, 27, Rue Amelot, Paris
From the front, January 6, 1917

Dear old Broken Nose,

If you see Véro, wish her a Happy New Year and say I'm very sorry she won't speak to me any more. Tell her if I don't come back, my last thoughts will be of her and all the happiness we had, really wonderful times. The money I gave you for safekeeping, give it to her. 'Tisn't much. I'd have so liked her to enjoy the easy life.

Old friend, I often think of you too, and the thrashings you gave me throwing dice on your counter, and the fun we had whenever you got out those seltzer bottles – that at least was some good fighting.

I'm getting transferred elsewhere, so if you don't hear from me for a while, not to worry, I'm in good health.

Well so long, say hello to everyone and long life to you.

Kléber

P.S. I can tell you, you'll be glad to hear, I met up with Biscuit and we're friends again. What fools we both were.

Francis Gaignard to Thérèse Gaignard
108, Route de Châtillon, Bagneux, Seine
Saturday, January 6

My dear wife,

I know you will be relieved to get this letter, but what can I say, I was not able to write to you for a month because I was sent to another regiment and it was very hard what with all the problems of moving around. Well, now I can wish you a Happy New Year that I trust will see the end of everyone's troubles. I hope that you were able to give fine presents to our little girls, to my dear Geneviève, to my beloved Sophie. I also hope that at the munitions factory they gave you your two days off so that you could rest at least, my dear wife, even though these holidays must not be very cheerful for you.

Do not be angry with me for what I am about to write, I am fit as a fiddle, but I would be happier to have this said. In case anything happens to me, you never know (look at my poor brother Eugène), do what you promised me, think only of our girls, me I will be beyond needing anything, and with all my heart I should like for you to find a good man so the three of you would live happily. At the end of this month, I will be thirty-one and you twenty-nine, soon it will be eight years we have been married. I feel they have stolen half my life away from me.

For once, since it is the New Year, embrace your parents sincerely for me. I hold nothing against them, you know that, but they should at least avoid speaking of certain things. It is because of the blindness of people like them that I am here, and my companions, too.

I must stop, fatigue duty is calling. I send you all my love, watch carefully over our dear little girls.

Thank you for being my wife.

Your Six-Sous

Benoît Notre-Dame to Mariette Notre-Dame
Les Ruisseaux, Cabignac, Dordogne
January 6, 1917

Dear wife,

Come spring, the work in the fields won't wait, so tell Bernay the deal is off unless it's all settled by early March. I have thought over his price. He's trying to sell us his manure too dearly. I think in spite of everything he will come around.

Say to my Titou I send him a big hug and tell him that nothing bad can happen to him as long as he pays close heed to his dear mama. As for me, I know there can be nobody better in the whole world. I love you,

Benoît

Ange Bassignano to Tina Lombardi
In care of Madame Conte
5, Traverse des Victimes, Marseille
Saturday, January 6

My Cream Puff,

I got no idea where you're at. Me, I can't say because of it's a military secret. I really thought my time was come but things are better now, I got hopes of getting out of this and may the Blessed Mother protect me once again, even though I'm a *favouille* as you well know. I never had no luck, that's for sure.

You remember us as kids, when we saw ourselves big as barrels in the mirror at the fair in Saint-Mauront? I feel my life has got twisted like that. Besides, I'm lost without you, I do nothing but mess things up. For a start that stupid run-in with Josso. Instead of that I should've left with you for America, like Florimond Rossi, the prettyboy over at the Bar des Inquiets, he hooked off so he wouldn't come to grief. We'd have made a pretty penny over there, it's full of millionaires. But like you always said, my Cream Puff, there's no going back.

I don't know what zone of operations you're wandering around in, looking high and low for me I'm sure, it worries me so much. I never needed you more than I do now tonight. Whatever happens, don't throw me over. Even back in prison, when you came to see me, you were my Sunshine.

I hope with all my heart I'll make it out of this and then I'll get you to forgive me all the unhappiness I caused you, I'll be so nice to you you'll pinch yourself hard to believe it and I'll kiss the bruises.

Ciao, my lovely Moonlight, my little Firecracker, my Heart

of Gold. Another fellow is writing this down for me as I hurt my hand and I'm not much good at writing anyway, but I put all my love in it.

I send you a kiss just like the first one, when we were kids, under the plane trees on the Rue Loubon. Long time ago, wasn't it, my Cream Puff?

Your Angel from Hell

The next letter is from Manech. It's identical to the one Mathilde received in early 1917, since both are in Esperanza's handwriting, but the colour of the paper and the arrangement of the lines are not precisely the same and this throws her off. For a few seconds, she can't help feeling that Manech has slipped even farther away from her.

Jean Etchevery to Mathilde Donnay
Villa Poéma, Cap-Breton, Landes
January 6, 1917

My love,

I'm not able to write today, so a fellow Landais is writing this for me. Your face is all lit up, I can see you. I'm happy, I'm coming home. I would like to shout out my joy on the road, I'm coming home. I would like to kiss you the way you like me to, I'm coming home. I must step lively. Tomorrow is already Sunday, and we're to be married Monday. I would like to shout my joy on the road by the dunes, I hear my dear old Kiki barking as he comes through the forest, you're with him, you're beautiful and all in white, our marriage makes me so very happy. Oh yes, my Matti, I'm coming towards you in this light, I feel like laughing and shouting, my heart is full of blue sky. The boat must be decorated with garlands, I'll take you to our spot across the lake, you know where. I can hear all those huge waves and your voice shouting your love for me into the wind: "Manech! Manech!" And I can see the candles burning in the wooden boat and the two of us lying on the nets, I'm going to run as fast as I can, wait for me. My love, my Matti, we will be married on Monday. My penknife cut our promise into the bark of the poplar down by the lake, it's so clear, yes, there we are.

I kiss you softly, so very softly, the way you like, and I can see your lovely eyes, and your mouth in the light, and you're smiling at me.

Manech

The Basque word for Jean is pronounced "Manech" but is written "Manex". Manech himself wrote it the other way on purpose, and Mathilde did, too. Esperanza may not have known this, but Mathilde doesn't think so, since he's from Soustons. She'll ask him. She definitely intends to go and see him again.

There's one last discovery to make in the packet: the letter from Captain Favourier. The paper and envelope are pale blue, the envelope lining is dark blue. The handwriting is not that of a teacher, even a teacher of the Lies called History. The writing is jagged, brutal, full of breaks, almost illegible.

But not quite.

Sunday, the 7th

Dear friend,

It's not yet dawn. I was so tired I went kaput before I could finish my story, and I find that very embarrassing.

So I was telling you, inspired by the cognac and my postage-stamp nostalgia, about Victoria Anna Penoe. To claim that at fifteen I was madly in love with the effigy of the greatest queen of all would be a euphemism. I was in despair over not being English or Australian or even from Gibraltar. I was so poor at that time, even poorer than I am now, and I could afford to treat myself to only the least expensive stamps bearing Queen Victoria's image. I was lucky enough, however, to have a handsome blue one from East Africa, and I naïvely imagined that Anna, the Indian currency in use down there, was my beloved's second name. As for Penoe, this is even better. It was a stamp I was able to admire only briefly, in a stamp shop, where other customers were busy fighting over it. This prize was already worth a great deal of money. Do you know why? The denomination was two pence – I'll leave you the thrill of discovering the place of origin – but an engraving error or a smudge during the printing had closed the c of "pence" into an o. Isn't that nice? Do you understand me now? So what am I doing here, of all places?

A little while ago, after I woke up, I went back to the trench. If it's any comfort to you, they'd managed to untie their bonds fairly quickly, they were digging in like moles. Twice – orders from on high, no doubt – the Boches tossed some grenades at random into the dark. Naturally our side had to reply with a few mortar rounds. Then all this foolishness died down. The only one who doesn't answer now from no-man's-land is the farmer, but that doesn't mean anything except that he has bad manners. I think they're all still alive.

This letter is to tell you I'll do everything I can so that they stay that way, including undertaking a surprise attack, something I'm reluctant to do. I hope, as you do, that the day will be quickly over and that at nightfall I'll receive the order to bring them back in.

Adieu, Sergeant. I would have liked to have met you at some other time, in some other place.

Etienne Favourier

Mathilde remains motionless for a short while, chin in hand, elbows on the table. Twilight fills the room. She reflects on the letters she has just read; striking images crowd her thoughts. She promises herself she'll reread them tomorrow.

Meanwhile, she lights her lamp, takes a few sheets of drawing paper from her drawer. She writes down what Daniel Esperanza told her, in black ink. She has a good memory. She tries to recollect the phrases he used. She listens carefully to the poor man's voice, she can almost still hear it, but she is even more attentive to what she saw as his narrative unfolded, saw as clearly as though she had lived through everything herself, and now it is all inscribed in her memory as though on a strip of film stock. For how long, she has no idea. That is why she's writing it down.

Later, Bénédicte knocks at her door. Mathilde tells her she's not hungry, asks to be left alone.

Even later, when she has finished, Mathilde drinks two or three swallows of mineral water, straight from the bottle, wriggles out of her dress, and manages to put herself to bed without any help. A moth has fluttered into her room and stubbornly insists on colliding repeatedly with her bedside lamp.

Mathilde extinguishes the light. Lying in the darkness, she thinks about Queen Victoria. She would like to find out where it came from, that stamp on which pence became penoe. She hadn't much liked Victoria, until this evening, because of the Boer War. She hadn't much liked captains, either.

Afterwards, she weeps.

Mathilde is nineteen years, seven months, and eight days old. She was born at the first glimmering of the dawn of this century, at five o'clock on the morning of January 1, 1900. This is very useful for calculating her age.

At three years, five months, and ten days, evading the watchful eye of her mother (who has always reproached herself for becoming embroiled in a silly argument with the lady across the landing over a cat that was peeing on her doormat), Mathilde climbed to the very top of a stepladder (five steps) and fell off. She later explained – so they tell her, she has no recollection of her exploit – that she had wanted to fly, the way she did in her dreams.

At the hospital, they performed every possible test on her. Apart from a cracked collar-bone that mended in a few days, she was uninjured. Not a single scratch. It seems she laughed delightedly in her bed, thrilled to be receiving attention from everyone.

Please, no tears: Mathilde never walked again.

At first they thought the problem might be rooted in a psychological shock, the frightening fall, or – why not? – her disappointment at discovering that in the air she was decidedly inferior to a sparrow. When further testing failed to turn up anything that might account for her mysterious infirmity, the medical authorities were on the verge of deciding that she'd grown fond of a subterfuge originally adopted to avoid being scolded. The last straw was when a skinny man with a beard offered the appalling suggestion that Mathilde, traipsing up and down the hall of the family apartment late at night, might have surprised Papa and Mama in each other's arms.

The papa in question is just over six feet tall, weighing close on sixteen stone. At the time of the accident, he was thirty-five years old and not a man to be trifled with. The unfortunate bearded gentleman, who received a smack in the face, is probably still wandering between Montparnasse Cemetery and the Rue de la Gaîté, where his erratic shambling along the sidewalk may earn him the occasional charitable coin.

Mathilde's father was not content with slapping a so-called psychologist, or with insulting doctors who "knew nothing outside of aspirin." He abandoned or severely neglected his work (a construction company) for months at a time, taking Mathilde to Zurich, to London, to Vienna, to Stockholm. She travelled widely, between the ages of four and eight, but without seeing more of the world than what can be glimpsed through train and hospital windows. Finally, her parents had to resign themselves. They explained to Mathilde, although she could hardly have failed to notice this, that the orders from her brain were no longer reaching her legs. Somewhere in her spinal cord there was a broken connection.

Then came the period when they believed in almost anything: spiritism, magic, sticking pins in dolls bought at the department store, four-leaf-clover bouillon, mud baths. And once, even a hypnotist. Mathilde, who was ten at the time, had suddenly stood up. Her mother claims she took a step, her father vouches for half a step, her brother Paul has an opinion but keeps it to himself. Mathilde collapsed in her papa's arms, and they had to call the fire brigade to revive her.

She was already quite proud, and had come to terms with her predicament as best she could. She refused to be helped by anyone in those places and situations where one is usually on one's own, except for her bath. She doubtless found herself in some difficulty now and again, she probably hurt herself a few times, but one learns from experience, and she has always been able to get about using her arms and hands, provided that some thought has been given to places where she might need to hang on to something.

Anyway, it doesn't matter. And the subject is boring. Mathilde has other lives, varied and quite beautiful ones. For example, she paints huge canvases she'll put on display one day, and everyone will see who she is. She paints flowers, only flowers. She loves white, black, passionate red, sky blue, soft beige. She has problems with yellows, but after all, so did Vincent, who greatly admired Millet. She will always see Millet's flowers as tender and cruel and full of life in the mists of time.

In her bed, where everything is possible, Mathilde often imagines she is the great-granddaughter of Millet. The rascal had left her hussy of a great-grandmother with a bastard child, a great gawky girl who wore her hair coiled in a chignon and who at the age of sixteen – after a brief stint as a lady of pleasure in Whitechapel and a repentant consumptive – had become infatuated with Mathilde's grandfather, who'd been unable to resist her charms. If there are those who doubt this story, it's just too bad for them.

The cats are another of her lives. Mathilde has six, Bénédicte one, and Sylvain another, which makes eight rascals in the house and a goodly number of kittens to be bestowed on deserving friends. Mathilde's cats are called Uno, Due, Tertia, Bellissima, Bandit, and Master Jack. They none of them resemble one another, except that they all put up with Mathilde, never giving her the slightest show of temper. Camembert, who belongs to Bénédicte, is the most intelligent but also the greediest of the gang and it would take a strict diet to make him slim down. Sylvain's cat, Mélusine, is a silly creature who won't even talk to Bellissima, her daughter, who is pained by this rejection and refuses to be separated from her mother, not even by a tail-hair's breadth. Mathilde, who always fears what the future will bring, wishes that cats lived longer.

There is a dog as well, at the Villa Poéma (a contraction of "Paul" and "Mathilde"). Old Chick Pea is a completely deaf Pyrenean sheepdog who barks when people leave, whiles away whole mornings chasing squirrels simply to keep them on their toes, and spends the rest of the time asleep, breaking wind. Each time she hears him, Bénédicte says, "Doggie fart, gladdens my heart."

Another of Mathilde's lives, during the war, was devoted to the children of the nearby town of Soorts, which had lost its schoolteacher to the army. First twelve, then fifteen pupils, ranging in age from six to ten, would come to the classroom Mathilde had set up in the villa. She taught them penmanship, arithmetic, history, geography, and drawing. In July of 1918, already widowed for more than a year by the loss of her fiancé, she had her class perform a snippet of Molière for their mothers, the mayor, and the local priest. Little Sandrine, cast as a woman mistreated by her husband, jumbled her lines at the spot where a neighbour, Monsieur Robert, intervenes on her behalf. Instead of "I happen to enjoy being beaten," she said, "And if I like it when he slaps me around, what's it to you?" And wham, she bopped Hector, one of the Massette boys, who was playing Monsieur Robert. Immediately clapping her hand to her mouth, she exclaimed, "No, that's not it. I don't want you sticking your nose into my business!" And wham, another slap. "No, that's not it, either. So what if I don't mind my husband beating up on me?" And still another slap. By this time the Massette kid was in tears, he hauled off and slugged her back, the mothers joined the fray, and the play ended in general mayhem, like Victor Hugo's historical drama *Hernani*.

Since the beginning of her "illness", in other words for more than fifteen years, Mathilde has performed gymnastics almost every day. Her mother or father or Sylvain exercises her legs. For a long time Monsieur Planchot, the bonesetter of Seignosse, came over on his bicycle three times a week, at nine o'clock sharp, to run her through a series of movements as she lay flat on her back or stomach, and to massage her shoulders, neck, and spine. He is now retired. Ever since the armistice, a swimming instructor from Cap-Breton has been performing the same service, with less punctuality but more imposing muscles: Georges Cornu is a splendidly moustached specimen who competed in local swimming championships in Aquitaine and served in the navy during the war. He doesn't talk much. At first Mathilde was deeply ashamed to have him pawing her all over, even her buttocks, and then she became used to it, as she had with everything else. It wasn't as bad as her hospital ordeals, after all. She closes her eyes. She lets herself be kneaded. She imagines that Georges Cornu admires her figure and is beside himself with desire. Once he told her, "You're certainly a good-looker, mademoiselle." After that, Mathilde didn't know whether she should call him my dear Georges, dearest Georges, or Jojo.

It's true that Mathilde isn't ugly. That's her opinion, at least. Like her mother, she has big green or grey eyes – depending on the weather. A straight little nose, long hair of a light chestnut colour. She gets her height from her father. Stretched out, she measures five feet ten inches. It seems she turned out this way because of all the time she has spent lying down. She has very lovely breasts. She's proud of them: they're heavy, well-rounded, and softer than silk. When she caresses her nipples she soon feels like making love. She makes love all by herself.

Like her imaginary great-grandmother, Mathilde is quite a girl. Before falling asleep, Mathilde fantasizes about being in all sorts of disturbing situations, each one more unlikely than the last, although they invariably reflect the same silly theme: she is the victim of a stranger – she never really sees his face – who surprises her somewhere in her underwear, is overwhelmed with desire for her, cajoles her, threatens her, undresses her, until she resigns herself to the inevitable or welcomes it wholeheartedly. The flesh is so willing. Mathilde rarely needs to develop her invented scenario through too many adventures before being carried away by pleasure, which is sometimes so acute, so imperious, that it seems to radiate even down her legs. She takes pride in this pleasure, and in being capable of it, which makes her – for a few instants of eternity – just like everyone else.

Not once, ever since the news of his disappearance, has Mathilde been able to bear the thought of her fiancé at such moments. And there are long periods when she's ashamed of herself and hates herself and resolves not to open her door to strangers. In the past, even before they had made love and during the months when he was at the front, she hadn't been able to see herself with anyone but Manech when she took her pleasure. That's how it is.

Then there are the dreams, the good ones and the bad ones. Sometimes she remembers them upon awakening. She knows she was running breathlessly through the streets of Paris, across the countryside, in the forest of Hossegor. Or else she steps off a train, in a foreign station, perhaps to find Manech, and the train leaves without her, carrying away all her luggage, and no one can tell her where the train is going, so it's all very complicated. Or else she's flying through the parlour of the house on the Rué La Fontaine, in Auteuil, where her parents now live. She skims along beneath the ceiling, between the crystal chandeliers, swooping up and down, performing so many aerial acrobatics that when she wakes up she's bathed in perspiration.

Well, that's enough. Mathilde has introduced herself. She could go on like this for hours, it would certainly be just as fascinating, but she's not here to tell the story of her lives.

Aristide Pommier is twenty-seven years old, with curly hair and severe myopia. He lives in Saint-Vincent-de-Tyrosse. He was assigned to the cookhouse in the same regiment as Manech in 1916. After the fighting in the autumn, he came to see Mathilde while he was on leave, bringing her good news of her fiancé, a smiling photo, and earrings Manech had obtained from some Tommies in a swap, he didn't say for what. To listen to him, all was for the best in the best of all possible wars. And then, rattled by unexpected questions, his cheeks flushed, his glasses steamed up, he changed his tune. He told them about the summer day when Manech was brought in from the front line, drenched in another man's blood and tearing off his own clothes, and he also told them of the court-martial for the self-induced jaundice, the judges' relative indulgence, the mysterious shaking fits.

A few months later, in April of 1917, when the Etcheverys had received confirmation of the death of their son, Aristide Pommier came home on leave to marry the daughter of his boss, a tree nurseryman in Seignosse. Mathilde was able to speak to him for only two minutes, outside the church. He was very sorry about Manech, a truly fine fellow. But the only fire he had seen during the war was that of his stoves. He hadn't been up at the front, hadn't heard a thing, and had no idea how it had happened.

Then he'd stood silently, in the rain that seals a lasting marriage, stuffed into a too-tight uniform he'd probably have to keep on even for his wedding night, just in case he had to rush back to the front, while Mathilde, naturally, said he was just a lickspittle, so there he was, motionless, his head hanging, his hair sopping wet, staring at a spot about an inch from his boot toes, taking all this abuse from a killjoy who had to put her oar in until Sylvain took the hell-cat away, away from it all, home.

Demobilized that year, Aristide Pommier returned to his job as a resin tapper, but once he became the old man's son-in-law, he fell out with his boss. They came to blows. The father-in-law cut his forehead open breaking Aristide's glasses with a head-butt. Bénédicte, who is Mathilde's *Landes Gazette*, claims that Aristide wants to emigrate with his pregnant wife and the two brats they already have. She adds a sentiment favoured by our gallant soldiers under fire: "No good can come of this."

Mathilde sees Aristide Pommier every now and then, when she is driven along the harbour or by the lake, but he merely touches his cap to her, turning aside his face and pedalling away on his bicycle. Mathilde no longer hates him, after what she has learned from Esperanza. She fully understands that his silence on his wedding day and throughout all these months has spared Manech's memory in his home town. She wants to see Aristide. She'll tell him that she knows. She'll apologize to him like the well-brought-up young lady she is when she's not busy calling people lickspittles. He'll realize that it's no longer necessary to hide anything from her.

Massaging her with his big swimmer's hands, Georges Cornu says, "Aristide? You won't find him today, he's off in the woods. But if you come to the water tournament tomorrow, you'll be able to fish him out of the canal. We're on the same team."

The next day, Sunday, Sylvain drives Mathilde to the banks of the Boudigau, unfolds her "scooter", and instals her in it beneath a parasol. People have come from miles around, crowds are everywhere, even on the wooden footbridge over the canal, which the police are trying to clear. There are lots of banners in gaudy colours, and plenty of noise. The adults shout, the children chase one another, the babies vegetate in their carriages under a tropical sun.

The boat jousts get under way. When Aristide Pommier, in white jersey and trousers, has fallen in the water enough times to be eliminated, Sylvain brings him over to Mathilde. He's soaking wet, except for his glasses. He's not a little proud of having been knocked over by all his opponents. "In this heat," he says, "it's a pleasure to lose." Mathilde asks him to push her to somewhere quieter, so they go over to a patch of shade beneath the pines. He squats down on his heels when he begins to talk.

I saw Manech for the last time around the middle of November in '16. It was at Cléry, in the Somme. I wasn't in his sector any more, but sad news travels faster than good through the field kitchens, so I wasn't surprised to see him brought in with his arm in a sling. I knew he'd got himself shot by a sniper on the other side.

They shut him inside a barn that was still standing. Three soldiers guarded him while they waited for the police to come and get him. About two in the afternoon, I said to my sergeant, "He's from back home, I've known him ever since he was a schoolboy lugging his satchel while I was already out working. Let me go and see him." So the sergeant said fine and I changed places with one of the three guards.

It was one of those barns you can see up north, built of good solid bricks, with thick beams going in every direction. A big barn. Manech looked really small inside it. He was sitting against a wall, in a spot of sunlight coming down through the gaping roof, with his wounded hand up close against his stomach. There was a kind of bandage on it, already dirty and soaked in blood. "How come they're keeping him here like this?" I asked the other two, but they didn't know.

Of course, I tried my best to comfort Manech. I told him it wouldn't be serious, they were getting an ambulance for him, he'd be well taken care of – that sort of thing. Besides, they'd got rid of the military tribunals months before, they wouldn't be too hard on him, he'd have a lawyer, they'd take his age into account. Finally he smiled, he said, "You know, Pommier, I hadn't any idea you could talk so well, you'd make me a pretty good lawyer yourself!"

The name of the lawyer he wound up with? Don't know. A while later, someone coming back from the village of Suzanne told me that all the Cornflowers in that group were represented by a captain in the artillery well up in legal matters, but I never learned his name.

I talked with Manech about a lot of things, about home, you, the trenches, about what he'd done because of a rotten sergeant who was always after him – what can I tell you? We talked about whatever came to mind.

The rotten sergeant? Him I knew. Name of Garenne, from the Aveyron. An ambitious show-off who thought about nothing but getting promoted. A real stinker, except that he was gung-ho about fighting. If he's still alive, he must have managed to snag himself at least two stars.

In the end it was some infantrymen who came to take Manech to the field hospital where he had his operation. Later I learned he'd lost his hand there. It's sad, but his sentence was even sadder. They read it out to all the sections. To tell you the truth, Mademoiselle Mathilde, I didn't think they'd do it, no one did, we were all sure old Poincaré would pardon them.

I don't know what happened. At the trial, there were twenty-eight of them, they all had wounds the authorities claimed were self-inflicted. Fifteen of them they condemned to death, probably because they were afraid many others would try the same thing if they didn't make an example of them. Poor Manech certainly picked the wrong time.

But even there, who can say? Three-quarters of my battalion fell four months later, at Craonne. Luckily, I wasn't with them any more, even in the cookhouse. They'd transferred me, because of my eyes, and I spent the rest of the war making coffins.

You mustn't be angry with me any more, Mademoiselle Mathilde. The reason I didn't say a thing to you, or to anyone, even my wife, is because I couldn't. When Manech went off with those soldiers, I hugged him, my heart felt so heavy for him, I swear to you. He whispered in my ear, "Whatever you do, don't tell them about this back home." He didn't have to ask, I'd never have breathed one word. Why would I have caused more pain to his poor mother, his father, or you? Anyway, people are so stupid, even around here. They haven't a clue what it was like. They would have said nasty things about Manech, and he didn't deserve that. So if he's dead too, then it's really the war's fault, like with all the others. Right?

When Mathilde returns to the hospital in Dax, Daniel Esperanza is in bed, in a room with pink wallpaper, wearing a nightshirt of the same unhealthy grey as his complexion. It's Tuesday, four days after their conversation out in the garden. Sister Marie of the Passion of Christ is not pleased to see Mathilde back again so soon. Her patient was worn out the last time. He's been coughing a great deal. Mathilde promises not to stay very long.

As she was leaving after that first visit, she'd asked him if there was anything he'd like. He'd replied sadly, "Nothing, thank you, I don't smoke any more." She has brought him chocolates. "Very kind of you," he tells her, "but I couldn't eat them, I'd lose my teeth." He thinks the box is quite pretty, though. He's perfectly willing to give his chocolates to the other patients, but he'd like to keep the box.

Before leaving the room, Sister Marie pours the candies into the kangaroo-pocket of her nurse's apron, tastes one, and declares, "They're good. They're very good. I'll keep a few for myself."

Mathilde has written down a list of questions. Esperanza watches her apprehensively as she unfolds her piece of drawing paper. He's propped up in bed by two pillows. The chocolate box, decorated with a picture of an autumnal forest glade, is displayed on his bedside table, obscuring the face of an alarm-clock that gamely continues tick-tocking.

First of all, why did he wait so long before revealing what he knew to her?

That spring, when he was still having trouble walking but had thought himself finally out of danger from the influenza, he had gone over to Cap-Breton in a gig to see Manech's parents. At the last moment, after searching hither and yon without finding their house, he'd given up his idea. He no longer knew what he was doing there or what comfort he might possibly give them. Then he'd driven his horse as far as the Villa Poéma, stopping in front of the white gate. Mathilde had been sitting in an armchair at the other end of the garden, painting, surrounded by her cats. She had seemed so young. He'd driven away.

Then he had fallen ill again. He'd told Sister Marie about his war experiences. Sister Marie is from Labenne, not far from Cap-Breton. Mathilde doesn't remember, but she saw Sister Marie many times when she was little and took hot-water baths with the children in the sanatorium. Someone had told the nun that after the armistice, Mathilde, like many other white widows, had taken steps to marry her lost fiancé. Sister Marie had persuaded Esperanza to come forward. There was no one better placed than he to verify that both Manech's last letter and his intention to wed Mathilde were authentic and sincere.

Mathilde thanks him. She feels no need to add that she has received, in Manech's own handwriting, dozens of letters just as convincing. Her project has run into more serious obstacles. Age, above all. Apparently Manech was old enough to get himself killed but not old enough to get married on his own decision. Now, the Etcheverys used to be fond of Mathilde, but ever since she spoke to them about her plans, they have been decidedly unwelcoming. The father – who sold his fishing boat but still owns an oyster bed in Lake Hossegor – is frankly convinced she's scheming to get her hands on his money. The mother – whose nerves have been sorely tried by the death of her only son – had a fit of hysterics and shrieked that she was not going to be robbed of him twice.

Mathilde's parents have proved equally short-sighted. Her father declared, "Over my dead body!" and her mother smashed a vase. Upon viewing a certificate obtained at a doctor's on the Rue de la Pompe, where their daughter had gone to obtain official confirmation of her irreparable condition, the two of them spent three whole hours collapsed in each other's arms, crushed by the weight of broken dreams. Her father would occasionally rouse himself to curse the bastard capable of taking advantage of a child's infirmity to satisfy his bestial desires. Her mother would shout, "I don't believe it! I don't want to believe it! Matti doesn't even know what she's talking about!" As for her brother Paul, ten years older than she is, married and the father of two idiotic brats, these things – as always – are quite beyond him.

This is why Mathilde has decided no longer to mention her resolution to anyone else. She's not about to start again with Esperanza. On January 1, 1921, in a year and four months, she will come of age. Then we'll see who buckles first, Mathilde or the others.

After her first interview with the former Sergeant she had realized, while writing down her notes, that he hadn't mentioned the name of a single officer who hadn't died since the incident at Bingo. For example, who was the CO who gave him his orders, in Belloy-en-Santerre?

Esperanza turns away. He has nothing more to add to what he has already said. He'd felt sorry for Manech, he finds it moving ("and even very beautiful") that a girl her age should be so faithful as to wish to marry him posthumously, but the names of those still living, who might be harassed over their unwilling involvement in this vile episode – these names shall never pass his lips. He was a soldier himself, respectful of his superiors, and a loyal comrade.

Is Célestin Poux still alive, as far as he knows?

He has no idea.

And his soldiers in the territorial army? And Corporal Benjamin Gordes? And the medical orderly in the ruined village?

He looks up at her slyly. His reply is witheringly precise: "Corporals are small fry, no one gives a damn about their testimony, so you couldn't prove a thing. Anyway, if you tried to use me to bring charges against the army, I wouldn't back you up."

Mathilde realizes that he has been doing some thinking about their first interview, too, and that it's useless to ask him the rest of the questions she has prepared. She asks them anyway.

Who defended Manech at his trial?

He doesn't know.

The name of the village where the court-martial was held?

No one ever mentioned it to him.

What happened to the other ten men who were condemned to death at the same time?

He shrugs.

Who was Captain Favourier's superior officer?

He doesn't even bat an eyelash.

Does he, personally, think that Manech could have been faking his condition?

No, absolutely not.

Was it Manech who asked him to write his first name phonetically?

Yes. Otherwise he would have written "Manex".

When he read and later recopied That Man's letter, didn't he feel, as she did, that it was somehow inappropriate?

He doesn't understand the word.

Here's a man sentenced to death, speaking to his wife for the last time. Unlike the others, he sends a very short message, barely a few lines, and then he devotes half of them to the price of manure and some transaction he has good reason to know will be concluded after he's dead and gone.

"Easy to see you never knew That Man," replies Esperanza. He was a brute – cunning, of course, but a brute almost six feet tall, taciturn, with ideas limited by the boundaries of his fields, a typical peasant. Besides, he, Esperanza, had only been looking for things in the letter that might be contrary to the interests of our army. As it happens, he'd been more concerned by Six-Sous's questionable allusions to pacifism. Thinking of the welder's wife and children, however, he'd finally given the letter to a post orderly.

Does he know anyone who was nicknamed Biscuit?

No.

When Esperanza says no, Mathilde can tell he's lying. She sees the surprise in his eyes before he looks quickly away, she senses the uncertainty of this "no" immediately covered by coughing. When she remains silent, staring fixedly at him, he adds, "I read the name in the Eskimo's postscript, that's all."

Mathilde doesn't insist.

When he and his territorials arrived at that crossroads in the trenches called Place de l'Opéra, how long did he stay with Captain Favourier in the shelter housing the telephone?

Again, he's taken aback, hesitates. Then: "About ten minutes. Why?"

Was the photo of the condemned men taken during that time?

He thinks that it would have indeed been the only moment when his soldier, the one named Prussien, could have taken the picture without him noticing.

Why did he make copies of the letters?

The letters might have been stopped by the censors or failed to reach their destinations for other reasons. He intended to make sure, once the war was over, that they had in fact been delivered.

Has he met, apart from Mathilde, anyone close to the other condemned men?

No. What with his wounds, and then his illness, he hadn't had the opportunity. If he went to Cap-Breton, it was because it wasn't far away. And then, he'd enjoyed driving a gig again. At present, he no longer has any desire to stir up old unpleasantness.

Was he promoted to sergeant-major, as his CO had given him to understand?

He nods uneasily and turns away as tears well up in his eyes. Mathilde doesn't want him to start snivelling again. She remains silent for a moment.

He's the one who returns to the subject. He says he ended the war as a regimental sergeant-major. In his hospital bed, in Paris, he was awarded the Croix de Guerre. Two tears spill from his colourless eyes. He wipes them away with his fingers, in an almost childish gesture. "It's true," he murmurs, "that does mean a lot to me." He looks over at Mathilde through more tears, uncontrollable tears; his parted lips are trembling. She senses that he's just on the verge of confessing something to her, but then he shakes his head and simply stammers, "I can't."

Later, when he has recovered a bit of composure, and some of his voice, he tells Mathilde she shouldn't think badly of him if he keeps certain things to himself. What would happen to him now, alone, worn out, useless, if he were to lose his pension? And what would she gain from learning those things? They have nothing to do with Manech.

"They would help me to find out the truth," replies Mathilde.

Esperanza sighs, "My dear girl," and says that she has better ways to spend her youth – especially given her lot in life – than to go chasing the wind. Her desire to marry a fiancé lost in the war is a noble sentiment, but she should put all bitterness aside. Bingo Crépuscule was one trench among thousands, the sixth of January in 1917 was one day in the horror of fifteen hundred others, and Manech one unfortunate soul among millions of unhappy soldiers.

"Except that he was still alive the next day," says Mathilde firmly, trying to impress him or perhaps simply beginning to show her irritation, "and he was alive out in front of that particular trench, and I don't have to find millions of soldiers, I need just one who can tell me what happened to him!"

They are both silent. She can hear the clock ticking away in the room. Propped up by two pillows, Esperanza is lost in his sad thoughts. Mathilde wheels her chair over to the bed, touches his old grey hand lying on the sheet. With a sweet smile, she tells him, "I'll come back to see you again." Mathilde often studies her own smile in a mirror. She can make it pleasant, nasty, sardonic, seventh-heaven, dim-witted, mischievous, captivating, ecstatic. The only thing she can't make it is happy. Well, somewhat happy, but not very. It's like school: one can't be good at everything.

As Sylvain pushes her wheelchair down a long white corridor, he says, "Be good, Matti, be good. While you were talking to your gentleman, I read in the newspaper that an aviator flew his biplane under the Arc de Triomphe. You know why? He was upset that aeroplanes hadn't participated in the Victory Parade. So, you see?"

Translation: Mathilde shouldn't be fretting over all this. Anyone who takes a good long look at people can easily see that cats and dogs – even silly creatures like Chick Pea – have more brains and more heart.

Taking her in his arms to seat her inside the car, Sylvain repeats, "Upset, I ask you! And in a biplane? Beneath an arch so damp and windy it'll give you pleurisy if you so much as walk under it!"

Mathilde laughs. She tells herself that it's true. If she had the talent of Millet or Van Gogh, or ten other lesser painters, she'd have the ideal model, a sergeant-major wearing the

Croix de Guerre, seated in the dappled sunshine beneath a stand of pines, or in a hospital room papered in pink and Spanish influenza. In a single image, the perfect illustration: all is vanity.

That evening, she hates Esperanza.

The Good Old Days

Thérèse Gaignard, the wife of the man known as Six-Sous, is thirty-one years old. She has a trim figure, naughty blue eyes, and fine, pale blonde hair. She now works as a laundress in Cachan, near Paris. She has a shop on a little square where the dead leaves from the plane trees twist and spin in the wind.

She knows that her husband shot himself in the left hand and was brought before a court-martial. One of his comrades in the trenches told her this when he came to see her after the armistice. She decided against trying to find out anything more. The official letter she received in April of 1917 bore the notation: *Killed in action*. She receives a pension, and she has two little girls to raise. She makes their dresses and hair-ribbons out of the same cloth, as though they were twins. For several months now she has been seeing another man, who would like to marry her. He's good to the children.

She sighs. "You take what comes. Six-Sous had a heart of gold. I'm sure he'd approve of what I'm doing."

She returns to her ironing.

She talks about Six-Sous. He'd been among those wounded at Draveil, in July of 1908, when the cavalry had charged the strikers at the sand pit and killed so many of them. He'd hated Clemenceau with a passion. He would be far from pleased to hear that murderer of working men hailed as Father Victory.

But you're not to imagine that Six-Sous thought about nothing except trade unionism. He loved bicycles and the dance halls along the banks of the Marne just as much as he did the General Confederation of Labour. He went along as a mechanic with Garrigou on the Tour de France in 1911, during that terrible July, the hottest anyone could remember. The night Garrigou won, Thérèse brought Six-Sous home in a wheelbarrow, dead drunk, all the way from the Porte d'Orléans to Bagneux. She was almost six months pregnant with their first child at the time. The next morning, he'd been so ashamed that he hadn't dared look at her, and hadn't wanted her to look at him, either. He'd spent much of the day with a napkin over his face, like the penitents of the Middle Ages.

She'd never seen him drunk except that one time. He didn't drink, except for a glass of wine at meals, and only because *she* thought it helpful to the digestion. During their courting days, she'd told him a proverb she'd often heard from her grandmother in the Vaucluse: "A glass of wine, taken with dinner, leaves Doctor's purse a little thinner." He wasn't the type to go wasting his salary gambling or drinking in cafés. People called him tight-fisted, just to tease him, but he wasn't stingy at all. When the pay envelope he handed over to Thérèse was lighter than usual, you could be sure he'd been helping out a friend. His favourite pastime was going to the

Vélodrome d'Hiver, where he knew all the cyclists and got in free. He'd come back from the stadium with his eyes shining and his thoughts in a whirl. "If we'd had a son," says Thérèse, "he'd have wanted to make a champion cyclist of him."

When Sylvain arrives to pick up Mathilde, the two little girls are home from school. Geneviève, eight years old, already knows how to press handkerchiefs with a small iron without burning herself. From her serious air of concentration, one can tell how proud she is to be helping her mother in front of Mathilde. Sophie, aged six, has brought in plane-tree leaves that she strips down to their skeletons. She offers Mathilde one of her creations.

Mathilde sits with Sylvain in the back seat of her father's car, a large red-and-black Peugeot, driven by the Donnay Constructions chauffeur, who's new and whom she doesn't know. She holds the stem of the denuded leaf between her thumb and index finger. If she'd had two children by Manech, she wonders, could she ever have wanted to forget him? She doesn't know. She doesn't think so, but then, of course, Thérèse Gaignard doesn't happen to have a father who was already earning a great deal of money before the war and is now earning even more, rebuilding ruined cities.

They return to Paris after nightfall. It's raining in Montparnasse. Mathilde watches the procession of shimmering lights through her streaming window.

"Poor, poor Six-Sous," she thinks. "As a certain captain once said to the man you called Esperanza, I would have liked to have met you at some other time, in some other place. You, I know, would pursue that hope until the truth was plain for all to see."

*

Mathilde had written to the wife of That Man, in the Dordogne. The letter was returned to her before she left Cap-Breton: *No longer at this address.* Mathilde, who was born in January, must have somehow – let the astrologers figure it out – inherited the stubbornness of Taurus or the obstinacy of Cancer. She wrote to the mayor of Cabignac. The village priest answered her letter.

September 25, 1919

My dear child,

The mayor of Cabignac, Monsieur Auguste Boulu, died this year. His successor, Albert Ducot, moved here after the war, during which he served honourably in the Medical Corps. Although he is a radical, our relationship is one of fraternal cordiality. This wise and impecunious doctor will accept nothing from the poor, who make up a large part of my parish. I have the utmost admiration for him. He gave me your letter because he never knew Benoît and Mariette Notre-Dame. It was I who married them in the summer of 1912. I knew Mariette when she was a child, and although Benoît didn't come to catechism class, I tried to teach him the glory of Jesus and Mary whenever I could catch him in the fields where he was ploughing. Both of them were foundlings. Benoît was abandoned a few kilometres from Cabignac, on the steps of a chapel called Notre-Dame-des-Vertus. That is where his name came from. It was a priest like myself who found him and carried him in his arms to some nuns of the Order of the Visitation, who became so attached to him they were later loath to give him up. Mounted policemen had to intervene. If you ever visit these parts, the old folk can tell you the whole story in complete detail.

A provisional monument to the dead was set up this summer in the town square, in front of my church. The name of Benoît Notre-Dame is there, among the sixteen names of those from Cabignac who died for their country. In 1914 we mustered fewer than thirty men who were fit to serve. So as you can see, the war has hit us hard.

My child, I sensed too much anger, too much rancour in your letter to our mayor. No one knows how Benoît Notre-Dame was killed in combat, but everyone around here is certain that it was a stiff battle: he was so big and strong that it would have taken hell to bring him down. Or else it was the will of God, what can I say.

Mariette received the terrible news in January of '17. She went immediately to see the notary in Montignac and put the farm up for sale, as she could not manage alone any more. She sold even her furniture. She left holding little Baptistin in her arms, seated in old man Triet's gig. She took two trunks and some bags with her. I said to her, "What are you doing? What will happen to you?" I was hanging on to the horse. She replied, "Don't worry about me, *Monsieur le Curé*. I still have my little boy. I've got friends near Paris, I'll find some work." Then, when I wouldn't let go of the reins, Triet shouted, "Get out of the way, priest! Or watch out that I don't give you a taste of my whip!" The old skinflint had lost his two sons and his son-in-law in the fighting, so he cursed God and insulted those who had returned from the war. It was he who bought the Notre-Dame farm. The notary has assured me that despite his reputation for stinginess, Triet gave Mariette a good price, probably because he respects misfortune more than money, now that he has had his own suffering to bear. So a ray of light may always pierce even the darkest soul, and I see this, my dear child, as a sign that the Lord wished to mark the occasion with his seal.

In April of '17 we received confirmation of Benoît's death. I forwarded the document to the temporary address Mariette had given me, a furnished room at 14, Rue Gay-Lussac in Paris. No one here has heard from her since then. Perhaps you might be able to learn of her whereabouts from the landlord at that address, and if you would let me know what you find out, I would be infinitely grateful. I should so like to learn what happened to her and the child.

Your obedient servant in Our Lord,

Anselme Boileroux
Curé de Cabignac

Mathilde also wrote to Tina Lombardi, Common Law's companion, sending her letter to the address he had used, in care of Madame Conte, 5, Traverse des Victimes, in Marseille. It is this lady who sends her a reply, in violet ink on a few sheets of paper taken from a school notebook. Decoded phonetically, each word studied under a magnifying glass, with a semblance of punctuation established, and thanks to the constant consultation of an Italian dictionary, this is what Mathilde was able to decipher.

Thursday 2 October, 1919

Dearest Mademoiselle,

I have not seen Valentina Emilia Maria, my goddaughter by affection, since Thursday 5 December of last year, in the afternoon, when she visited me for the last time the way she did before the war, bringing me a pot of chrysanthemums for the tomb of my father, my sister, and my husband, all deceased, a whipped cream cake, some tomatoes and some peppers, and also fifty francs she left in the sugar tin without telling me so as not to hurt my pride.

She seemed much as usual, not happy not unhappy, and to be in good health. She wore a blue dress with white polka dots, very pretty it was but short enough to see her calves, you know the kind. She told me it was all the fashion but I am certain you do not wear dresses like that, you are surely respectable and educated, except perhaps for disguising yourself on Mardi Gras as a trollop, but I don't think so. I showed your letter to my neighbour Madame Sciolla, and also to Madame Isola, she and her husband run the Bar César on the Rue Loubon, a sensible and highly regarded woman, I assure you, and both of them told me, "You can tell that she is quite a proper young lady," and said I should answer for Valentina because I don't know where she is, not now and not for months. So that's what I'm doing.

Above all, dearest mademoiselle, do not be ashamed of my writing on my account, I never went to school, being too poor, and I came here to Marseille, with my widowed father and my sister Cecilia Rosa in January 1882, at fourteen years of age, coming from Italy, and my poor sister was deceased in 1884 and my poor father in 1889, who was a mason and held in great esteem by all, and I had to work without rest. I married Paolo Conte Saturday 3 March, 1900, at thirty-two years of age, and he was fifty-three and he also had worked without rest for twenty years in the mines of Alès. He died of lung trouble Wednesday 10 February, 1904 at two in the morning, so we weren't even married four whole years, it's a shame, I promise you, because he was a fine man, he came from Caserta where I myself was born, together with my sister Cecilia Rosa, and without the joy of having a single child, yes, it's a shame. After, it's my heart that started giving out and here I am at fifty-one, not even fifty-two, an old woman who can hardly ever go out now, I get winded just in going from my bed to the cookstove, you can imagine my life. Luckily I have good neighbours, Madame Sciolla and Madame Isola. I am supported by the municipality thanks to Madame Isola who petitioned for me, I have everything I need. And so do not think I want to complain to you, my poor mademoiselle who has lost your beloved fiancé in the war, I have my pride and I send you my most sincere condolences, together with Madame Sciolla and Madame Isola.

I was always fond of Valentina Emilia Maria since she was born 2 April, 1891. Her mother died bringing her into this world and I had already lost both father and sister and not yet married a husband. I would surely tell you these things better if I did not have to write them, but you can imagine my pleasure when I was twenty-three and I rocked her in my arms, especially since her father Lorenzo Lombardi thought only of drinking and picking fights, hated by all the neighbours. She often escaped to my place to sleep her fill, so you may well think, is it any wonder things went wrong with her? At thirteen, fourteen years old, she met this Ange Bassignano, who had not had any better life than hers, love conquers all.

I take up this letter again the next day 3 October, because yesterday I gave out, my heart was thumping too hard. You must not think Valentina Emilia Maria, my goddaughter by affection, is a bad girl. She is very good-hearted on the contrary, before the war she never missed her weekly visit to me, and always presents and also fifty francs or even more in the sugar tin, when my back was turned, so as not to wound my pride. But she fell in with misfortune when she fell for that wretched Neapolitan, she followed him in his disgrace and lived the high life until he flew into a murderous rage against another local tough in a bar in Arenc, and stuck a knife in his back, it gave me such a turn when I heard this.

After, she went every Saturday to see him in Saint-Pierre Prison and he never lacked for anything with her, I promise you, no more than usual, on account of she's the one who supported him since he was fifteen and already thought he was quite something. And after that, in 1916 when they sent him off to war, she followed him too, wherever he went, because they had a secret code in his letters to her to say where she could find him, can you imagine their love and what she turned into, an army whore. She even told me he'd found at least fifty fools that paid him for her as a wartime pen-pal and when they went on leave, she took all their money. And even worse things he made her do, always for money. But what good is money to him now, after he died like a dog, probably at the hand of French soldiers? What dishonour for his mother and father if they had lived to see that wasted life, but luckily they never knew him as anything but an adorable little boy, a real cherub. They died when he was four and he was raised by some Piedmontese, people of no account who let him run wild, and I who am as kind as could be, I promise you, when the police came to tell me he was dead at the front and gave me the notification, I cried, but I said good riddance. It wasn't for him I was crying, I promise you. He was a poor lost child but he became a devil for my goddaughter.

Now I'm coming to what you wanted to know from Tina, as you call her, because I felt within my rights to open your letter, as I always do, because she asked me to open everything when I don't know where she is, it might be the authorities or the police, so as I can answer them. The first time we learned this Ange Bassignano had gone missing in the war, it's me who heard this, already from the police, on Saturday 27 January, 1917, about eleven in the morning. Meanwhile, on Tuesday 16 January I received the last letter that the Angel from Hell, as he himself said, sent to Valentina. I was that astonished to receive it, because since he'd left the prison, I was no longer his post office, and astonished also at his sweet words, but he was a liar through and through and I think those sweet words were only there for that secret code with my goddaughter, like I told you.

At that time, I had a postal address for Valentina Emilia Maria: A.Z.1828.76.50, nothing more, because she went all over the army zone of operations, but it was at least five weeks old and she never stayed long in the same sector. I sent the letter anyway and she received it, she told me later, and so she found the trail of her devil and learned of his fate.

She told me it had happened in the Somme and it was all over for him. She told me so when she came back to Marseille, it was in my kitchen, on Tuesday 13 March, 1917. She was thin and pale and tired of everything. I told her cry, why don't you cry, poor dear girl, it will help you, but she told me she did not feel like crying but like blowing out the brains of everyone who hurt her Nino, that's what she called him. After,

I did not see her awhile but she wrote me a postcard from Toulon to tell me she was fine and I was not to worry. Finally the official death certificate, brought by the police, that was on Friday 27 April, at the end of the day. That is when I said good riddance to bad rubbish. On the notice there was: *Killed in action, January 7, 1917,* but not where they buried Ange Bassignano. As you can well imagine I asked the policemen, but they didn't know. They told me certainly with many others.

I wrote to Toulon, and in June, when she was able, my goddaughter came back to visit me. I was pleased to see that she had put on some weight and some colour and especially that she did not want to talk any more about her Nino. After that and almost every month until the Thursday 5 December, 1918 that I told you about she came here with presents and treats, we would have dinner together in the kitchen, and one day too I went out with her, I hung on to her arm, we went to eat at the Bar César because Madame Isola had made pig's trotters for us, a true delight, there's not a better cook in the whole neighbourhood of Belle de Mai, or Saint-Mauront, or all up and down the Boulevard National.

I have no idea where my goddaughter is now. I received for my birthday in February of this year a card from La Ciotat. Afterwards someone said she had been seen in Marseille with the girls who work the Panier, the area overlooking the old harbour in Marseille, and then that she was in a brothel on the road to Gardannes, but if she doesn't tell me herself I don't believe anyone, it's easy to talk behind someone's back.

I take up this letter again 4 October, having left off last night for the same reasons of fatigue. My eyes will not stand reading it over but I hope you will be able to understand my nonsense. Now I'm worried the post office won't take such a thick letter, the longest I wrote in all my life. In a way it has done me good, I don't know how to say this to you, and when I see my goddaughter again, because I will see her again, I will take the liberty of sending you her address and until then I wish only the best for you, and tell you again of my sincere condolences, together with Madame Sciolla and Madame Isola.

Au revoir and yours very truly,

Madame Veuve Paolo Conte, née Di Bocca

The bar Little Louis owns on the Rue Amelot is a long room with dark woodwork. It smells of aniseed and sawdust. Two lamps shed their light on walls and a ceiling that haven't seen a fresh coat of paint in a long time. Behind the zinc counter, above a row of bottles, are hung photographs of boxers from before the war, posing with their fists at the ready, their expressions not so much threatening as intrigued by the camera. All the photos are in varnished wooden frames.

"The Eskimo made those frames for me," says Little Louis. "And also the model of the sailing ship over there, across the room. She's a bit shabby now, but you should've seen her when he gave her to me in 1911, a real beauty, an exact replica of the *Samara* that had taken him and his brother Charles, in their salad days, from San Francisco to Vancouver. He was clever with his hands all right, the Eskimo."

Little Louis has pulled down the iron shutters; it's nine-thirty in the evening, his usual closing time. He told Mathilde, on the telephone, "It'll be quieter that way, we'll be able to talk."

When she arrived, wheeled in by Sylvain, there were two

customers still at the counter, who were promptly urged to drink up. Now he comes over to the marble table where she sits, he's carrying a plate, an open bottle of wine, and a saucepan containing his supper, some warmed-over mutton stew. He offers to share his meal with Mathilde, but even just to be polite, she couldn't swallow a mouthful. As for Sylvain, he's gone off to eat in a brasserie he spotted earlier, all lit up on the Place de la Bastille.

Little Louis well deserves his nickname, but he has thickened around the waist. "At this point," he says, "if I were still in the ring, I'd be drawing middleweights. The least little nobody would be wiping up the canvas with me. It's hard to keep your weight down when you're running a bistro."

He's amazingly light on his feet, however, when he goes back and forth between his counter and the table to fetch two glasses, half a baguette, and a Camembert in its box. His step is elastic, springy, but one can surmise that even in his trimmer days he must have taken a lot of punishment. He has a flattened nose, cauliflower ears, and a battle-scarred mouth. His smile is a grimace liberally flecked with gold.

After he has sat down and tucked one end of a checked napkin inside his collar, he pours a glass of wine, which he offers to Mathilde. To get the polite formalities over with, she accepts. He fills the other glass, swallows a mouthful to rinse his mouth, and smacks his lips.

"You'll see," he says, "it's not bad. I have it sent from Anjou, that's where I come from. I'm going back there as soon as I've saved up a big enough nest egg to take the rest of life easy. I'll sell this damned joint and I'll live in a wine cellar, with one or two pals to keep me company. You know, I've seen many things in my life, but I can tell you, nothing counts more than wine and friendship." He grins with an air of false contrition and adds, "Excuse me, I'm talking rot. It's just that you make me a little nervous."

Then he fills his plate, eating his stew while tearing off chunks of bread to mop up the sauce. As he eats, he tells Mathilde what she wants to know. She has drawn her "scooter" up to the table. Out in the street, no noise disturbs them, not even a passing car, not even the rowdy shouts of revellers who are too fond of wine and friendship.

It was a widow from the Patriotic Committee, one of the "ladies in black", who came to the café at the end of January in 1917 to tell Little Louis that his friend was dead. She had just come from the building on the Rue Daval, not two steps away, where the Eskimo had had his carpentry workshop in the courtyard and his room up under the eaves.

Grief-stricken, Little Louis had collapsed onto a chair, to the astonishment of some customers he'd just been regaling with the story of one of his most glorious exploits. That evening, all alone, he'd got drunk and wept as he reread the Eskimo's last letter, received the week before, and to finish off the night, he'd reduced one of his café tables to smithereens, cursing fate.

In April, a municipal employee had brought him the official document: *Killed in action, January 7, 1917.* The man had wanted to know if the Eskimo had had any relatives, even distant ones, who should be notified. Little Louis had told him he wasn't aware of any. The Eskimo had left his older brother, Charles, back in America, but he hadn't heard from him in a very long time.

That evening, in an effort to lift his spirits, Little Louis had gone out with one of his mistresses. They'd gone to a restaurant near Place Clichy, after walking out of a movie before the end, because Little Louis hadn't had the heart for it. He hadn't had the heart for anything else, either; he'd accompanied the lady home, but just to her door. Tears streaming down his cheeks, he'd walked back to his café, where he'd holed up to get drunk by himself, to reminisce by himself. If he didn't break a table this time, it was because they're expensive, and anyway, it doesn't help.

No, he'd never heard anything more, later on, about the circumstances of Kléber Bouquet's death or the place where he was buried. No army friends ever turned up to visit him. At the beginning of the war, some soldiers had occasionally dropped by when on leave to bring him news, a letter, a photograph, but these visits had tapered off, the regiments were constantly being reshuffled, perhaps they were all dead, maybe they were prisoners, or simply tired of being the bearers of bad tidings.

Little Louis often saw Véronique Passavant – the Véro mentioned by the Eskimo in his last letter – and he still sees her now and then. She sometimes comes at closing time, to have a cup of coffee near the stove, talking over old times and shedding a few tears. She was already living with Kléber in 1911, the year when Little Louis hung up his gloves at the grand old age of thirty-nine and bought his bar, after taking a terrific drubbing from Louis Ponthieu. He'd never touched knee to canvas in his life, not even against the heaviest hitters, but in that bout he'd practically worn out the seat of his trunks. The next three years had been what he and Véro refer to as the good old days. During the week, Kléber would pop in several times a day for a quick refresher of chilled white wine, his face and workshirt covered with sawdust. In the evening, he'd often go out to the music-halls with Véro, who'd be dolled up like a marquise. He was very proud of his flashy girlfriend, whom he called his wife in front of others. In fact, even without any official piece of paper, they'd joined together to love and cherish each other all their lives, until they were torn apart by the war.

But guess what happened! In 1916, Kléber was still paying rent on the workshop and his room, so that he could come home on leave and find everything as it should be. He had more leaves than many others did, perhaps because he was so charming and ingratiating, perhaps also because he'd been mentioned in the regimental dispatches for bringing in some prisoners. He spent a good half his days of so-called rest and relaxation in bed with Véro, and the rest in various establishments catering to those looking for a bit of fun, including some in which he'd never have dared set foot before the war. As soon as he arrived home, probably as he headed up the stairs, he'd strip off his uniform and not wear it again until it was time to return to the front. He was something to see, arm in arm with that minx of his, swaggering about in his tweed jacket from London, his boater tipped casually back on his head, a long white scarf around his neck – people took him for one of those flying aces.

It has to be said as well that Véronique Passavant is what's called a fine specimen. Tall, well endowed in all the right places, with black hair down to her waist, big saucy cat's eyes, a complexion to drive respectable ladies wild with jealousy – really, a gorgeous specimen. She's twenty-seven years old. The last time she came to chat with Little Louis, in July of this year, she was a salesgirl in a ladies'-wear shop in Ménilmontant, he doesn't know which street it's on or where she lives. But she'll definitely be back to see him again soon, and he'll put her in touch with Mathilde.

Whatever it was that came between them when Kléber was home on leave that time in 1916 is still a mystery to Little Louis, as neither one of them ever spoke to him about what happened. He assumed it was a lovers' quarrel, regrettable, but only temporary. When Véro had come running, on that nasty January morning in 1917, having just learned from someone in the neighbourhood that her lover was dead, Little Louis had made her read the Eskimo's last letter out loud, and had asked her what it was all about. She was in tears, on her knees, in a state of collapse. She had lifted her face to him, a face made ageless by grief, and cried, "What does it matter, now? Do you want me to choke on my own remorse? What makes you think I hadn't promised myself I'd throw my arms around him on his next leave? Forgiving everything, yes, everything!" This in front of five or six customers who hadn't had the decency to make themselves scarce, so enthralled were they by the misfortunes of others, but Little Louis had tossed them out.

Some time later, after she had calmed down, sitting dry-eyed at a table near the stove, Véro had said, "In any case, Kléber made me swear not to say anything to anyone." Little Louis had let the matter drop. If Mathilde wants his opinion, Kléber had a weakness for women, a not uncommon failing, and was too frank to be careful about such things. While he was on leave that summer of '16, he must have fooled around a bit on the side, and then admitted this to Véro, who'd been so upset she'd packed her things and left him. That's how he, Little Louis, sees the situation, at least when he avoids tying his brain in knots over the details, two of which he finds distinctly bothersome. In the first place, Véro loved Kléber too dearly to have remained bitter for so long over a simple passing fancy. Secondly, Kléber didn't confide in him, in Little

Louis, whom he trusted with everything, even his savings, so either he was ashamed or else, and this is more likely, he was protecting someone. But, and would Mathilde please excuse his bluntness, when there's tail involved, there's no knowing.

While Little Louis is finishing his meal, Mathilde feels cold and moves closer to the stove. At one point, he'd said something – she can't remember exactly what it was – and she'd felt a chill. Or had she been struck by an image, when he'd got up to rummage through a drawer and had brought her some mementoes of the Eskimo he'd collected to show her: photos from America and the good old days, photos of the war, the last letter. Mathilde hasn't yet decided whether she should tell Little Louis she has a copy of that letter, or tell him about the horrible circumstances under which it was written, but as it turns out, there's no need for pretence: she feels as though she were reading the letter for the first time.

Through that clumsy handwriting, all slanted to the left, through the miserable spelling of a street urchin, there suddenly comes to her the image of a bound soldier, pitiful, shivering with cold, turning around at the top of a trench ladder to ask if he might try to protect someone even more pitiful than himself.

Now, after setting his glass and Mathilde's down on the table nearest to her, Little Louis sits smoking a cigarette. There's a faraway look in the eyes beneath those heavily scarred brows. Mathilde asks him about this Biscuit mentioned in the postscript of the letter.

"You must be reading my mind," Little Louis tells her with a grim smile. "I was just thinking of him."

Biscuit, another long story.

He was – because the poor soul didn't come back from the war either – the most engaging man, a tall bean-pole, quite thin, with quiet blue eyes and chestnut hair that was growing sparse. People called him Biscuit because of his biceps, his "biscottos", muscular marvels that Little Louis (who wasn't a big gorilla, after all) could have easily encircled with a single hand.

Biscuit had been Kléber's pal since the floods of 1910, when the two of them had saved an old woman from drowning. They'd hawked furniture together, meeting every Saturday at the intersection of Faubourg Saint-Antoine and Avenue Ledru-Rollin to sell small pieces they'd made, chests of drawers, console tables, and the like. The Eskimo had a way with wood – just look at the model of the *Samara* across the room – but Biscuit! Mathilde couldn't begin to imagine the talent that man had: hands the like of which will never be seen again, the hands of a magician. The other hawkers didn't even bother being jealous.

On Saturday evening – not every week, because he had a wife and five children and he probably got what for when he let his supper get cold on the table – Biscuit would come along with Kléber to the café, where they'd have a little fun, take turns standing rounds, and split up their day's earnings. At those moments, it was Little Louis who was jealous of Biscuit, and he freely admits it. Not spitefully, of course, because Biscuit was a fine sort, never underhand, never raising his voice in anger, and he was a good influence on Kléber. Yes, a good influence. It's thanks to Biscuit that Kléber began to put aside some savings, a hundred francs here, two hundred francs there, which he entrusted to Little Louis so as not to spend the sum foolishly. Whenever he received a deposit, Little Louis would stash it in a biscuit tin decorated with wild flowers, which he kept in his safe-deposit box at the bank. When he handed the money over to Véronique Passavant, as the Eskimo had asked him to in his letter, she hadn't wanted to take it, she'd wept and said she didn't deserve it. In the very bar where Mathilde is sitting now, Little Louis had drawn himself up to his full height of five and a half feet, and strong in the knowledge of a promise given, match in hand, he had sworn if she didn't put those bills into her handbag then and there, he would burn them all and even eat the ashes so that nothing would be left of them. In the end, she'd taken the money. It was almost eight thousand francs, not enough to assuage her grief, but a tidy sum nevertheless.

And what do you know, the Good Lord works wonders: in the war, Kléber and Biscuit, both born in the same neighbourhood, wound up in the same regiment, and soon in the same company. The Marne, the Woëvre, the Somme, Verdun, they went everywhere together, and when one came home on leave, he'd bring news of the other man, and he'd try to tell the customers about the trenches, but he'd nurse his glass and gaze sadly at Little Louis, obviously anxious to change the subject, because, you see, it's not easy to talk about the trenches, the noise, the filth, the stench, but in spite of everything they're alive, more alive than any other damned place, and no one can understand this unless he's been there, with his comrades, up to his ears in mud.

With these bitter words, Little Louis falls silent for a good minute.

And what do you know, the Good Lord botches the job: in the summer of 1916, he's forgotten which front it was, the beautiful friendship fell apart. Kléber and Biscuit couldn't stand each other any more, they fought all the time over trifles, a pack of Gauloises bleues, a tin of bully beef, or whether Fayolle or Pétain took better care of his men. Then they avoided each other, no longer on speaking terms. When he was promoted to corporal, Biscuit changed companies, and soon regiments. He never came back to the bar. He died, it seems, in a bombardment, while he was being evacuated from some front or other where he'd been wounded.

The Eskimo must have told Little Louis Biscuit's real name when he introduced his new friend to him one Saturday in 1911, but Little Louis can't remember it, and the other customers who knew him probably wouldn't either. He was simply Biscuit. His workshop must have been somewhere in the neighbourhood, on the other side of the Bastille. In any case, Little Louis had been glad to learn that God does exist, after all, that before dying, each off on his own, the two men had become friends again.

When Sylvain knocks outside on the iron shutter, it's past eleven o'clock. Mathilde takes one last look at the photos of the Eskimo while Little Louis goes to get the crank to lift the shutter. The breeze that enters carries the scent of rain. Mathilde wonders if she should tell Little Louis what she has learned from Esperanza. She decides not to. It would only give Little Louis bad days and worse nights.

In the photographs, the Eskimo is posing with his brother Charles under a giant tree in California, a sequoia. Here they are in a covered wagon, with Charles holding the reins. Here they are again, out in a vast expanse of snow, with a town or village of wooden houses off in the distance, and the Eskimo, born Kléber Bouquet in the 11th arrondissement of Paris, is waving two great handfuls of white fox pelts. He has a solemn look on his face. If Mathilde's calculations are correct, he is eighteen years old, because he has noted on the back of the picture, in writing steadily slanted to the left: Dawson, Klondike, 16 January, '98. Nineteen years later, almost exactly to the day, his fate caught up with him in the snows of the Somme.

In the photo that Mathilde likes best, or finds most moving, the Eskimo is doing his laundry in a cantonment. The sleeves of his collarless shirt are rolled up to the elbows, he's wearing an army cap, and he's looking towards the camera. He has kind eyes, a handsome moustache, a strong neck, and broad shoulders that inspire confidence. He seems to be telling Mathilde – and she wants to believe this – that he managed to protect Manech, unbeknownst to anyone; that he was too tough, too experienced, and too much of a survivor to let the boy die.

Queen Victoria's Tuppence

NOVEMBER

Mathilde's father, Mathieu Donnay, employs as his legal adviser an affable and attentive lawyer, Pierre-Marie Rouvière, who is fifty years old, quite handsome in spite of his bald pate, and a man reputed to be as tireless in the defence of males in need as he is devoted to the conquest of females in distress. He has known Mathilde since she was a child, when he won her over with *calissons d'Aix*, the irresistible marzipan sweets. When Mathilde arrived in Paris in early October, she consulted him in his capacity as the family lawyer, telling him her story in his office with its velour-covered walls.

At the first mention of Bingo Crépuscule and Place de l'Opéra he threw his arms in the air and called the entire thing a grotesque farce. Five bound soldiers, dragged all the way to a front-line trench and tossed over the barbed wire to the enemy – and in the snow, no less! It was outlandish, it was simply one of those morbid and unfortunately not always unprejudiced tales that had flourished like weeds all through the war.

Esperanza? The poor man was just a pathological liar *in extremis* who was trying to embellish his biography and was already backing away from his story because he knew he'd gone too far. The photograph of the condemned men? It didn't prove a thing, it could have been taken anywhere. Manech's letter and the identical copy? It could have been dictated under entirely different circumstances. Favourier's letter? A fake, like the forged document that had convicted Dreyfus. While they were on the subject, this Captain Favourier might himself be a complete fabrication.

Nevertheless, giving the benefit of the doubt to the reality of this court-martial, since this point has been corroborated by a fellow soldier in Manech's regiment, Pierre-Marie Rouvière had written down in a black-leather-covered notebook embossed with his initials – "All this remaining just between ourselves, on a strictly friendly basis" – the names of the people and places Mathilde mentioned to him, and he promised to make inquiries, to do his best to clear up this rather far-fetched story.

Since their discussion, he has telephoned Mathilde twice at home in Paris, first to check on the name of the medical officer who attended the five prisoners in the destroyed village (Santini), then to make an appointment for four o'clock this afternoon at her house on the Rue La Fontaine.

Rain courses down the window panes. Pierre-Marie is smoking Turkish cigarettes in a long ivory holder. He's wearing a black tie, which has been his habit ever since the armistice, in memory of an actress who died that day and whom he had deeply loved. His clothes are gloomy. His expression is gloomy. The normally cheerful morning room, so lovingly arranged by Mama, has become quite gloomy.

First of all, Mathilde must swear that what she is about to

hear will never be revealed to another soul. To obtain this information, Pierre-Marie has had to trade upon his friendship with a staff officer who has put himself greatly at risk by divulging what he knows, information that Pierre-Marie has assured him will be kept strictly confidential. Mathilde, perfectly aware of what a liar she is, promises without hesitation.

The lawyer sits down. He produces some folded papers from the inside breast pocket of his jacket. In the course of the last five weeks, he has had several meetings with this officer, who shall remain anonymous, and whom he calls My Officer Friend, as though this were his real name. They had lunch together today and reviewed what they had learned. Although certain of Esperanza's statements have been confirmed by documentation or testimony they have collected, they both remain convinced that his story is a fabrication, that the doddering old fool told Mathilde things that couldn't possibly have happened at Bingo Crépuscule. They must certainly have had better things to do in that trench, on the sixth and seventh of January in 1917, than to throw condemned prisoners over the parapet to save a few French bullets.

The morning room brightens. Mathilde can see daylight through the rain-streaked windows. She sees the flames flickering in the pink marble fireplace, and even the sudden flash of gold on the lawyer's signet-ring when he unfolds his papers. Then Bingo really did exist?

He looks at her, he nods, he says yes, there is no doubt about it, and no doubt about some of the other details in Esperanza's story.

Bingo Crépuscule was the name of a German trench occupied by our forces in October 1916, number 108 in a sector of the front on the Somme, near Bouchavesnes. In January 1917, the trench marked the junction between the French and British troops. During the day and night of Sunday, January 7, it was the scene of heavy fighting. Beginning on January 8, British soldiers were brought in to replace our troops in that area, in accordance with an agreement reached in the autumn by the commanders of the two Allied armies, which precludes any connection to the events that interest Mathilde. It is quite true that Etienne Favourier, a thirty-five-year-old history teacher, was in command of the half-battalion stationed in trenches 108 and 208, first- and second-line positions, on Sunday, January 7, 1917.

It is quite true that Lieutenant Jean-Jacques Estrangin, twenty-five years of age, was the leader of the company positioned in Bingo Crépuscule, which did include corporals Urbain Chardolot and Benjamin Gordes, as well as infantryman Célestin Poux.

My Officer Friend has personally consulted the casualty list of January 7. The names of the fifty-six men killed include those of Favourier and Estrangin, while Benjamin Gordes was indeed among the seventy-four wounded.

Here the lawyer stops, giving Mathilde a long, pensive look as he removes his spectacles. Then he says, "There's something else, my poor Matti."

Among those listed as killed on the casualty list drawn up on Monday, January 8, by a sergeant (the highest-ranking survivor in this battered company), under the heading "Detached to the battalion on January 6," are Kléber Bouquet, Francis Gaignard, Benoît Notre-Dame, Ange Bassignano, and – "I'm sorry, that's just how things are" – Jean Etchevery.

Mathilde wheels her chair over by the fire. Without turning around, she forces herself to say, "Go on. I'm listening."

It is quite true that the medical officer, Lieutenant Jean-Baptiste Santini, aged twenty-seven, was killed in a bombardment at Combles on January 8, 1917. His immediate superior at the field hospital does not recall ordering him, two days earlier, to go and attend any wounded men condemned to death. When questioned by My Officer Friend, this rather well-known doctor told him flatly, "Really now, if something like that had happened, I would certainly have remembered it." He was even more categorical on the subject of the unknown medical orderly who is supposed to have accompanied Lieutenant Santini. "What, you say there was an orderly there as well? Two men, one of them a doctor, to change five dressings? Are you joking? I would never have given such an order, it's absurd!"

It is also quite true that in January of 1917 a regiment of dragoons was billeted in the same sector as the destroyed hamlet, Tancourt, where the prisoners would have been taken and put in Esperanza's custody. But My Officer Friend has looked into the records of this regiment. He is certain that no escort assignment of this kind was reported for Saturday, January 6. Unless Esperanza mistakenly identified some other soldiers as dragoons, which is highly unlikely, given his three years of battlefield experience, we must once again dismiss his allegations as sheer fantasy.

Pierre-Marie has spoken on the telephone with the chief surgeon at the hospital in Dax, but was unable to talk to Esperanza, who is now too ill to come to the phone. The poor man is completely bedridden, hardly says a word, and remembers nothing, aside from a primary school teacher he had when he was little. He calls her name every night, and cries.

The commandant of Esperanza's battalion in January 1917

died that same year, not in the war, but home on leave, from a heart attack at the end of a family meal. His widow has never heard him speak of Bingo Crépuscule, or of the five men condemned to death, or of anything else in that vein, it seems, as she hated listening to his war stories.

There. That would have been all of it, except that Pierre-Marie has just learned the most important part at lunch that very day, something that in his opinion erases all doubts and puts a definite end to the matter.

The trial did indeed take place. In the elementary school of Dandrechain, near Suzanne, in the Somme. Twenty-six soldiers and two corporals from one corps, who had all mutilated themselves in the same way within such a short period as to pose a severe threat to army discipline, were brought before a court-martial on the twenty-eighth and twenty-ninth of December, 1916. Fourteen soldiers and a corporal, one Francis Gaignard, were condemned to death, while the others received twenty to thirty years' hard labour.

Folding up his papers again, Pierre-Marie suddenly rises and comes over to the fire, facing Mathilde, who says, "I don't see how this puts an end to the matter, when that's precisely where it all begins."

"Wait, Matti. I haven't finished. How do you think we learned these specific details?"

She assumes there must be transcripts from these courts-martial, some written records in the army archives.

No, My Officer Friend has not been able to find (not yet, at least) the minutes or any other trace of the trial at Dandrechain. But he found better: the "captain in the artillery well up in legal matters" mentioned by Aristide Pommier after his water-jousting revels. The very man who defended Manech.

At this, Mathilde is speechless, her heart is in her throat, she stares at Pierre-Marie wide-eyed and open-mouthed. He nods several times, pleased at her reaction, saying, "Oh yes, yes, Matti. My Officer Friend found him."

Manech's case was pleaded by an attorney from Levallois, who no longer practises law and now lives on a small private income and his invalid's pension, in a stone-built house, surrounded by his books and cats. He lost a son at Eparges, a leg in Champagne, and his wife in the Spanish flu epidemic. My Officer Friend met this man at his home yesterday afternoon and heard from his own lips what happened at the trial. He left with an important piece of news, a revelation he'd saved until his meeting with Pierre-Marie today over lunch: on January 2, 1917 – that's four days before the events at Bingo Crépuscule – all fifteen of the condemned men were pardoned by President Poincaré, who commuted their sentences to terms at hard labour. Manech's counsel for the defence was notified of this pardon on January 4 in his quarters, but the authorities involved must have been informed even earlier, by telegram. Why should anyone believe Esperanza's cock-and-bull story now?

After Mathilde has had time to gather her thoughts, she replies, "I shouldn't like you to think I was insulting your Officer Friend, but does he have proof this notification actually existed?"

Leaning towards her, in a voice suddenly so strong and resonant that Mathilde draws back in surprise, Pierre-Marie announces, "I saw it!"

The former attorney entrusted the document to My Officer Friend. Pierre-Marie examined it at noon this very day. He read the names of Jean Etchevery and the fourteen other condemned men. He read the reasons adduced. He read the commutation of the sentence and the date and the signature of Raymond Poincaré. Can she possibly think there would be a single French commander who would disregard this signature?

She doesn't think that, no. But what if the pardon arrived too late? What if the prisoners were already on their way? They'd told Esperanza of an exhausting, aimless journey lasting two days and two nights before they arrived at that village in ruins – Tancourt, that was the name? – where he took charge of them.

Pierre-Marie shakes his head, he sighs over such a stubborn desire to persuade oneself of the unbelievable. A reprieve arriving too late! How can she explain the fact that they didn't execute the men as soon as their sentence had been passed, as had always happened when the military tribunals were in operation? Precisely because since the suppression of the military tribunals, the law forbids all executions, even those upheld upon appeal, until the President of the Republic has had a chance to exercise his right of reprieve. Therefore, his decision was awaited. It could arrive sooner or later, but never too late. He repeats, "Never, it's obvious."

He must see from Mathilde's face exactly what she thinks about things that are obvious. He sighs again. Then he says fine, he's perfectly willing to play the devil's advocate.

"Let's admit that Esperanza is telling the truth. Let's admit that his mission was to take five men condemned to death – five wounded, exhausted men – to that front-line trench. I'll tell you, if I had to make a case here, this is how I'd present the situation. The commanders of the units in which the same offence has been committed twenty-eight times in sixteen days want to make an example of these men, and that's that. They have a presentiment of the wave of disgust, indiscipline, and mass insubordination that swept through our entire army in the spring, if some voices in our Chamber of Deputies are to be believed. Rather than wait for the President's decision, they divide the condemned men into three groups of five, they send them off to three different fronts, they lose track of them. It's of no importance that they'll be reprieved, for they'll already be dead. That will show everyone what a heavy price must be paid for doing what they did. They can't be executed legally? Fine. They're tied up, tossed into no-man's-land, and those across the way will finish them off. When it's all over, they're added to the regimental casualty lists. Even their families won't know a thing. *Killed in action.* And all those who had anything to do with this business – officers, NCOs, territorials, dragoons, train conductors, medical officers, truck drivers – they're scattered in every direction, they're engulfed by the war. Many will die, and dead men tell no tales. Others will keep quiet, to keep out of trouble, to keep their pensions: cowardice can be mute as well. After the deliverance of Armistice Day, when the survivors return to their homes, they'll have other things to tell their wives, children, and friends than the shameful story of a certain snowy Sunday in Picardy. What's the use? It would only tarnish the single image they cherish: they fought well, their children admire them, their wives go on and on in the grocery store about how their men single-handedly captured fifty prisoners in the most ferocious fighting at Verdun. So there's no one left but honest Daniel Esperanza, among the thousands of men in the Bouchavesnes sector on the sixth, seventh, and eighth of January, who has the courage to say, What I saw was murder, the flouting of our laws, the army's contempt for civilian authority."

Eager to interrupt the lawyer, which his opponents in court are said to manage only with considerable difficulty, Mathilde applauds weakly.

"Bravo," she says, "but you don't have to convince me, that's just what I think. Apart from a few gaps here and there, that's precisely the way things must have happened."

"Gaps?"

Once more Mathilde wouldn't like to appear doubtful of his Officer Friend's sincerity, so she will say rather that he has discovered only truths he finds convenient. If he had access to the regimental files, then it wouldn't have been too difficult for him to locate a few survivors of Bingo Crépuscule and question them.

"By what right?" bursts out Pierre-Marie. "And under what false pretext? If just one of them complains of being harassed or even simply starts talking wildly all over the place, what would we do?"

He brings a chair over in front of her and sits down.

"You're most ungrateful, Matti," he says sadly. "This man took great risks to help me, solely for friendship's sake. He can't do any more. He did speak with an artillery captain and the wife of a territorial army commandant and a medical officer. He did so because he knew he could rely on their discretion, as they could rely on his. As for the rest of it, if you think he discovered only 'truths he finds convenient' – and convenient in what way, I'd like to know – may I point out that he did not conceal from us those truths he finds disturbing, if only to his soldier's pride. I know him well and have known him for a long time. He must not have felt relief from his own misgivings until just this morning, when he had the presidential pardon in hand and could verify the effect it had had."

He leans forward, one hand on Mathilde's shoulder, and says, "I would have liked to keep this to myself, Matti, so as not to deepen your sorrow with vain regrets, but the two other groups of prisoners, who ended up at different fronts, were contacted and returned to Dandrechain, where they were told their sentences had been commuted. The ten of them are still alive today, breaking rocks in the penal colony in Guiana."

Mathilde bows her head and remains silent.

"Matti," says Pierre-Marie, "my little Matti, be reasonable. Manech is dead. What would it do to his memory even if, against all likelihood, you turned out to be right?"

He gives her a peck on the cheek, smelling of lavender and tobacco, and stands up to leave. When she looks over at him, he's reaching for his raincoat, which he'd draped over an armchair.

"Give me the name of that attorney in Levallois."

He shakes his head, sorry, impossible. He puts on his coat, his grey angora scarf, his grey felt hat, picks up his cane.

"You see, Matti, this war produced not only tons of bullets and bombs but almost as much again in paperwork. It would take months, probably years, to track down all these records, gather them together, sift through every one. If you won't be convinced, at least be patient. And careful. These days, it can prove quite dangerous to disregard certain taboos."

As soon as he is gone, Mathilde has her fountain pen and some drawing paper brought to the morning room. She makes a written record of the conversation she has just had so she won't forget a thing. Rereading her notes, she finds that she really has learned quite a bit, but only about two distinct periods of time: before Sunday the seventh of January, 1917, and afterwards. As for this Sunday itself, Pierre-Marie has only confirmed what she already knew, that there was fighting, that many soldiers were lost. Actually, she is even better informed than he is. She thinks of Manech building a snowman out in no-man's-land, of an aeroplane brought down by a grenade, of Six-Sous singing the song of the Paris Commune for anyone willing to listen. Of "sheer madness". She tells herself that she'll have to go on being mad all by herself.

That same evening, at dinner, she eats a chicken drumstick with her fingers, without saying a word, her thoughts elsewhere. She is seated at one end of the large table, facing her father, whom she loves with all her heart. To her left, Mama, whom she loves dearly. To her right, her brother Paul, who is rarely in her thoughts but whom she finds tolerable, and her lump of a sister-in-law, Clémence, whom she finds intolerable. The two monsters, Ludovic and Bastien, eight and six years' worth of nastiness, have long since gone off to wet their beds.

"Is something wrong, Matti?" asks her father.

"Nothing's wrong."

"When this blasted newspaper strike is over," he says, "I'll pay for your advertisement, it will be your Christmas present."

"Fine."

She wants to publish an ad in the major daily and weekly newspapers, as well as in those servicemen's magazines where everyone's looking for everyone else. She has written it out like this:

BINGO CREPUSCULE

(Trench in the Somme, Bouchavesnes sector.)
Reward for information concerning
JANUARY 6, 7, and 8, 1917

as well as Lieutenant Jean-Baptiste Santini, Corporals Urbain Chardolot, Benjamin Gordes, Private Célestin Poux, and any serviceman at this place on this date. Write to: Mlle Mathilde Donnay, Villa Poéma, Cap-Breton, Landes.

She has no doubt she will receive hundreds of letters. At night, in bed, she imagines herself at Cap-Breton, busy going through them. There are so many that Bénédicte and Sylvain must abandon kitchen and garden to come and help her. Everyone is living on sandwiches, the nettles are having a field day, the lamps burn late into the night, and one morning, one fine morning . . .

"What are you thinking about?" asks Mama.

"A hundred sous if you can guess."

"Oh, I know perfectly well whom you're thinking of."

"You win the prize."

Mathilde asks for some wine. Her father is the only one who has wine at meals. He keeps the bottle near his place. He rises and goes over to pour Mathilde a glass. As he does so, the Intolerable One feels obliged to remark, "You've taken to drinking wine now?"

"A glass of wine, taken with dinner, leaves Doctor's purse a little thinner," replies Mathilde.

"Wherever did you hear that?" asks her father, who returns to his seat without commenting on the impudence of his daughter-in-law.

Mathilde tastes her wine and replies, "It's the considered opinion of the Vauclusian grandmother of the wife of the mechanic of the 1911 Tour de France champion Garrigou."

"How about that," observes her father, amid general but silent consternation. "Could you just run through it again?"

"Backwards or forwards?"

"Either way."

Mathilde drinks a little of the wine and takes a deep breath.

"Garrigou, the winner of the Tour de France in 1911, had a mechanic, the mechanic had a wife, the wife had a grandmother in the Vaucluse who claimed what you asked me to tell you where I'd heard it."

"She's drunk already," says Mama in blank dismay.

"Matti was eleven in 1911," says Paul. "How can she know who won the Tour de France?"

"Oh, I know lots more stuff," counters Mathilde. She drinks a sip of wine and turns to her brother. "Take the same year, 1911. Who won the featherweight boxing match between Louis Teyssier and Louis Ponthieu? Go on, take a crack at it. You'll win another louis, a gold one, if you guess correctly."

Paul shrugs to show he's not interested in boxing and hasn't a clue.

"What about you, Papa?"

"I never bet money."

Mathilde drains her glass, smacks her lips, and announces, "It was Louis Ponthieu, whose real name was Louis de Reygnier-Ponthieu. The intrepid Louis Teyssier, better known as Little Louis of the Bastille, was well and truly trounced."

She gazes thoughtfully at her empty glass. "That reminds me," she says, "we'll have to stock up on wine from Anjou. It's my favourite."

Then she sighs; she'd like to go to bed. In Paris, her bedroom is upstairs, and it's a whole circus routine to get her up there. Before the war, her father installed a small lift without walls: it disfigures the entrance-hall, works only half the time because the little pests put it out of order, and takes forever to climb – huffing and puffing – three metres, with a clanking of chains that is absolutely hair-raising. And what's more, Mathilde cannot operate it by herself. Someone downstairs must chock the wheels of her chair, then go upstairs to await her arrival and unchock them again, if he or she hasn't fallen asleep in the meantime.

Often, as on this evening, Mathieu Donnay simply carries his daughter upstairs to her bed. He removes her shoes and stockings. Once she has stretched herself out, Mathilde can take care of the rest. She's a born contortionist.

As he massages her feet and ankles, her father tells her, "I ran into Rouvière a little while ago. He'd just been to see you. He told me how well you were looking."

"What else did he tell you?"

"Nothing. That times are hard. That the second round of voting will give us a legislative assembly that won't immediately fall apart. But you? What did you want to talk to him about?"

"Stamps," replies Mathilde.

Mathilde's secretiveness is hardly news to her father, who doesn't let it upset him any more.

"Fancy that. You've been taking an interest in rather a number of things lately. Bicycling, boxing, the wines of Anjou, now postage stamps."

"I'm improving my mind," agrees Mathilde. "You should try it, too. I'm sure you'd be quite unable to tell me the name of a single boat plying between San Francisco and Vancouver in 1898. Or to explain to me what a *favouille* is, or even how the names of foundlings are chosen."

He laughs. "You're pulling my leg. But what does all this have to do with postage stamps?"

"Ah, that's a mite trickier, even for me. You're not going to believe me."

"But of course I'll believe you." And all the while he's busy massaging her tootsies.

"Well, last week I read word by word, line by line, page by page, more than half a catalogue in English, as big as that, to find out which Queen Victoria stamp has one of her two secret names, Penoe."

"What's the other one?"

"Anna."

He smiles; his eyes grow wide and dreamy with nostalgia, as though he'd once been a ruthless tease with a memorable Anna, in his younger days, when he was poor and lived in the Latin Quarter.

"Papa, you're silly when you don't listen to me."

"Then I'm never silly."

"Four whole days it took me!"

It's true. Last week, Mathilde spent four days in the hospital for so-called routine examinations, between which troublesome procedures she indulged in an orgy of philatelic arcana.

"And you found it?"

"Not yet. I'm only up to the letter L in the catalogue. To be precise, I'm in the Leeward Islands, a British colony in the Caribbean, north of Martinique and east of Puerto Rico. You see, they're very instructive, postage stamps."

"Why do you need to know such a thing?"

He has stopped massaging her toes. He's already sorry he asked the question. He knows his Matti (at least he thinks he does) better than anyone else. He knows that once she has gone so far (tonight, to the Leeward Islands), she'll keep on going, and that it's time to heave to. Behind the mocking attitude she affects towards everything, which can get out of hand if she's given a free rein, will always be a lifetime of unshed tears.

"You couldn't invent something like that," replied Mathilde. "And things that cannot be invented are very useful for distinguishing between what's true and what's false. In October, when I went to see Pierre-Marie, if I'd known about this tidbit, I could have shut him up in no time."

She motions to her father to come closer. He sits down near her on the edge of the bed. She wants him to come even closer, to put his arms around her. He puts his arms around her. He, too, smells of lavender water and fine tobacco, but she likes it, it's reassuring.

Looking up at the ceiling, she says, "A history teacher sends a letter to a merchant of Bordeaux wines, a letter that contains this puzzle: What is the place of origin of a stamp that reveals the second secret given name of Queen Victoria? Now Pierre-Marie says right away that the letter's a fake, that the plonk seller sent it to himself."

"You have to compare the handwriting in the two letters."

"I did. They're not alike. But I don't know anything about the history teacher's handwriting, except for this letter. Suppose the plonk seller simply disguised his own?"

Papa thinks about this, with his daughter's cheek resting against his shoulder, and then he says, "You're right, Matti. If your wine merchant isn't up on his stamp lore, then the letter really is from the history teacher and Pierre-Marie is an ass."

At those charming words, Mama knocks on the bedroom door and makes her entrance.

"You haven't even finished your dinner," she chides her husband. "We're sitting around like waxworks, waiting for you so that we can have dessert." And to Mathilde she says,

"What are the two of you cooking up behind my back?" She says this all the time, to exorcise the foolish feelings of guilt and anxiety that torment her simply because her daughter plunged off a stepladder at the age of three.

Later, alone in her bed, on the verge of falling asleep, Mathilde hears shouting downstairs. She thinks she recognizes the voices of her father and Sylvain, but that's not possible, they've never had an argument. She must be dreaming already. The voices grow faint. She watches the flames die down in the fireplace. She dreams of a vast field of yellow wheat, as far as the eye can see. A man is watching her as she draws near him. She hears the crunching of wheat straw beneath her own feet, but now she is surrounded only by flowers, big yellow daisies spreading everywhere, which she tramples underfoot. The man has vanished. The flower stems have grown so thick she can no longer see a thing. She realizes she has made a mistake, she should never have tried to walk across the field like this, they were really sunflowers, now she can clearly see that, sunflowers taller than she is, surrounding her, she's crushing their thick stems with furious kicks, the bruised stems are bleeding a milky liquid, but she will never, she's too weak, she'll never be able, her white dress is all dirty, she'll never be able to . . .

As soon as she opens her eyes in the morning – after dreaming that she won't be able to something or other (which is hardly a new experience for her) and lots of other silliness as well that she no longer remembers – she sees something new in the half-light of the room, sitting on the table where she draws, writes, and sometimes weeps: the very shabby model of a sailing vessel that plied the waters between San Francisco and Vancouver before she was even born, the *Samara*.

Smiling, she lets her head fall back on her pillow. Lord,

she tells herself, her father and Little Louis must have had a merry old time last night.

That afternoon, she sends Sylvain to return the *Samara* to the bar on the Rue Amelot, with a note thanking the former boxer for lending it to her for a few hours, and above all for allowing her father to surprise her once again.

On the way home, Sylvain makes a detour, stopping before the house on the Rue Gay-Lussac where Mariette Notre-Dame stayed in a furnished room with her little son Baptistin in February of 1917.

The landlords remember her well, even though she stayed there only three or four weeks. Her room was on the second floor. She was allowed to use the kitchen to prepare her child's meals. They invited her several times to eat with them, but she always declined the invitation.

According to their description, Mariette Notre-Dame was a very young woman – hardly more than twenty – with big, sad eyes and light hair worn in a chignon. She was rather pretty but did nothing to show herself to advantage. She had just lost her husband in the war, and after telling them this when she first arrived, she never spoke of it again. She was not very talkative. Her hands alone revealed that she was from the country and had worked hard from an early age. She went out only to buy what she needed or to take the child to the Jardin du Luxembourg. Baptistin, whom she called Titou, was eleven months old and already toddling about. Twice Mariette had taken her son and gone out for the day "to see friends". Those were the only times the landlords ever saw her in something other than the grey and black dress she usually wore.

Early in March, she told them she would be leaving soon, saying that her friends had found work for her and would let her stay with them until she could find new lodgings. On the morning she left the house, after insisting on paying for the "inconvenience in the kitchen", she called a taxi for the Gare de l'Est, but did not say which train she was taking or leave any forwarding address, "not having one yet to leave". In any case, she never received mail. The taxi driver roped her trunk on the roof of his car, tucked the bags and suitcases wherever he could, and off she went with her little boy. That was the last they'd seen of her.

Two months later, in May, a letter arrived for her from the Dordogne. The landlords kept it a long time, more than a year, thinking that Mariette Notre-Dame might one day chance to be in the neighbourhood and stop by to see them. Then they decided to open it, and found the official notification of the death of her husband, aged thirty, killed in action. They thought it was very sad, yes, very sad, but since the poor little lady had already been sufficiently informed of her misfortune, the letter had ended up in the kitchen stove.

In the train taking her and Sylvain back to Cap-Breton, Mathilde reaches the letter M in her English stamp catalogue. She slumps heavily against the banquette. She feels vaguely cold, as she always does when her heart beats faster, but it's a good feeling, even better than winning at cards, and she's filled with pride, glad of her own perseverance. As the train rushes along, drawing ever closer to the Landes, she gazes out of the window with an entirely fresh sense of confidence.

Sylvain hasn't seen Bénédicte in six weeks. He's missed her more and more – he's even missed their squabbling. Now they're almost intimidated by each other. "I'd forgotten what a handsome fellow you are!" Bénédicte tells him. And he, great strapping man that he is, he has no idea what to do with himself. He tears off his tie and stiff collar, smooths his reddish moustache with the back of his hand, grins like an utter fool, and looks everywhere but at Bénédicte.

Mathilde is reunited with her cats, who aren't in the least intimidated and are perfectly happy tagging along after her wheelchair. And she rediscovers the taste of the salt air, the view from her windows of the dunes, where Manech kissed her and held her close, desiring, desired, a girl like any other.

On her first night back home, sitting at her real table, in her real bedroom (which thank God is on the ground floor), surrounded by her photographs and her cats, she writes on a sheet of drawing paper:

> *Variant of the number 4 of Mauritius, a blue 2 pence printed in sheets of 12, in 1848. Due to a slip of the engraver's burin, the seventh stamp on the sheet contains the spelling error, which reads PENOE instead of PENCE.*
>
> *Whether in pristine or badly worn condition, these two little pence are today worth a fortune.*

And towards the bottom of the sheet, she writes:

> *A casualty list can be altered. From now on, stick to Captain Favourier's letter. At dawn on Sunday, all five of them are still alive.*

The Mahogany Box

Véronique Passavant
16, Rue des Amandiers
Paris
January 12, 1920

Mademoiselle,

I stopped by on Saturday, the day before yesterday, to see Little Louis and wish him a Happy New Year. He told me about your talk with him, one evening last autumn, and repeated to me more or less what he had told you.

First let me say about the split between me and Kléber Bouquet, the Eskimo we called him, that I wouldn't want there to be any misunderstanding because I loved him truly, with all my heart and soul, and I have suffered greatly from my stubbornness with him. But I was sure that on his next leave we would make it all up again, I never thought to see him killed in the war. To reassure me he would always say he had connections and would never be sent where the fighting was worst, and then it did seem so impossible to me that he should die, and besides there are nights when I still don't believe it and I'm going to tell you why.

This I didn't tell Little Louis because what point is there in causing him more pain, but a woman came to see me early in March in 1917, where I work, and she's the one who told me what I think you have already known for a long time, mademoiselle, and what you didn't want me to tell Little Louis either, this business about Kléber shooting his hand and being sentenced to death.

This woman I mentioned had just come from the combat zone where her own man had been sentenced the same way, with still another three as well, so I suppose your fiancé must have been one of those. The woman told me they weren't shot but taken up to the front line to be killed by the Germans. The rest of what she knew she kept to herself, what she wanted was to find out from me if I'd had news of Kléber or if I'd seen him alive since January, hiding out somewhere or some such thing. I told her absolutely not. You can imagine she didn't believe me and I cannot blame her, for if Kléber were alive to my knowledge I would surely hold my tongue.

Still she did know more than she was saying to be asking me all those questions, so I think she was hoping her own man was still alive, as you are hoping for yours and I for mine. Have I got that right? That must be it, since you came asking questions too, from Little Louis and then later your father woke him up in the middle of the night to grill him again, pretending he didn't know anything, unless you have kept even your own family in the dark.

Now it seems to me we are in the same boat and that we ought to open up a little more, at least to each other. That's what I wanted to say to you. Little Louis told me you cannot walk because you had an accident when you were small, I can see you cannot travel about so readily, poor lady, but at least you can answer this letter, it's surely easier for you to write than for me, without much education as I guess you know by now. But I am not stupid and I would like both of us to put our cards on the table.

Me, it's just a feeling I have, and only sometimes, that my Kléber is still alive. I have no reason, not one, not even the smallest, to doubt he died in January of '17, it's only that woman who got me all confused with her story. What I think is she didn't know if her man was alive or not but she has learned something she's not saying that proves one at least of the prisoners was able to escape. If I have got it right, there were five. To show you I'm being straight with you, I will tell you the one small thing in her story that gives me a spark of hope for Kléber is that there was snow where they were sent to get killed, so I think he had one more chance than the rest to stay alive for he has lived through snow and cold much worse than that. It isn't much, but you must know yourself how hard one clings to anything at all.

Maybe this woman with the Midi accent also came to see you? Please tell me, and if you know more than I do, speak sincerely. I am most anxious to hear from you, so please don't let me wait long. Little Louis told me you were a decent sort. Please don't keep me suffering in suspense.

Véronique Passavant

Mathilde is moved by the grief of this woman, whose situation so closely resembles her own, but, suspicious as ever, she writes back to say that she has no idea what Véronique is talking about, that she will be in Paris sometime during this spring or summer, and they will see each other then.

She writes next to the excellent Madame Paolo Conte in Marseille, encouraging her to get in touch with her "god-daughter by affection", Tina Lombardi, who followed her ill-fated Nino from pillar to post.

While she's at it, she writes to Pierre-Marie Rouvière as well, urging him to find out what coded destination corre-sponded to postal address 1828.76.50 in the zone of operations in January of 1917, but she changes her mind while verifying the number in Madame Conte's letter, and tears up her own.

It's late morning now, and quite chilly.

The window panes of the living room are misted over, so that she cannot see the ocean from the villa. Her cats watch as she consigns the scraps of her letter to the flames in the fireplace.

"To hold one's tongue," she says to them, "now, that is good counsel, for once. Don't you think I'm right to be par-ticularly wary of anyone who gives me such advice?"

Uno couldn't care less. Due's in a quandary. Tertia and Bellissima wander off to take a nap over by the stone statue of the Virgin, a souvenir of a visit Mama and Papa made to Toledo, where, in 1899, on a night of Castilian rapture and in a sudden reflowering of affection, they made Mathilde all in one go.

Bandit and Master Jack alone follow her back to the big table where she often spreads out – while Bénédicte sulks – the letters and sheets of drawing paper that serve neither for drawing nor for happiness but instead fill a large mahogany box with gilded corners, like a sailor's sea-chest. Where Manech ever got the idea to buy such a thing Mathilde just doesn't know, which goes for Mama and Papa's statue of the Virgin as well. People are strange.

Mathilde tosses Véronique Passavant's letter into the box,

closes the cover carefully, so as to let sleeping sorrows lie, and says to Bandit and Master Jack, "If you get down from this table right now, I'll tell you – and only you – a secret." Since the cats don't move a whisker, she adds curtly, "It's a very secret secret." They look at her with expressionless eyes, peculiarly blank and neutral – really, you'd swear they were cat's eyes – and then they saunter together on their velvet paws over to the edge of the table to jump down.

Leaning forward, clutching her wheelchair with one hand and patting Manech's mahogany box with the other, Mathilde lowers her voice to pique the cats' interest.

"This casket contains the story of one of my lives. And you see, I tell it in the third person, exactly as though I were someone else. Do you know why? Because I'm afraid and I'm ashamed of being only me and of not being able to get to the end of it."

The end of what? she then wonders, watched by four imperturbable eyes. She doesn't know. Luckily, the cats seem to have an inkling, for they need no explanation and stroll off to a quiet corner where they can contemplate the passage of time at their leisure.

Leprince Hardward
3, Rue des Dames
Paris
January 25, 1920

Mademoiselle,

Today is Sunday so I can take this time to write to you, it's about your advert in *Bonhomme*. I'm telling you straight out I don't want any money, I'm no lowlife that takes advantage of people's unhappiness looking for their missing loved ones. I went through the whole war in the infantry, except for 1918 when I was in hospital on account of shrapnel wounds in my leg, then they transferred me to the field artillery, which wasn't any better because gunners have it just as bad as regular footsloggers, and now I hear only half as well as I used to, but that's another story.

What I want to tell you is I knew that trench you asked about, except not at the same dates. I was there at the end of November 1916, after the colonial troops had taken it from the Boches, and I don't think you'll mind if I correct you on your mistake here because it wasn't Bingo but Bing au Crépuscule, I remember perfectly the wooden sign the boys before us had nailed to a supporting beam, I can still see it, and the poor devils had written that because in October, when they were digging the tunnels, the sniper fire was probably something terrible around nightfall.

As for the names you listed, if it's the same person, I knew a soldier name of Célestin Poux, not from my regiment, but I do believe there could not have been two like him in that war or it would be common knowledge, and our side would have won or lost a lot sooner. He was the biggest finagler and scrounger I have ever seen, they called him the Terror of the Armies. He would have stolen oats from the horses' feedbags to trade for wine for his platoon, he invented platoons that didn't even exist, he brought the dead back to life so he could strip the field kitchens bare. As you can imagine, his comrades thought the world of him, and was he clever – no one ever saw through him. At Verdun, I heard, he made off with a roast leg of mutton, white bread, wine and liqueurs, an entire supper for some lucky stiffs on the general staff. And he'd answer back as innocent as you please, "It's all a pack of lies."

In '18, in the artillery, I heard him talked about again, at Saint-Mihiel: three cases of tobacco, our army smokes and some milder cigarettes for the Americans. When those cases arrived they held sacks full of sawdust. Célestin Poux, you bet I remember him. He was from the Ile d'Oléron, he had blond hair, blue eyes, and a smile to fool the fiercest quarter-master-sergeant. When he asked you for the time, if you told him, it was just like kissing your watch good-bye.

Anyway, I heard tell of him in Saint-Mihiel in '18, which means he'd already made it safely through an awful lot, and given as he was always the kind to land on his feet, if you look around over by Charentes, I'm sure you'll discover he's still alive, but as for that trench, I wasn't there on the dates you said so I don't know anything, except that the Porridges came in to relieve us around about then, and what with all the confusion, that Célestin must have fleeced them properly.

I hope you find your loved ones, mademoiselle, and if you ever get over my way, don't hesitate to come and see me.

Yours truly,

Adolphe Leprince

Madame Paolo Conte
5, Traverse des Victimes
Marseille
Saturday 31 January, 1920

Dearest Mademoiselle,

I am very upset, I promise you, at answering your letter, I cannot sleep at night over it, what with me being torn between you and my goddaughter Valentina who does not want to hear of me writing to you for any reason at all, and she would not even give me her address for fear I would send it to you. So until she comes to see me again, and now when will that be I wonder, as she had a fit and left me all in a rage on account of I was pushing her too hard, I can do nothing, nothing, only fret and worry myself.

That I am answering you is because I showed your letter to Madame Isola, the friend I told you of who is so sensible and esteemed by all, and she said to me what a pity you poor dear and that I would torment myself to death if I did not tell you how things are. Lying does not pay but costs both pride and peace of mind.

So here it is. I saw Valentina again on Sunday the ninth of this month, after more than a year she had been gone, and it was early in the afternoon, she wore a coat of midnight blue velvet with a beaver collar and matching muff and bonnet, they must have cost an arm and a leg, but certainly they were a Christmas present, she was all chic and pretty and looked happy, cheeks red with the cold outside and her lovely black eyes shining, I was that happy to see her again and kiss her, I had to sit down. To me she brought presents too, a woollen blanket from the Pyrenees, slippers, oranges from Spain, and a little cross of real gold I wear since then around my neck, even at night, oh yes I was happy, you cannot imagine. Then I went and spoiled everything, everything, I gave her your letter of October and I told her I had answered you. She flew up like the mistral into a fury, she told me: "What business is it of yours? Don't you see this upper-class girl with her fancy words, she's only trying to hoodwink us?" And other things I cannot say, very unkind to you, as I am myself most certain that in your letter you are speaking only the truth to her, your poor fiancé had known Ange Bassignano in the war and you wanted to talk to her, that's all.

And so she did not stay with me even one hour and her cheeks were red now with anger not the cold, she walked up and down my kitchen with great clacking of heels, there I was on my chair not wanting to cry, but in the end I could not help myself, and she said to me with her finger under my nose: "Go ahead and cry, Godmother Bianca, it don't help one bit. Do you see me crying? I told you one day I'd blow out the brains of everyone who hurt my Nino. Now have you ever, ever known me to change my mind?"

She so frightened me I could not recognize her face anymore, I could not recognize my goddaughter, I said: "But what are you saying, what are you saying, have you gone mad? How did this lady ever hurt your Neapolitan with his evil star?" She shouted: "I don't give a damn about her, but I got nothing to say to her! That way she can't repeat nothing! I don't want you answering her no more, it's my business, not yours! If she writes again, you just do this!" On that she took the poker to lift the lid on my cookstove and in went your letter that she crumpled up into a ball with a meanness I never I swear did suspect was in her, even when she was fifteen and got on her high horse each time someone tried to tell her a thing or two.

Then she said she had affairs to attend to on the other side of town, she kissed me standing there in the doorway but her heart wasn't in it, I listened to her heels going clackety-clack downstairs, I went to the kitchen window to watch her go off down the pavement, she made me cry she was so small from up above and precious with her beaver collar and her little hat and muff, I do so fear I will never see her again, never.

I take up my letter again this Sunday morning, my eyes cannot take writing so long any more, you must know that by now. Last night it still pained me to think of Valentina and the angry scene she made, but this morning the neighbourhood is full of sunshine, I tell myself that spring will bring her back, I feel better and a great weight is lifted now I have told you the truth. You ask me, in your letter, why I wrote in October of Ange Bassignano: "He died like a dog, probably at the hand of French soldiers." Because it just slipped out, because I cannot imagine he would die except as I saw him live, I know I should not speak of him like this, especially with the cross I wear around my neck, but I cannot help it, I never believed he died attacking the enemy with a bayonet like you see in pictures, he was way too lily-livered for that, he must surely have pulled as usual one of his nasty tricks or done something awfully stupid somewhere and they just shot him for good this time, and of course they wanted to keep it quiet because it would hurt morale and put a stain on the flag.

For Valentina's note I wrote you about also and you ask me to explain, that she had found the trail of her Nino in a sector of the Somme and it "was all over for him," I cannot promise you that is exactly how she said it, but that was her meaning, that it was a closed book and we would talk no more about it, that is in fact what happened those other times she visited, not a word was said of this again.

When my goddaughter comes back to see me, I promise you, dearest mademoiselle, I will tell her the truth too, that I have written you, even if she flies in a rage against me once more, for I know she has a good heart and I will manage to calm her suspicion, you will see she deserved better of life than she got and all the hurt that has been done to her, but that is the lot of everyone, unfortunately.

I send you my kindest thoughts and my best wishes for the New Year, together with Madame Isola and Madame Sciolla.

Yours very truly,

Madame Veuve Paolo Conte, née Di Bocca

Pierre-Marie Rouvière
75, Rue de Courcelles
Paris
February 3

My dear Matti,

I do not approve of the initiative you have taken in publishing that notice in the newspapers. Neither do I approve, even though I understand it, of your father's regrettable indulgence toward you. I took the liberty of telling him so and I want you to know this.

Since our last meeting, I have thought things over very carefully. Although it does seem to me, after all, that mishaps, delays, difficulties in communication, even ill will at one level or another could have allowed this horrendous miscarriage of justice you believe has taken place, I find it even harder to understand what benefit you hope to derive from making this tragedy public. You seem to be behaving as though, against all evidence, you were refusing in some purely visceral way to accept Manech's death. I respect the tenacity of your love for him, and as I am above all your friend, it is not my place to argue against such perseverance. What I have to tell you is something much more simple, and more brutal, I'm sorry to say. You must never forget that despite the presidential pardon, Jean Etchevery is still under sentence of life imprisonment. If by some miracle, by some unheard-of divine reward for your persistence, you were to see him again one day, you would bitterly regret having brought wide public attention to this affair, for he would then be forced into hiding to avoid incarceration for life in a convict prison.

I ask you, I beg you, my dear, whom I know to be so impulsive but so level-headed as well when necessary, to cancel any further publication of that announcement and to observe the greatest caution from now on. Rely on me and on me alone for the truth you seek. You must understand that if a single one of these five men managed to escape, you will represent a danger to him, and this obviously includes Manech. You must also realize that those who participated in one way or another in this injustice have every motive to keep it secret, and can only be your enemies.

I hope I have made myself clear. I send you my love, as I have ever since you were a child.

Pierre-Marie

Mathilde replies that she is no longer a child, that's all.

Olivier Bergetton
Maker of Mechanical Toys
150, Avenue de la Porte-d'Orléans, Paris
Monday, March 15, 1920

Mademoiselle,

I was acquainted with a Corporal Gordes. If he is the man you speak of, it was in the Somme, between Combles and the wood of Saint-Pierre-Vaast. I was a post orderly, and although I belonged to another regiment, I took some letters for him and his infantry section in the autumn of 1916, because it made me sick that their mail was being held up, for reasons I will not mention, except that once again it was because of a piece of stupidity on the part of some NCO. Gordes was a rather tall man, as I recall, with thinning hair, and somewhat sad. I mean that he seemed even sadder than the rest of us, but other than that the corporal was very well thought of.

I shouldn't like to cause you any sorrow – and above all do not send me any reward, I've never been one for that kind of thing – but I do believe he was killed during the period mentioned in your advertisement, because someone who was with me told me, one day in January of '17: "You remember the tall corporal who slipped you his letters? He was killed in a bombardment." But since I never knew the first name of this Gordes, perhaps he isn't the one you're looking for.

Célestin Poux, in any case, absolutely has to be the same one, there couldn't possibly be another like him with that name. We called him Toto the Soldier, or the Pest, or Justa Bit More. All the lice in that war put together can't have sucked as much blood as he did from army supplies. It was in the same sector, during the autumn and winter of 1916, that I knew him. One time, I heard, he bet the fellows in the canteen an entire cauldron of soup that he could make it disappear while they had their backs turned and counted to ten. And before they'd turned around again, he and two pals and the steaming cauldron were gone. Afterwards the cooks said, "Well, of course, we did it on purpose, it was all arranged beforehand." But I don't believe it, and neither do the others who heard this story, because with Célestin, nothing else mattered besides getting grub for his platoon. We'd have all liked to have him looking out for our bellies.

Unfortunately, that's all I can tell you. I wasn't at the place you mentioned in that notice in the magazine *Footsloggers*, and I never heard tell of it. But one thing is certain, if it really is my Célestin you're looking for, even if he hasn't made it home yet, he'll be back some day. If the Boches took him prisoner, that's why they began starving to death and sued for peace. If the poor soul is dead, put a lock on your pantry door all the same.

I send you my regards, mademoiselle, and I will certainly write you if I learn anything new.

Olivier Bergetton

Germain Pire
Investigations of All Kinds
52, Rue de Lille, Paris
Tuesday March 23, 1920

Mademoiselle,

I am not replying to your advertisement in *Le Figaro* expressly to offer you my services, although the great majority of my clients have professed complete satisfaction with my efforts on their behalf.

I simply wish to inform you, free of charge, that last year I numbered among my clients a certain Madame Benjamin Gordes, whose husband, a corporal in the infantry, had been listed as missing at the front in the Somme in January of 1917.

You will understand that as professional discretion prevents me from informing you of the results of my investigation, I can only give you the address of the sole person able to do so, should she agree to this: 43, Rue Montgallet, Paris.

Of course if you feel I may be of any use to you in your own difficulties, please feel free to contact me regarding my schedule of charges.

Yours sincerely,

Germain Pire

Madame Veuve Alphonse Chardolot
25, Rue des Ardoises
Tours
March 28, 1920

Mademoiselle Donnay,

I am the mother of Urbain Chardolot, who was a corporal in 1916, was made sergeant in June of 1918, was wounded in Champagne on the twenty-third of July 1918, and died while being evacuated from the front.

Urbain was our only son. My husband died of grief at the age of fifty-three at the beginning of last year. He survived the death of his adored son by only a few months, leaving me alone.

I think that you too have suffered the loss of a loved one, and that is why you placed a notice in *L'Illustration*, which I do not read, simply because I can no longer bear to read any newspaper for fear I will come across something horrifying. I do not wish to think about the war ever again. A relative showed me your appeal for information, however, and I am writing to you because you mention my son's name there, as well as a time and place he spoke of briefly when he was on leave at the end of January 1917.

Two weeks earlier, on the sixth of January, Urbain had been in a trench on the Somme nicknamed Bingo. They brought up from the rear five French soldiers condemned to death because they'd shot themselves in the hand. These men were tossed, with their arms tied behind their backs, into the area between that trench and the German one. My husband, who was a pharmacist, a sensible man and proud of our army, could not believe this story, and I myself did not wish to hear it. I remember that Urbain shouted, "Your heads are stuffed with lies, you don't understand any more, we lost half our company because of this damned mess!" Later, when he had calmed down, he told us, "You're right, I must have dreamed everything, and also that I saw the five of them lying dead in the snow, except that at least one of them, if not two, was not the person I'd expected to find there."

I know, mademoiselle, that what I am writing to you is terrible indeed, but these are my son's own words. He never mentioned this affair again in front of me. Perhaps he spoke further of it to his father, during that leave or his last one, in March of 1918, but I do not know.

You are doubtless the sister, friend, or fiancée of one of

these condemned men. Believe me when I say that I was tormented by this thought before I decided to write this letter, but I have told you exactly what my son told us. For love of him, I am prepared, if necessary, to confirm my testimony in the presence of witnesses, whoever they might be.

I feel I may embrace you with all my heart, as one who shares your grief.

Rosine Chardolot

Mathilde promises herself to answer this letter soon. But not right away. Hope is swelling so violently inside her, she mustn't lose control of her emotions.

That evening, however, she writes the following on a sheet of drawing paper, while Bénédicte sits sulkily on the bed, waiting to help her retire for the night.

In March 1917, Tina Lombardi questioned only Véronique Passavant, the Eskimo's mistress.

If she had met or even tried to contact Mariette Notre-Dame, the priest in Cabignac would have remembered this, and so would the landlords of the furnished rooms on the Rue Gay-Lussac.

And she did not speak, quite obviously, with the "upper-class girl" whose letters she so cavalierly tosses into a stove in Marseille.

What did she learn, during her search for the truth, that made her fear or hope the Eskimo was still alive?

Urbain Chardolot said: at least one of them, if not two.

*That one, Tina Lombardi has good reason to believe,
is the Eskimo. The second she hopes desperately will turn
out to be her Nino.*

The next day, as soon as she has dressed herself and had her
morning coffee, Mathilde writes, farther down on the page:

*What could serve to distinguish between the Eskimo and
the four others, at Bingo?*

*The wounded hand? For three of them, it's the right one.
For two, the Eskimo and Six-Sous, it's the left.*

*The colour of their eyes? Manech and Six-Sous have
blue eyes. The others have dark eyes.*

*Age? The Eskimo is thirty-seven, Six-Sous is thirty-one,
That Man is thirty, Nino is twenty-six. In Esperanza's
photo, taken in the trench, exhaustion and despair have
made them all look the same age.*

And still farther down:

*Right. The German's boots. And Tina Lombardi was
wrong, the Eskimo was no longer wearing them.*

Madame Elodie Gordes
43, Rue Montgallet
Paris
Sunday April 11, 1920

Dear Mademoiselle,

I was not able to reply to you earlier through lack of time,
for I work all week in a dressmaking shop and at home my
children give me no rest.

As Monsieur Pire has written to you, I was obliged to seek help from him in February of last year so that I could collect my pension as a war widow. My husband Benjamin Gordes was reported missing on January 8 of 1917 at the front in the Somme, that is all I knew until Monsieur Pire took up my case. As I have told you, I have no time for anything, even though I never go to bed until late at night because of all the housework and laundry. It was impossible for me to continue my efforts on my own, so I preferred to sacrifice part of my savings. Luckily Monsieur Pire had not lied to me and my sacrifice was not in vain. Today my husband is officially deceased. He was wounded in the head during an attack and he was killed in a bombardment on January 8 in 1917 at the field hospital where he had been taken for treatment. The hospital register and eyewitnesses, medical orderlies and other wounded men, have sworn to this.

My husband's last leave was back in April of 1916. I do not remember hearing him speak the names of Chardolot, Poux, or Santini, but this is not surprising since he changed regiments in August and perhaps he did not meet them until afterwards. In his letters he spoke only of his children, not of his comrades or the war. I have read over his letters of the autumn and winter of 1916 and I did not see a single name.

That is all, mademoiselle, I cannot tell you any more, save that I am sincerely sorry that your fiancé met with the same fate as my husband.

Very truly yours,

Elodie Gordes

Emile Boisseau
12, Quai de la Râpée
Paris
June 15, 1920

Mademoiselle,

While I was waiting for my turn at the barbershop, I found a copy of *La Vie Parisienne* that was a few months old and I saw your advertisement looking for information. I have no idea what it's worth, but I've got something for you. I knew Benjamin Gordes very well, we were in the same company in 1915 and 1916, before he became a corporal and was transferred to a different regiment. When the war was over, I heard he didn't make it, well of course he wasn't the only one. Anyway, I knew him, although he wasn't a good friend, just someone I'd say hello to whenever we ran into each other somewhere. On the front line all that matters is your own platoon, that's just the way it is, and he wasn't in mine. Besides, he wasn't very gabby. His only real pal was a soldier he'd known before the war, a carpenter like he was, a very easy-going fellow, that one. The two of them stuck together and didn't mix much with the others. Benjamin Gordes was a tall skinny man about thirty years old, with long arms and legs, they called him Biscuit. The other one, he was a bit older but didn't look it, and I never even learned his name, they called him Bastoche, at least in the beginning, because a lot of the fellows in the regiment were from the neighbourhood around the Bastille in Paris, but later he was called the Eskimo, on account of how he'd gone looking for gold in Alaska. Anyhow, they were inseparable, in good times and bad, real pals, but then things started to go wrong, no one knew why.

Well, war can get the better of just about everything, I know. In June of 1916, I came to Paris on leave with the Eskimo and a few others. It's when we got back that I heard they'd had some kind of falling-out. And then things got right out of hand, and quickly too. One evening in a billet they even came to blows. I didn't see it myself, I'd be a liar if I said so, but the Eskimo, who was the heftier of the two, he managed to pin Biscuit on the ground and he shouted at him, "Benjamin, just calm down now, or I won't be responsible for what happens! Whose idea was it, damn it all, why are you blaming me?"

After that they avoided each other, they wouldn't look at each other, and whatever the grudge was between them, it was eating them both up inside. We tried to figure out what was going on, naturally, we even asked the Eskimo, but he just told us to mind our own business. At the end of the summer, Benjamin Gordes was promoted to corporal, he talked to the major and got transferred to another sector of the Somme. He died in '17, I heard, but his old pal didn't wind up any better, in fact he finished worse. He wounded his left hand with another soldier's gun, by accident, he said, and when you knew him, you could believe it, because he wasn't the type to do that on purpose, but they arrested him anyway and a court-martial sentenced him to be shot.

It's a sad story, I know, but I swear on my word of honour that it's true. That's all I can tell you about Benjamin Gordes. I don't know about any of the other people you mentioned with regard to the reward, and I never heard of Bingo whatever-you-call-it. The trenches I saw in the Somme and all over Picardy, they were always called Cemetery Alley, Dead End Street, This Way Out, or The Shells Drop Inn, picturesque maybe, but not too cheery. Anyway, that's how it goes.

If you think my information is worth something, I'll leave any reward up to you. I do a bit of work here and there, mostly selling fish along the dock or unloading barges, but it's not making me filthy rich, so whatever you can send along will be just fine with me. And I have to say, I enjoyed thinking over the old days again, even if they were rotten ones, because when you come right down to it, I have no one I can talk to about them.

Good luck, mademoiselle, and thank you for whatever you can send me.

Emile Boisseau

Mathilde sends two hundred francs and all her gratitude. She is so excited that her hand trembles slightly as she writes on a fresh sheet of drawing paper:

> *A new piece of the puzzle is falling into place.*
>
> *Véronique Passavant walks out on the Eskimo while he is home on leave in June 1916.*
>
> *Benjamin Gordes, called Biscuit, has a fight with this same man when he returns from leave and then arranges to be transferred to another regiment so he won't have to be around him any more.*
>
> *What is his state of mind when he meets him again at Bingo, a man condemned to death? The Eskimo claims they were reconciled. But what if this reconciliation was only a hypocritical gesture, or an expression of momentary pity on Benjamin Gordes's part? What if he took advantage of the situation to satisfy his private grudge?*

In any case, on that snowy Sunday, Benjamin Gordes definitely had some effect on the Eskimo's fate, and there-fore on the fate of the other four as well.

The reason behind their quarrel doesn't seem very hard to guess, but as Little Louis says, "When there's tail involved, there's no knowing."

The Woman on Loan

JULY

The storm breaks over Paris the instant Elodie Gordes, wearing a blue cotton dress, steps out of her apartment building on the Rue Montgallet. She runs through the rain to the car in which Mathilde sits waiting. Sylvain opens the door for her and helps her inside, then hurries off through the rain himself to seek shelter in the nearest bistro.

Elodie Gordes is a timid woman of thirty with a rather pretty face and light hair. Since she lives on the fifth floor, Mathilde's apology for having made Elodie come downstairs is simply a matter of form.

"Oh no, it's nothing," she replies. "The gentleman told me about your unfortunate condition."

Then, nothing else. She sits very straight on the car seat, looking down at her knees, biting her lips with a martyred air. To coax her into opening up a little, Mathilde asks her how many children she has. Five, four of whom are from Benjamin Gordes's first marriage. She adds, "It doesn't make any difference."

She retreats back into her shyness. Mathilde looks through her handbag for the photograph Esperanza gave her of the five prisoners and shows it to her. Elodie gazes with wide eyes at the picture for a good while, her lips parted, slowly shaking her head. The blood has drained from her cheeks. She turns to Mathilde with a frightened look and exclaims, "I don't know him!"

"And just which one is it you don't know?" asks Mathilde. She places the tip of her index finger on the Eskimo. "That one?"

Elodie Gordes shakes her head more vigorously, staring straight in front of her, and suddenly opens the door to get out of the car. Mathilde holds on to her arm and sees her eyes filled with tears.

"Then it's because of you that your husband and his friend Kléber had that quarrel?"

"Let me go..."

But Mathilde won't let her go. "I absolutely must know what happened, don't you understand? They were together in that damned trench, and my fiancé was with them! What happened?" Now she as well is blinded by tears, shouting, "What happened?"

But the other woman keeps shaking her head, without saying another word, already halfway out of the car in the driving rain.

Mathilde lets her go.

Elodie Gordes dashes across the street, stopping at the doorway of her building to turn around. For a few seconds she looks over at Mathilde, who has dragged herself across the seat to the open car door. Elodie walks slowly back, heedless of the storm, with her dress soaked and her hair plastered to her face. In a flat, tired voice she tells Mathilde, "It's not what you think. I'll write it down for you. I'd rather. I'll write you. Have the gentleman come and get my letter Sunday night." She touches Mathilde's cheeks with two wet fingers, and walks away.

That year, in another of her lives, Mathilde has her first exhibition of paintings in a Parisian art gallery. She's obviously a complete unknown, but her papa is not, and one of his business acquaintances is a banker in a great hurry who must think he's in a flower shop at the *vernissage*, for he buys camellias, roses, sunflowers, lilacs, and a whole field of poppies for his office. He compliments Mathilde on her "nice touch", assures her she'll go far, very far, he has "a good nose for such things", he's truly sorry to be in such a rush but he's leaving that very evening for the Riviera, the trunks aren't packed and the train won't wait. She receives more sincere congratulations from the elderly lady who is delighted with the petit fours, because she can hardly remember, even before the war, tasting such delicious ones "in places where they are free of charge". In short, this exhibition can be considered a promising success.

One afternoon out of every three, so as not to have too much of a bad thing, Mathilde has herself driven to the gallery on the Quai Voltaire, where she spends an anguished hour or two studying the people studying her paintings. The expressions of the solitary visitors are so doleful or contemptuous and the murmured remarks of the couples are so mocking that Mathilde wishes she could take everything down, go home, and dream henceforward only of posthumous fame. No one ever leaves the gallery, however, without signing the visitors' book. She even sees some of them wrinkling their brows in concentration as they add a brief comment: "A real talent for floral architecture"; "A youthful Romanticism in the sorrowful implacability of the blues"; or, "I feel as drained as if I'd just returned from an amorous escapade in the country." Still, there were a few who expressed some reservations: "Poor flowers, they never hurt anyone, and now look at them!" Or, "What rubbish!" The owner of the gallery – a Monsieur Alphonse Daudet who did not write *Les Lettres de Mon Moulin* but named his establishment after the book anyway – inks out the harsher comments and claims they are the work of jealous colleagues.

It's amid this reassuring and reverent atmosphere, one afternoon in July, that Mathilde reads a letter Sylvain has brought over from the Rue La Fontaine. The letter is from Sister Marie of the Passion of Christ, in Dax. Daniel Esperanza is dead. He was buried in a cemetery near the hospital. He no longer had any friends or relatives. The only other mourner at the funeral, besides the priest and Sister Marie, was Madame Jules Boffi, the widow of his former corporal. It is Madame Boffi who was given the dead man's few personal belongings and mementoes, but several days before his death, he had picked out a photograph to be sent to Mathilde which she now holds in her hand, a photo taken in his youth, one day at the beach, when he wore his hair and moustache à la Max Linder, a photo he hoped would show her that he wasn't boasting when he said he'd once been a fine figure of a man.

While he waits for her, Sylvain stands with his hands in his pockets, craning his neck to study the paintings, although he knows each and every square inch of them even better than she does. Mathilde tells him she doesn't feel like going home for dinner, she'd rather go with him to some restaurant in Montparnasse and afterwards have one of those white rum drinks that make your hair curl. Sylvain tells her that's the spirit, it'll do her good, and himself as well, because it's too bad she has agreed to sell off her flowers like some street vendor; it makes his heart ache to see them go, especially the poppy field, et cetera.

Well, this evening they have a choice artistic subject for discussion, so to hell with yearnings and regrets.

Elodie Gordes
43, Rue Montgallet
Paris
Wednesday, July 7

Mademoiselle,

I thought it easier for me to write you and here I have started this letter over a good three times now. I do not understand how what hurts me so much in the telling will be of use to you, or what it has to do with the death of your fiancé, but you say it is vital and I felt such sorrow in you, the other day, I would be ashamed to make you suffer even more by remaining silent. Only I beg of you, do not speak to anyone of what I will tell you, as until today I have not revealed these things to another soul.

In that photo of those bound soldiers I was much distressed to see Kléber Bouquet, but when I said I did not know him it was only half a lie. Before the war, for more than three years my husband spoke often of him, as they shared the money they earned every Saturday at the open-air market where they hawked their furniture, but I never saw him. I did not even know his name, for my husband called him the Eskimo.

Now, so that you will understand me, I must speak of certain matters, and these above all I beg you to keep secret because the happiness of the children is at stake.

When he returned from military service Benjamin Gordes was going on twenty-three years of age and was hired by a cabinet-maker in the Faubourg Saint-Antoine, where there was a book-keeper working, a little older than he was, Marie Vernet. He grew fond of her as the days went by but he had no hopes on her account, she had been living with a married stockbroker for four years, who could not or would not be divorced, and she already had three children by him, not acknowledged of course. This was in the spring of 1907. A few months later Marie Vernet was in the family way again so her employer sent her away as others before him had done.

In October of 1908 Benjamin rented a small workshop on the Rue d'Aligre and set up for himself. He slept on a mattress right there in the shop, with all the furniture he made around him. That is where Marie Vernet came looking for him in need of work in January or February of 1909. She was now quit of her stockbroker, for he was murdered outside his own front door one day, they never learned who did it, probably someone he had driven to ruin. Benjamin married her in April and adopted the four children as his own. He always spoke of her to me with affection, but Marie Vernet was never one to have any luck for long. Married on Saturday, she was rushed to the hospital the following Wednesday with acute appendicitis and expired that night, just like my own mother when I was sixteen.

As for me, before my path crossed Benjamin's, I had not

had much luck either. When my mother died my only relative was an uncle, her brother, but there had been a falling-out between them and they had not been close for years. He was the one who took charge of me. I left school two years short of the *baccalauréat* to work in the haberdashery he ran with his wife on the Rue Saint-André-des-Arts. I had a tiny room across the courtyard behind the shop. Except for going to buy bread from the baker nearby, this courtyard was almost my whole world for a few months. But you do not need to go far, sometimes, to find what fate has in store for you. In the spring of 1909, about the time when Benjamin was left a widower with four children, I met a mason hired for some work on the stairwells in the building. I was seventeen, he was twenty. He was forward, had a way with words, whereas I was always painfully shy, but he was sweet to me, and it was the first time I had ever felt at ease with someone. I did not hold out against him long.

He would come to my room on the sly and leave before dawn. Twice we went walking of an evening along the Seine. One Sunday he showed me a Paris I did not know, the Champs-Elysées, the Trocadéro, and we went up the Eiffel Tower. Another Sunday I waited for him at Place Saint-Michel, he had managed to borrow a car, he took me out to the countryside over by Poissy. We stopped at an inn for lunch, in Juziers, and that afternoon we rented a boat to row over to a pretty little island, all green out in the middle of the river. This was already the end of our affair. It had not lasted two months. I told him on that island that I was going to have a baby, he brought me back to Paris, and I never saw him again.

My aunt and uncle were not particularly kind or unkind to me, they took me in because they were my only family and someone had to. After my little Hélène was born, I think they were relieved that I wished to go off on my own. The doctor who attended me at the Hôpital Saint-Antoine helped me find employment with room and board. While I was taking care of my baby, I was to look after the children of Benjamin Gordes, too. He had entrusted them up to that time to the care of his sister Odile in Joinville-le-Port, six years older than he, a confirmed old maid who could not abide them any longer. So I went to live where I still am today, in the apartment on the Rue Montgallet that Benjamin had rented for himself and Marie Vernet. It has a dining room, a kitchen, two bedrooms and a toilet. I slept with the children in the biggest bedroom, overlooking the street, Benjamin Gordes in the other.

Everyone who knew him will tell you my husband was a good and tenderhearted man, close-mouthed because he had taken some hard knocks in his time, without much education to speak of but a master at woodworking. A real artist, and this is but the plain and simple truth of it. When I came to work for him he was only twenty-five years old but already was taken for much older, because he was sober in conduct, temperate in all things, and thought only of the children. Now I think this love for them sprang from a vague foreboding that he would never have children of his own, which is how things did turn out.

Marie Vernet's four little ones, Frédéric, Martine, Georges and Noémie, then aged two to six years old, adored their father, it was all smiles and jubilation when he came home in the evening from the workshop on the Rue d'Aligre, and tears when he stayed out late now and again on a Saturday with his friend the Eskimo and I wished to put them to bed before his return. Benjamin loved my baby Hélène just as much as his four, and her first word, in her cradle, was of course "Papa". During the six months I cared for his household before he asked me to marry him, we were already living practically as man and wife though we weren't sharing the same bedroom. I was the one who received the weekly house-keeping money and listened to all his troubles, the one who went out walking with him and the children on Sunday, and I was the one who did his laundry, prepared his breakfast and his lunch box. We were married on September 10, 1910, and Benjamin adopted Hélène as his child. Since he was somewhat ashamed of remarrying so soon and the company of others has always been a torment to me, we invited only his sister and my aunt and uncle to the town hall. As it happened, none of them came, so we had to pull our witnesses in off the street and give them a tip.

As I knew even then, the next four years were the best years of my life. I will not claim that I felt for Benjamin the longing that threw me into the arms of my mason, but I loved him ever so much more, we were in agreement on all things, we had lovely children, and easily enough to live on, we made plans for a holiday by the sea, which neither of us had ever seen. At eighteen, nineteen, most girls have other dreams, but not me, nothing made me feel safer than the routine and even the monotony of our daily lives.

As I write this the children have been long abed, today is Friday, making it two nights ago that I began this letter. I feel worry and trepidation as I come to what you desired to know all in an instant, that day of the thunderstorm, like a bolt from on high. No doubt I cannot help putting off the telling, but there is something else too, I am trying to make you understand that ours was a folly like many another which would never have come to pass without the war. The war destroyed everything, even Benjamin Gordes, and finally the Eskimo, and simple good sense, and me.

In August of 1914, grief-stricken as I was knowing he might never return, I was relieved to learn from his first letter that my husband had met up in his regiment with his friend from the furniture market. He had always spoken of the Eskimo with a fondness I felt in him for no other. He admired him for his steadiness, his cheerfulness, his air of adventure, and most likely he felt admired in return for his skill as a cabinet-maker. One proof of how deep this friendship went was that when mobilization came, Benjamin, as the father of five children, should have been assigned to the territorial army and remained back at the home front to repair roads or train tracks, but no, he insisted on going off with the rest of his regiment. He told me: "I would rather be with the Eskimo than with some lot of old men who'll get bombarded anyway. As long as we can be together, I'll not feel so afraid." Perhaps it gnawed at his conscience, I admit, to be excused for children that were his in name only. That was him all over, more's the pity.

I will not dwell on what those terrible years were for me, you have certainly lived through the same heartache. Apart from the children, my days were given over to waiting. Waiting for a letter, waiting for the official daily bulletin, waiting for the next day to come so that I might spend it waiting. Benjamin had never much taken to writing, for he stupidly feared to make a fool of himself, still he did not ever let me go long without news, though of course we were at the mercy of the post office. I already told you he did not speak of the war to me, which is true, but the longer the war lasted, the more sadness and discouragement I could feel in his letters. His spirits lifted only when he mentioned the

Eskimo, and that is how I learned his name. "Yesterday I went with Kléber to see a show, some entertainment for the troops, we laughed heartily." "I must go, duty calls, Kléber and I take on two unwary grenadiers in a game of manille." "Remember, in your next package, to send some shag for Kléber, always puffing away on that pipe of his." "Kléber has it on good authority, we will soon be going on leave."

Leave. This word came up again and again. In fact, Benjamin's first leave was after the fighting in Artois, at the end of July 1915. That made it almost one year to the day he had been gone. To say he was a changed man does not come close, for he was not the same man at all. Doting on the children one moment, shouting at them the next for making too much of a racket. And then he would sit silent at the table after meals for a long time, finishing up his bottle. He hardly ever touched wine before the war and now he had to have his bottle at noon and suppertime. One day during that week at home he went over to his workshop and returned after nightfall unsteady on his feet and smelling of drink. I had put the children to bed. That was the evening I first saw him cry. He could not stomach any more of the war, he was afraid, he had a terrible sense that if he did not do something, he would never come home again.

The next day, sober once more, he held me in his arms, he told me: "Don't be angry with me, I've taken to drink like some others because out there it's the only way I can keep going. I never thought to see the day I would do such a thing."

He left. His letters grew sadder still. I found out later that his regiment was in Champagne during the autumn and winter, and outside Verdun in March of 1916. He came home on leave on April 15, I remember it was a Saturday. He was more thin and pale than ever, with something dead, yes, something already dead in his eyes. He had stopped drinking. He saw the children growing up without him, he tried to take an interest in them but they quickly wore him out. He told me, in our bed where he no longer felt desire for me, lying in the dark: "This war will never end, the Boches are being mass-acred and so are we. You don't know what courage is until you see the English fight, but their courage is not enough, nor is ours, nor is the enemy's. We are drowning in mud. It will never end." Another night, when I lay huddled close to him, he said: "Either I desert and they catch me or I need another child. When you have six children, they send you home for good." After a long silence, in a changed voice, he said: "You understand?"

Do you understand? I feel sure you understand what he meant. I am certain you are already laughing and making fun of me as you read this.

Please excuse me. That was a foolish thing to say. You are not laughing at me. You would like your fiancé to come home, too.

That night, I told Benjamin he had gone mad. He fell asleep. Me, I could not. He came back to it the next day and the others as well, whenever the children could not hear us. He would say: "You will not be deceiving me, because I am the one asking you to do it. And what difference can it make since the other five are not mine in any case? Would I want such a thing if my blood were strong enough to give you the sixth child? Would I want this if I were free of all ties and a fatalist like Kléber?"

He had said the name: Kléber.

One afternoon we were outdoors, we had left the children for an hour with the downstairs neighbours, the two of us were walking along the Quai de Bercy, and he told me: "You must promise me before I go. With Kléber, it doesn't bother me. All I can see is that then I would be out of it and we would be happy, as though the war had never been."

The day he left, I went with him to the station. At the Gare du Nord he kissed me through the bars of the gate, he looked at me, I had the terrible feeling I did not know him any more. He said: "I understand, you feel you no longer know who I am. Yet it really is me, Benjamin. But I cannot survive any longer, save me! Promise you'll do it. Promise."

I nodded to say yes, I was weeping. I watched him trudge away in his uniform, a dirty blue colour it was, carrying his helmet and haversacks.

I am telling you about my husband, and about myself, not about Kléber Bouquet. And yet it was Kléber who told me, later on, what I would come to believe: you take what comes, when it comes, you do not struggle against the war, or against life, or against death, you pretend, and the only master of this world is time.

Time only made Benjamin's obsession worse. What he could no longer bear was how the war went on and on. All he spoke of in his letters was the month when Kléber would be on leave. All he wanted to know from me was what my best days would be to conceive a child.

I wrote him: "Even if it takes, there would still be eight or nine months to wait, the war will be over by then." He wrote back: "What I need is hope. If I could find reason to hope again for eight or nine months, that would already be something." And Kléber told me: "When we were in Artois, Benjamin lost heart to see all those dead bodies, the horrible wounds, and the butchery of Notre-Dame-de-Lorette and Vimy, across from Lens. Poor Frenchmen, poor Moroccans, poor Boches. They tossed them into carts, one after another, as though they had never been anything at all. And one time there was a fat fellow up in a cart packing in the corpses, arranging them so they would take the least amount of space, and he walked all over them. So Benjamin yelled at him, calling him every name in the book, and this man jumped on him and they fought rolling around on the ground like dogs. Maybe Benjamin had no heart left for war, but he had courage enough to tangle with a big lout trampling on the bodies of fallen soldiers."

Mademoiselle, I do not know if I am making clear to you what I mean, that nothing is ever black or white, because time turns everything to grey. Today, Sunday, July 11, having written this letter by fits and starts, I am no longer the same person I was last Wednesday when I was so afraid to speak to you of these matters. Now I tell myself that if my memories can help you, the pain they cost me is a small price to pay. To be frank, there is something for me in this as well, I am no longer ashamed, it is all as one to me.

Kléber Bouquet arrived on leave in June of 1916. On June 7, a Monday, he left a note in my mailbox saying he would come by the following afternoon and if I did not want to see him, he would understand, I had only to hang a coloured cloth in a window facing the street. The next morning I took the children to their Aunt Odile in Joinville-le-Pont, telling her merely that I had some things to attend to and might be busy for a few days.

At around three o'clock in the afternoon, watching from the window of my bedroom, I saw a man stop on the pavement across the street and look up at my building. He was in light-coloured summer clothing, wearing a boater. We looked at each other for a few moments, stock-still, both of us, and I could not bring myself to give him the slightest sign. Finally he crossed the street.

I did not open the door until I heard his footsteps reach our landing, then I went to the dining room. He came in, taking off his straw hat, almost as ill at ease as myself, saying simply: "Hello, Elodie." I replied hello. He closed the door, came into the room. He was as Benjamin had described him to me: a robust man with a placid face, a frank look in his eyes, with brown hair and moustache, and the large hands of a carpenter. The only thing missing from the portrait was his smile, but this was quite beyond him, while as for me, I leave you to imagine. We surely seemed like two foolish actors at a loss for their lines. I have no idea how, after a few seconds when I no longer dared look him in the face, I was able to say: "Do sit down, I've made some coffee."

In the kitchen my heart was pounding, my hands were shaking. I brought out the coffee. He was sitting at the table, he had placed his boater on the sofa where my sister-in-law Odile sleeps when she stays with us. It was a hot day but I did not dare open the window for fear we might be seen from the building next door. I said: "You may take off your jacket if you'd like." He thanked me, he hung his jacket on the back of his chair.

We drank our coffee sitting across from each other at the table. I could not bring myself to look at him. Like me he did not want to speak of Benjamin or the front, which would naturally remind us of him. To relieve our embarrassment he recounted his younger days in America with his brother Charles, who had stayed behind there, and also his friendship with Little Louis, who had been a boxer and now owned a bar where he staged Seltzer-bottle fights with his customers. I looked up just then and saw his smile, it was childlike and comforting, this smile truly did change him wonderfully.

Next he asked me if he could smoke a cigarette. I went to fetch him a saucer for an ashtray. He smoked a Gauloise bleue. He was silent now. We could hear children playing outside. After only a few puffs he put out his cigarette in the saucer. Then he stood up and said in a gentle voice: "It was a ridiculous idea. But we can lie to him, you know, pretend we did. Maybe it will give him some peace of mind out in the trenches."

I did not answer. Still I could not look him in the face. He took up his boater from the sofa. He said: "Leave a message for me with Little Louis, Rue Amelot, if you wish to speak with me before I go back." He went towards the door. I stood up as well, I was there before him to keep him from leaving. After a moment, when I looked him finally straight in the eye, he pressed me against his shoulder, his hand was in my hair, we stood like that without a word. And then I pulled away from him, I went back into the dining room. Before he had arrived I had tried to prepare the bedroom, by this I mean to remove whatever might remind us of Benjamin, but I had given up this idea and did not wish to go with him into that room or the children's bedroom.

Without turning around, I took off my dress by the sofa and everything else as well. As I did this he kissed the back of my neck.

That evening he took me to a restaurant on Place de la Nation. He smiled at me across the table and I felt that nothing was quite real, that I was not truly myself. He told me of a prank he had played with Little Louis on a stingy customer, I was not listening carefully to what he said, too busy looking at him, but I laughed to see him laughing. He told me: "You should laugh more often, Elodie. The Inuit, the people we call Eskimos, they say when a woman laughs a man should count the teeth she shows, for he will take the same number of seals on his next hunt." I laughed again, but not long enough for him to count on more than five or six in the bag. He told me: "No matter, we'll order something else, I never did like seal."

Walking me home in the darkness of the Rue de Sergent-Bauchat, he slipped an arm around my shoulders. Our steps echoed in an empty world. No suffering anywhere, no tears, no mourning, no one anywhere or any thought for tomorrow. On the front step of my building his large hands were holding mine, his boater was tipped back on his head, he told me: "If you asked me to come up it would make me happy."

He came up.

The following afternoon I went to his place, on the Rue Daval, a room beneath the eaves. His workshop was down in the courtyard.

The day after that, Thursday, he came back to my flat for lunch. He brought red roses, a cherry tart, his trusting smile. We ate our meal naked, after making love. And we made love all afternoon. He was taking the train in the morning. He had told the truth to the woman he had lived with before the war, and she had left him, taking all her belongings I had pretended not to see the day before. He said: "These things always work out in the end." Time ... I do not know if I loved him, if he loved me, outside of the laughable interlude I have described to you. Today I remember the last time I saw Kléber. He was on the landing just about to go downstairs. I stood at my door. He tipped his boater, he smiled, his voice was so low it was almost a murmur, he said: "When you think of me, show him many seals. You'll bring me luck."

I believe you understand what followed, at least what

Benjamin made of those three days, since you asked me in the car, in the pouring rain, if I was the reason they quarrelled. They quarrelled because we are people, not things, and no one, not even the war, can change that.

I did not get pregnant. Flying in the face of everything, Benjamin was stubbornly jealous, or he became that way. He must have pushed Kléber to the limit and so heard truths that were unbearable. And once again, time did its work. Benjamin's questions in his letters, after he learned he had gained nothing in lending me to his friend, were like a hail of bullets: how and where I had undressed, had it upset me to be possessed by another, how many times during those three days, in what position, and above all, aching, throbbing, that obsession with finding out if I'd shared his pleasure. Yes, I had shared it, from the first time to the last. I can certainly tell you: that had never happened to me before. My mason? I had naïvely imagined I felt the woman's share of it, less than what one finds stroking oneself in bed. Benjamin? To please him, I would pretend.

The hour is late, the gentleman who was with you will come for this letter. I think I have told you everything. I never saw Benjamin again, I never saw Kléber again, and in 1917 I found out by chance, which makes such a bad job of things, that he was not ever going to come home either. Now I work, I raise my children as best I can. The two oldest, Frédéric and Martine, help me as much as they are able. I am twenty-eight years old, I wish only to forget. I trust in what he said, the man of my interlude: the only master of us all is time.

Adieu, mademoiselle.

Elodie Gordes.

Mathilde rereads this letter twice on Monday morning, after having read it twice the night before, when Sylvain brought it to her. On the back of the last page, which is blank, she writes:

Adieu?
We'll see.

Elodie Gordes
43, Rue Montgallet
Paris
Thursday, July 15

Mademoiselle,

I was much moved by your understanding and your words of comfort. The questions you ask me are more than a little confusing, but still I will do my best to answer them.

I did not know that my husband ran into Kléber again in his new regiment and patched up his quarrel with him. His last letter is from New Year's Day of 1917. If he had seen Kléber again before that date he would certainly have written me so.

I did not know that Kléber was killed in the same sector as my husband and at about the same time.

When I said I heard of Kléber's death "by chance, which makes such a bad job of things", I did not mean the woman who lived with Kléber and left him because of what happened between us. I don't know anyone named Véronique Passavant. I learned of his death through the woman who runs the bakery on the Rue Erard, the biggest gossip in the neighbourhood. One April day in 1917 she told me: "That pal of Monsieur

Gordes, the one who hawked furniture and was called the Eskimo, the Boches have done for him too. I got it from my nephew who hangs about in that bar Little Louis has on the Rue Amelot."

If Kléber wrote to Little Louis that he and my husband were friends again, I am glad of it, and I am certain that this could not be a false reconciliation, for they were neither of them false-hearted or sly.

Benjamin would never ever in any way have taken advantage of a "sudden opportunity" to revenge himself on Kléber. Anyone knowing them both would understand that is just impossible.

On the contrary, whether they were reconciled or not, I am certain Benjamin would have helped his friend and done everything in his power to save him.

As for your question that bewilders me about their shoes, yes, I do think they could have worn each other's. My husband was tall but Kléber almost matched him. If I had it in my heart to laugh, I swear to you that when I read that part of your letter, the neighbours would have heard me surely.

I think I have told you everything about the results of Monsieur Pire's investigations. However, I was very happy to telephone him today from where I work to tell him he may give you all the information he gathered about my husband's death.

Please believe me, mademoiselle, I hope you find what you are looking for even though I cannot understand what that could be. With all my sympathy,

Elodie Gordes

Germain Pire
Investigations of All Kinds
52, Rue de Lille, Paris
Saturday July 17, 1920

Mademoiselle,

Following our conversation yesterday in the art gallery on the Quai Voltaire, I studied the file on Benjamin Gordes very carefully.

As I told you, I did not personally conduct the inquiry into this matter, but my associate, who in this case was my brother Ernest, took scrupulous notes on all the evidence he was able to collect. As you can easily understand, our efforts at the time were intended only to prove the fact of Corporal Benjamin Gordes's death, nothing more, and our investigation was limited to this end.

Nevertheless, I am able to shed some light on several points of interest to you.

On Monday the eighth of January in 1917, the French field hospital at Combles was situated in half of a two-storey building at the north of the village, near a rail line laid down by military engineers. The other half of this building was occupied by the British. This place had already suffered extensive damage from both the enemy's artillery and ours, during the offensives of 1916. The bombardment on that day, between eleven o'clock in the morning and two in the afternoon, caused part of the second floor, on the French side, to collapse. The death toll, in the ruins and near vicinity, was thirteen, including both soldiers and hospital personnel.

Lieutenant Jean-Baptiste Santini, a medical officer, does in fact appear on the list of those killed.

Shortly before the bombardment began that morning, Corporal Benjamin Gordes had arrived at the hospital, along with others wounded in the violent fighting at the front line. He had a head injury, which is attested to by the admissions register, and was due to be evacuated to a hospital in the rear. His body had remained unidentified until our investigation, and his identity was established thanks to the testimony of the survivors we were able to locate and interview. There are three of them: a nursing sister of the Order of Saint-Vincent-de-Paul and two wounded men who saw Gordes before the collapse of the building.

The detail about which you questioned me yesterday and which had gone clean out of my head, if indeed it was ever there, which I doubt because I would have remembered it, is this: Corporal Benjamin Gordes, as all three witnesses confirm, was wearing German boots. He wore them in the trench for extra warmth, and had been wearing them when the sudden attack began.

I cannot help wondering about this point, in fact I wonder if you would help me out in this instance. You wanted me to assure you that Corporal Benjamin Gordes was indeed wearing German boots that day – but how did you know this in the first place?

I still believe, mademoiselle, that you should be more open with me. Who knows if I might not speedily solve the problem you prefer to keep to yourself? I can find absolutely anyone. I've had a great deal of practice. If you're worried about my fees, that matter could be quickly settled. As I told you, I'm enormously fond of your painting. Since a melancholy black dot appended to its title card tells me the field of poppies has already been sold, I would be content with the mimosas by the lake, the canvas with that poplar whose trunk bears the letters MMM. You see that nothing escapes my notice.

My expenses as well, of course. But I eat very little, seek modest lodgings, drink only water, and tip quite sparingly.

Think about it.

Even if you don't think about it, please believe that I congratulate you sincerely on your talent and will follow your career with interest.

I will long regret not having that field of poppies to brighten my life.

Germain Pire

He's a sprightly little man with lively eyes, thinning but carefully smoothed hair, a moustache like a circumflex accent, and decidedly old-fashioned taste in clothes. In the middle of the summer, Monsieur Pire is wearing a frock coat, a stiff collar, a large, floppy bow tie, a bowler hat, and white spats. Perhaps the artistically flowing tie is intended to give this array a final Bohemian touch. In his youth, he confesses with just the right amount of wistfulness, he had himself "dabbled in painting". As an amateur, naturally.

At the far end of the narrow art gallery, he sits down facing Mathilde, so close that their knees almost touch. Producing a small, worn notebook that has clearly seen better days, he writes down the name and birth date of Tina Lombardi, as well as the list of all the places where someone might have seen her over the last three years: Marseille, Toulon, La Ciotat, a brothel on the road to Gardannes.

"Well now," he remarks, with a saucy twinkle in his eye, "here's an investigation that will make a change from wartime tragedies. But don't worry," he adds immediately, "I shan't be sampling the wares myself. I never mix business with pleasure."

As a reward for his efforts, if they are crowned with success, Mathilde will give him a painting, but under no circumstances can it be the mimosas, which are there only to be seen and which she intends to keep for herself. He rises and makes another tour of the premises, peering through his pince-nez and sighing heavily in front of each canvas. After some indecision, he finally selects a bank of Parma pink hydrangeas against a background of pines.

His expenses as well, of course.

As he is leaving, he tells Mathilde, "Perhaps you will feel more confidence in me when I've located that unsavoury woman for you. Why don't you explain frankly what this is all about?"

Mathilde replies that she intends to keep that for herself too.

He's already on the pavement, standing just outside the gallery's front door. "I'll show you what a good sort I am," he says. "At no extra cost to you in flowers, I'll take my cue from your newspaper advertisement and find that soldier, Célestin Poux, for you as well."

Mathilde can't very well do less than put him on the right track. "As far as I know, if he's still alive, he's about twenty-five years old, he has blond hair and blue eyes, and he comes from the Ile d'Oléron. He was in the same company as Benjamin Gordes."

Monsieur Pire writes all this down, leaning his old notebook against the gallery's plate-glass window. Leaving his pencil in the notebook, he wraps a rubber band around the whole thing.

"Your hydrangeas are as good as blooming in my home even as we speak, young lady," he says. To show how determined he is, he pats the top of his bowler with the flat of his hand, shoving it down almost to his eyebrows.

On another evening, Véronique Passavant comes to see Mathilde at the house on the Rue La Fontaine. The Eskimo's sweetheart is indeed the fine specimen Little Louis had described. Wearing a dainty straw hat trimmed with a whisper of azure tulle that matches her dress, she sips shyly at her glass of port, intimidated by her surroundings, perhaps, as well as by an infirmity of which she had been aware beforehand but that she now sees with her own eyes. Luckily, her uneasiness does not last long.

The woman who came to question her at the shop where she works, in March of 1917, did not give her name. She was young and pretty, albeit somewhat common, a brunette with dark eyes. She was wearing a skirt and coat short enough to reveal her shapely calves, and the sort of large-brimmed hat favoured by women confident of their allure. She spoke rapidly, with a certain suppressed vehemence; her accent showed her to be from the Midi.

Her interest in the five condemned prisoners was limited to her own man and Kléber Bouquet. She never once mentioned any of the others. She kept repeating, "I beg of you, don't lie to me. If your man has contacted you, tell me so. They're in hiding together. I'll get them out of this fix, the two of them." She seemed certain that the Eskimo had survived. "Have you any proof?" Véronique had asked. The other woman had replied, "As good as." She said of the second survivor, "According to what I've heard, it must be my man. But he was in bad shape, and I hate to think what might have happened to him."

And then, without bothering to wipe away the tears, she had wept, her weary face bent towards the floor, there in the storeroom at the back of the shop, where Véronique had taken her unexpected visitor. When she finally realized she would not obtain even the slightest scrap of hope from Véronique, she had shouted, "If you're keeping something back because you don't trust me, then you're a lousy bitch, no better than the bastards who did this!" And with that, she'd left.

Now, in the morning room so cheerily decorated by Mama, it is Véronique Passavant who has started to cry.

"If Kléber were alive he'd have let me know somehow, I'm sure of it. In '17, because of that madwoman, I got to imagining all sorts of things, I waited and waited, but three and a half years . . . It's impossible, she put ideas in my head that were just as crazy as she was."

She dabs at her eyes with a little white handkerchief and tells Mathilde, "Your fiancé would have found a way to let you know, don't you think, if he'd still been alive these past three and a half years?"

Mathilde, who isn't lying, gestures with her hands to show that she simply doesn't know.

She does not want to talk about Manech's confused state of mind when he was taken to Bingo. That's not something that would have prevented her from finding him, on the contrary, after Esperanza's revelations, her first thought had been to make inquiries in all the hospitals, both civil and military. There were more than thirty soldiers who had been neither identified nor claimed by their families after the armistice and who had lost either their memories or their minds. Ten of these thirty or so men were around Manech's age. Seven of these ten had brown hair. Three of these seven had blue eyes. But none of these three had lost a hand or an arm in the war.

Sylvain, who had gone anyway to Châteaudun, Meaux, and Dijon to see these last three men, had taken dispiritedly to calling Mathilde's initiative "Operation Dwindling Hope", until she'd lost her temper one night and pounded on the table while the crockery danced.

Still, the hospitals hadn't completely exhausted that line of inquiry. What if Manech had been taken prisoner, suffering from amnesia, and been cared for after the war by some kind people in Germany? And what if Manech, having recovered his wits, were still afraid to come forward, for fear of implicating his parents or Mathilde if he were to be recaptured? And what if Manech, with or without his memory or his mind, had wandered in a daze, famished, until he'd finally found refuge somewhere – and another Mathilde?

She tells Véronique that even if she has no chance of ever seeing her fiancé again, she wants to know what happened to him. Because what transpired between those two enemy trenches on that snowy Sunday is all that matters to her now. As for everything else, she'll make the best of it, she doesn't feel that it's important, or even quite real.

Her wheelchair, for example. That's not a reason anyone should feel sorry for her, in fact she often forgets it altogether. She gets around the way she has grown used to getting around, so she thinks no more about it than Véronique does about her legs. And when she does think about her wheelchair, it's bound up with all her memories of Manech.

Other things, ordinary daily routines, they don't interest her. Still less whatever interests everyone else. She has no idea what's going on in the world, she doesn't even know if there's a new President of the Republic, since the one whose name she can't remember fell from a moving train, in the middle of the night, in his pyjamas. Is that really true?

Véronique manages a faint smile and a brief nod, and her black curls bounce softly beneath the rim of her straw hat.

Later, when twilight is fading in the windows, she says to Mathilde over her second glass of port, "I'd like to tell you what made me break with Kléber, but he had me swear I'd never breathe a word."

Mathilde answers in the same tone, almost in the same slangy Parisian accent, "Mustn't talk about it, if you promised not to." And adds, in a more serious voice, "Anyway, I already know. I'm sure you can guess from whom?"

Véronique stares at her with big dark eyes, then looks away and nods again, with the slight pout of a scolded child.

"It didn't help me discover much of anything, either," admits Mathilde with a sigh. "You see, I've got too much imagination sometimes. I'd be perfectly capable of making a huge fuss over a pair of boots."

Véronique doesn't bat an eyelash. She takes a ladylike sip of her drink, with a faraway look in her eyes. "I feel so at ease with you," she says. "If it were up to me, I'd sit here forever."

But it will soon be time to leave this fool's paradise, and three days later, Mathilde is plunged into a hell darker than any she has known since she first learned of Manech's death.

The exhibition of her paintings is over, the bags are packed for her return to Cap-Breton with Sylvain, and just as she is about to sit down at the table for her last meal with the family – no, I don't hate you but how I'd like to strangle a few of you! – she receives a telephone call from Pierre-Marie Rouvière. The telephone receiver is lying on its side on a console table, and as Mathilde approaches, alone, it appears more and more sinister, until she is alarmed by the very touch of it when she picks it up. Or perhaps, when she later remembers this moment, Mathilde will simply imagine – quite sincerely – that she felt this sense of foreboding.

Pierre-Marie has just learned from My Officer Friend of a cemetery in Picardy where Manech and his four companions were interred, each of them beneath a cross bearing his name, in March 1917. Their bodies had been recovered at that time, after the German withdrawal, in the same spot in front of Bingo where they had died two months earlier. On Monday the eighth of January, they had been summarily buried with their clothes and identity tags in a shell crater and covered with a tarp by some charitable British soldiers.

"Little Matti," says Pierre-Marie, "I'm sorry to hurt you this way. You knew that he was dead. Whenever you like, I'll drive you there myself, with Sylvain."

Long after he has hung up the phone, Mathilde sits in her wheelchair with her forehead resting on the table, still holding the receiver which she tries blindly to replace in its cradle and finally lets drop to the end of its wire. She does not cry. She does not cry.

The Mimosas of Hossegor

Mathilde is ten and a half years old. As for Manech, he has just turned thirteen on June 4. He's on his way home from school, wearing shorts and a jersey, with his satchel slung over his shoulder. He stops in front of the iron fence surrounding the Villa Poéma. He sees Mathilde for the first time, sitting in her wheelchair across the garden.

Why he decides to pass by the villa on that particular afternoon, well, that's a mystery. He lives beyond Lake Hossegor, he has no reason to go home this way. In any case, he's there, he watches Mathilde through the bars, and then he says, "You can't walk?"

Mathilde shakes her head. Unable to think of anything to say, Manech goes away. A minute later, he comes back. Something seems to be bothering him. "Have you got any friends?" he asks. Mathilde shakes her head. He says, without looking at her, clearly ill at ease, "If it's all right with you, I'll be your friend." Mathilde shakes her head. He throws a hand up in the air, shouting, "All right, then!" And off he goes once more.

This time, she doesn't see him again for at least three minutes. When he reappears on the other side of the bars, God knows what he has done with his satchel, he's got his hands in his pockets, and he's putting on a relaxed, superior air.

"I'm pretty strong," he says. "I could cart you around on my back all day long. Hey, I could even teach you to swim."

" 'Tisn't true," she replies haughtily. "How could you do that?"

"I know how – with floats, to keep your feet up."

She shakes her head. He puffs out his cheeks and whistles soundlessly. "I go fishing with my father on Sundays. I can bring you back a hake big as this!" He spreads his arms to show a fish about the size of a whale. "You like hake?"

She shakes her head.

"Bass?"

Same response.

"Crab claws? We get a lot of them, in the nets."

She turns her chair around and pushes the wheels along – now she's the one who goes away.

"Snobby Parisienne!" he yells after her. "And to think I almost fell for you! I smell too fishy, is that it?"

She shrugs, ignoring him, heading for the house as fast as she can go. She hears Sylvain, off somewhere in the garden, shouting, "Hey, kid, you looking for a kick in the pants or something?"

That night, in bed, Mathilde dreams that her little fisherman walks her along the road by the lake, through the forest and the streets of Cap-Breton, and the ladies in their doorways say, "Don't they make a charming couple, the two of them, just look at that infectiose friendship!"

When she learns that "infectiose" is not a real word, she'll imagine the ladies saying, "Just look at that infectible friendship," and, later on, "that infected love.".

He returns the following afternoon, at the same time. She's waiting for him. This time he sits on top of the low wall just outside the fence. He doesn't look at her right away.

"I've got loads of friends in Soorts," he announces. "I don't know why I bother with you."

"Could you really teach me to swim?" she asks.

He nods. She rolls her "scooter" closer, touches his back so he'll look at her. He has blue eyes, and such curly hair. They shake hands ceremoniously through the bars.

He has a dog and two cats. His father has a fishing boat in the port. He has never seen Paris or Bordeaux. The largest city he knows is Bayonne. He has never had a girl for a friend before.

Perhaps it's that day, perhaps it's some other day, that Bénédicte comes out on the terrace and says to Manech, "What are you doing out there? Do you take us for savages? The gate's open, come on in."

"So that redhead can give me a kick in the pants?" he replies.

Bénédicte laughs. She calls Sylvain, who tells the boy, "I don't much like being called a redhead, you know. Keep it up and I'll really park my foot in your behind. You're the Manech belongs to the Etcheverys in Soorts? Then your father would thank me, he must owe you a few kicks in the backside. Well, come in, then, before I change my mind."

Friendships that get off to a bad start, they say, are the ones that prove most infectious, and Bénédicte, Sylvain, even Chick Pea – who's exactly one year old – quickly come down with this virus. Bénédicte serves the new friends a hearty snack almost every afternoon. She thinks a good appetite is the mark of a well-brought-up child. Sylvain is willing to admit that Manech, who will complete his elementary education in two years, is a dutiful and hard-working son, who helps his father with the fishing and his mother, who has a delicate constitution, with all the housework.

Summer vacation begins. When he's not out at sea or cutting wood for the winter, Manech takes Mathilde to the lake. They have a favourite spot, on the side closest to the ocean, almost directly across from the Auberge des Cotis. Between the road and the sand is a thicket of trees and shrubs, with mimosas that flower even in the summer. They never see anyone else there, apart from a bearded stranger who turns up on Sundays in city clothes and a straw hat, and who has a fisherman's hut and a boat a little farther along the shore. Manech calls him the Bogey Man, but he's not a bad sort.

One time, Manech helps him pull his nets out of the lake and gives him advice on how to catch more fish. The Bogey Man is astonished at the expertise of such a young fisherman, and Manech proudly tells him, "I was born underwater, so naturally I know my way around." Now the Bogey Man has caught the virus, and simply waves and calls a greeting whenever he sees Manech on his property.

The first summer, the second. It seems to Mathilde that it was during the second summer that she decided to learn to swim. Manech made cork floats to go around her ankles, and he stepped out into the lake with Mathilde hanging on to his shoulders. She doesn't remember swallowing any water. She felt a joy and a sense of fulfilment such as she had rarely known before. She was able to float, to move forward on her stomach using only her arms, and she could even turn over on her back to swim that way, too.

Yes, that second summer with Manech, the summer of 1911

and the terrible heat wave. While she's swimming around, Gustave Garrigou, "The Dandy", followed by his faithful mechanic Six-Sous, wins the Tour de France. Mathilde hasn't the slightest hint of breast, or even a bathing suit, for that matter. The first time, she goes in the water wearing only her drawers, which are of white cotton with a slit crotch for peeing, so as you can imagine, she's quite the bathing beauty. After that, since it takes years for the drawers to dry, she simply wears her birthday suit. Manech goes in mother-naked, with everything proudly on parade.

Just getting to the Bogey Man's property is already an adventure. Manech pushes the "scooter" as far as he can along the dirt road, until the ground becomes too rough. Then he carries Mathilde piggyback through the thicket, pushing away obstructing branches with one hand, until they reach the edge of the lake, where he sets her down in the sand as gently as he can. Then he returns to hide the wheelchair, in case someone should start wondering about it and raise a hue and cry all across the Landes. After their swim, when Mathilde's hair is dry again, it's the same tomfoolery in reverse.

One evening, when Mama gives Mathilde a kiss on the neck, she tastes salt on her lips and licks her daughter's upper arm in dismay. "You fell in the ocean!" she exclaims.

Mathilde, who never lies, answers, "Not in the ocean, too many waves there. In Lake Hossegor. I wanted to commit suicide, but Manech Etchevery saved me. And while he was at it, so that I wouldn't drown myself later on, he taught me to swim."

After Mathieu Donnay, also alarmed, has come along with them on one of their excursions to see how well she manages, Mathilde is equipped with a decent bathing suit, as is Manech, who becomes the proud owner of a white suit with navy-blue stripes, shoulder straps, and a crest over the heart that reads: *Paris, fluctuat nec mergitur.* When Manech asks Mathilde to translate, since she's already studying Latin, she replies that it's not interesting, and detaches the crest from his suit with her teeth and nails. Afterwards, you can see where it was removed, which displeases Manech, who claims his new suit doesn't look brand-new any more.

Latin. When summer vacation is over, Mathilde goes back to her classes with the Sisters of Divine Mercy, in Auteuil. The school is so close to her house that she could go there in her wheelchair, like a big girl, but her father – who is the son of a poor farrier up north in Bouchain and who has just purchased the town house on the Rue La Fontaine "with my own money" – takes pride in having her driven back and forth by his chauffeur, nicknamed Speedy, for she never bothers to remember his real name. She is a good student in French, history, science, and arithmetic. She sits in the back of a classroom, facing the centre aisle, where she has a double desk all to herself. The Sisters are very nice; the girls aren't unbearable. She watches from the sidelines during the breaks. What she hates the most is when a new girl arrives and wants to prove how kind she is: "Let me push you," or, "Do you want me to toss you the ball?" and all that blah-blah-blah.

After a second stay in the hospital in Zurich, in 1912, Mathilde asks to be allowed to live permanently in Cap-Breton, with Sylvain and Bénédicte, and Chick Pea, plus Uno, Due, and Tertia. Two teachers share the week's classes at Poéma, three hours each day: a former seminarian who has lost his faith and a retired private-school teacher (a revanchist regarding Alsace-Lorraine, anti-Red to the hilt, so prudish she hides her teeth when she smiles), one Mademoiselle Clémence (nothing in common with the Intolerable Sister-in-law of later on), who requests, as payment for her efforts, a candle in church on each anniversary of her death, a debt that Bénédicte and Mathilde will never fail to repay, when the time comes.

Early in the summer of 1912, Manech completes his elementary education. Now he goes out fishing every day, because the Etcheverys are not rich and his mother's medication is very expensive, but as soon as he returns to port, he runs straight to the villa to "walk" Mathilde. They go off together to their spot on the lake shore, to the mimosas, to the boat the Bogey Man lets them use. Manech poles the boat along, taking Mathilde on a cruise to the canal. She sits aft, right on the bottom of the boat, gripping the sides with both hands.

Come autumn and winter, she sees Manech on days when the ocean is too rough for fishing. Sometimes, with the donkey Catapult hitched to his father's gig, he takes her home to see his parents. His father is a gruff fellow, but good-hearted; his mother is sweet-tempered, quite slender, almost frail – she has a heart murmur. They raise rabbits, chickens, and geese. Manech's dog, Kiki, is a Breton spaniel, white with russet patches. He's much more lively and intelligent than Chick Pea. As for the two cats, Mathilde finds them rather inferior to her own, but still, they're both a handsome charcoal colour, and she's partial to anything feline.

Manech teaches Mathilde to tie sailor's knots with bits of rope: sheepshank, bowline, granny, cat's-paw, clove hitch, trefoil. In return, she teaches him card games she has learned from Sylvain: Bouillotte, Russian Bank, Red Dog, Pinochle, and especially the game they both love the best, Snap. When you have a card that exactly matches the number of points showing on the table, you rake in all the cards, shouting, "Snap!" and you put a big chestnut next to your pile for a marker. When Manech loses, he grumbles, "This is a stupid old game," and when he wins he says, "Have to think fast to play this one."

Another year – 1913, probably, because Mathilde's breasts are growing fast and she has her period – they find an exhausted tortoise on the lake-shore road, doubtless off on a pilgrimage to Santiago de Compostela. They adopt it and name it Snap. Unfortunately, they feed it too well, and it's even more devout than Mademoiselle Clémence. As soon as it's feeling fit again, it sets out on its adventures once more.

And the ocean, the great, terrifying ocean of crashing waves, frothing bursts of snowflakes and pearls – Mathilde goes swimming there, too, hanging on to Manech, clinging to his neck almost tight enough to strangle him, shrieking her head off with fright and pleasure, battered by the tumbling waves but always eager for more.

When he carries Mathilde piggyback over the steep dunes after their swim, Manech is chagrined to find he must set her down on the sand and catch his breath. It's during one of these forced halts, a few days before the outbreak of war, in the summer of 1914, that Mathilde leans over to plant a consoling kiss on his cheek and impishly lets her lips glide over to his. This new arrangement is so clearly superior to the old one that she wonders why she waited so long before trying it out, and as for him, even his ears have turned beet red, but she can tell he's not displeased.

The summer of the war. For her brother Paul, a married man for the last few months, with the first kid already on the way, it means a post in the commissariat at Fort Vincennes. He's a lieutenant in the reserve army. At the dinner table, the Intolerable Clémence adopts a peremptory tone: she knows, having heard it from a pork-butcher who delivers sausage to one of the top brass at headquarters ("I'm sure you know who I mean"), that peace will be proclaimed in one month to the day, before there has been any actual fighting, and that William and Nicholas have already signed a secret pact approved by the King of England, the Archduke of Austria, and God knows who else, perhaps the Negus of Abyssinia, so all this drum-beating is simply a ploy to save face. Even Chick Pea – who hasn't yet begun farting all over the place, otherwise he'd have let fly a stinging retort – decides it's time for a stroll around the garden.

That August, Sylvain goes off as well, a quartermaster, but his work involves supplies for the navy and takes him no farther away than Bordeaux. Once a month until 1918, he'll be able to show up at the Villa Poéma to hear Bénédicte tell him what a handsome man he is, especially with that red pompom on his cap.

Manech's father and Mathilde's are both too old for the war, and even those with lots more brains than Clémence can't believe it will last so long that Manech, who has just turned seventeen, will have to go.

The summer of '14 remains for Mathilde the summer of those first kisses, and first deceptions. In front of Bénédicte and Mama, she and Manech work so hard at appearing innocent they seem practically retarded. They talk to each other only about silly little things, or about nothing at all, going off adventuring with Catapult instead.

The summer of '15 is a time of fear and jealousy, because it's not long before Mathilde learns from her *Landes Gazette* that Manech has been seen on the main beach of Cap-Breton with a blonde from Liverpool named Patty, five years older than he is and already divorced, with whom he's probably playing other games besides Snap and stolen kisses. Bénédicte, with naïve cruelty, insists that a boy his age should be gaining some experience, knowledge that will stand him in good stead later on when he marries some local girl. She tells Mathilde not to be angry with him if he comes less often to take her "out for a walk".

"What do you expect?" she says, busy with her ironing. "He's growing up, and with his good looks, I'd be quite surprised if he hadn't set tongues wagging about him by now."

When Mathilde reproaches Manech for not coming all week long, he looks away sheepishly, saying he has a lot of work to do. When she tries to kiss him, he turns away again and says they mustn't do that any more, he's ashamed of deceiving Mathilde's parents when they've been so kind to him. When she accuses him of fooling around behind her back with some snotty English girl, he takes Mathilde home without another word and leaves, looking grim.

In bed, Mathilde is left to amuse herself by imagining the torments she'd like this blonde hussy to suffer. One day, catching sight of her on the wooden bridge in Hossegor, she races towards her in the wheelchair, runs over her feet, and bumps her into the canal to drown. Another time, she goes after her in the Hôtel du Parc and shoots her dead with Sylvain's big revolver. But the best time is when she masks her hatred with honeyed words and convinces her to slip behind the German lines in the service of His Majesty. Patty Potato, betrayed by her ex-husband, is arrested as a spy by uhlans sporting the death's-head insignia, tortured, raped ten times, disfigured by sabre cuts, and finally – with great shrieks – torn apart by four regimental horses, exactly as Mathilde has read about in her history books.

Luckily for the horses and the sweet repose of the implacable seeker after justice, August comes to a close, and the poor intended victim disappears before these plans can be carried out. In September, when English girls are hard to find, Manech returns to Mathilde, who prefers not to bring up irritating subjects any more. The two of them find their way back along the straight-and-narrow path to the mimosas once again. Manech forgets his scruples long enough to kiss her the way she likes to be kissed, and one evening he kisses her breasts, which he finds very lovely. Torn between shame and delight, Mathilde feels as though she were going to die.

It isn't until early in April 1916, however, when Manech learns that his age group has been called up, that they free themselves, in their common despair, from the semblance of a childhood friendship that is already deeply compromised. Despite a chilly wind, they lie entwined and weeping on the sand; they swear that they love each other and always will, that nothing can separate them, not time, or the war, or bourgeois taboos, or the scheming of blondes, or the treachery of small stepladders.

A bit later, when everything is at flood tide, Manech carries Mathilde to the hut belonging to the Bogey Man, whom they haven't seen for two years, and who must be at the front, like everyone else. Manech sets her down on a pile of nets, undresses her a little, she feels somewhat panicky but doesn't dare say a word because it seems such a solemn moment, he kisses her all over, her face is flushed, and so is his, then it hurts the way she thought it might during her nocturnal musings, but not too much, after all, and then again, she feels as good as she had hoped, too, and even better.

Another evening, they return to the hut, where they make love three times, laughing a lot in between – about everything, about nothing – and then they straighten their clothes, comb each other's hair with their fingers, and Manech carries

Mathilde outside in his arms. He sets her down in her wheel-chair and tells her from now on they're engaged, may they burn in hell if they lie to each other, and she says fine, and they swear to wait for each other and to be married when he comes back. To seal their promise, he gets out his pocketknife, one blade with a whole bunch of useless accessories, and he leaps into the thicket, making his way to a big silver poplar growing in the middle of the jungle. He cuts something into the trunk, and when Mathilde asks what, he says, "You'll see." When he has finished, he clears away the brush to make a path for the wheelchair. He's like a savage, dripping with sweat, his face and hair covered with twigs, scratches all over his hands, but he's happy.

"After that," he shouts, "I deserve a dip in the lake!"

He pushes Mathilde to the poplar. He has cut the letters MMM into its trunk, so that forwards and backwards, either way, it reads "Manech's Marrying Mathilde" and "Mathilde's Marrying Manech."

Now he tears off his shirt and runs away to take a header into the lake. He calls out brrr, it's freezing, but he doesn't care, he's not afraid of death any more. He swims. In the evening silence, in the great calm that reigns all around her and in her heart as well, she no longer hears anything but the rhythmic movements of her lover's arms and legs. With her finger she traces the letters carved into the poplar's bark: MMM.

They have a short while longer to love each other in the hut, she's not sure exactly how long, she doesn't remember any more. Perhaps six or seven days. He goes off to the depot in Bordeaux one Wednesday, on the fifteenth of April, 1916. Since he's leaving very early, around four in the morning, and he has promised to come and kiss her good-bye at the Villa

Poéma, Mathilde won't go to sleep and spends the night in her chair. Bénédicte is up before four to make the coffee. Manech arrives, wearing an overcoat that belongs to his father and carrying a wicker suitcase. When he kisses Mathilde for the last time, Bénédicte sees clearly how naïve she has been, but she looks away without saying anything, and so what?

Manech had been hoping to wind up in the navy, like his father and uncles before him, like Sylvain, but in 1916 it's foot soldiers they need. After three weeks of training, in Bourges, he is sent to the front. First as reinforcements at Verdun, then in Picardy. Every day Mathilde writes a letter, and waits for one. On Sundays, the Etcheverys come to the villa, looking ten years older, in the little cart drawn by Catapult. Together they make up a package into which they'd like to put everything, food, drink, the roof, the fire, the lake, the wind off the Atlantic that would bring in the Americans, everything, even packs of gold-tipped cigarettes his mother insists on stuffing inside the socks she knits, because even if Manech doesn't smoke, this way he can always make some new friends.

He writes that everything's fine, everything's fine, that he's hoping to come home on leave, that everything's fine, he'll be home on leave soon, everything's fine, everything's fine, dear Matti, everything's fine, until December, when suddenly there's no word from him, but Mathilde keeps telling herself that everything's fine, he hasn't written but that's because he hasn't had time, everything's fine, and Christmas goes by, and in January 1917, she finally receives a letter that someone else has written for him, she doesn't understand, he says things that are so beautiful but so strange that she doesn't understand, and one morning, on Sunday the twenty-eighth, Sylvain arrives from Bordeaux, he kisses Bénédicte and he kisses

Mathilde, so sadly, he's having such trouble finding words that he frightens them, at the station he met someone coming back from Soorts and he heard terrible news, and he has to sit down and he twists his cap with the red pompom in his hands, and Mathilde sees his eyes suddenly fill with tears, he looks at her through the tears and tries to tell her, he tries to say . . .

Be good, Matti, be good.

JANUARY 1921

No one will be surprised, after that evocation of those long, hot summers, to hear that Mathilde, who came of age three days ago, rushes to buy – without haggling over the price, and "with my own money" (consisting mainly of all her New Year's presents, carefully hoarded since childhood, and the proceeds from her paintings now flowering in the offices of Papa's banker friend) – one hectare of land for sale on the shore of Lake Hossegor: the property of the Bogey Man, who never came back from the war, leaving behind a jungle which the deceased's three sisters are quite glad to see the last of, despite the lovely mimosas there.

With the ink barely dry on the deed of purchase, the price paid, the three sisters thanked with grateful pecks on the cheek, Mathilde has her father and Sylvain drive her from the notary's office in Cap-Breton to the scene of her adolescent amours. The hut is still there, at least what's left of it, and the poplar, the silvery poplar, has weathered all winds. Now that she's grown up, Mathilde would be willing to tell all, but her father turns down the offer, saying, "Spare me your memories. What I like about this place are the mimosas and this tree with the sentimental triple M that hints at what many fathers, for I'm not the only one, cannot bear to imagine. And then they get used to it."

He has carried Mathilde there in his arms, while Sylvain has taken charge of her sturdy new wheelchair, a practical, improved version invented for the paralysed veterans of the war. Which shows, claims the Intolerable Clémence, that war is always useful for something.

It is a crisp, clear day. Mathilde is sitting near the poplar, her plaid blanket over her knees, while her father wanders through the thicket, and Sylvain heads down to the shore to leave them alone. Every so often, Mathilde touches the letters announcing her marriage to Manech. The gulls ignore these solitary humans and congregate on the sandbanks that have emerged from the middle of the lake.

"Well, why not?" exclaims Mathilde's father after a long consultation with himself. He returns to where his daughter is sitting and announces that he will build her a large villa designed entirely with her happiness in mind, so that she may live by the lake with Sylvain, Bénédicte, and the cats. He will leave Poéma, if that's all right with her, to Paul and his family. It's all right with Mathilde, but the mimosas must not be touched, and the same obviously goes for the poplar. Her papa shrugs. "There are times," he tells her, "when you really are a *favouille*."

She laughs, asking him how he knows that. Some of his construction workers are from Provence, he replies, and they explained to him that a *favouille* is a little crab that's not too bright – which is unusual in our supposedly ancient ancestry – so that in Marseille, Bandol, or Saintes-Maries-de-la-Mer, calling someone a *favouille* means the person is basically a bonehead.

He then summons Sylvain to tell him of his plan to build

a house there, without disturbing the silver poplar or harming even a single mimosa root. As Sylvain is an experienced gardener, what is his opinion?

"The mimosas," opines Sylvain, "can be moved. As for the poplar, it's near the edge of the property, so it's not in the way."

Monsieur Donnay shakes his hand heartily.

"Thank you, Papa," says Mathilde. "Now at least, in the summer and at Christmastime, I won't have to put up with my brother's wife and your revolting grandsons."

And Sylvain adds, quite innocently, "Matti's right. And Bénédicte's going to be pleased as well."

The next day Mathilde and Sylvain take the train to accompany the rest of the family to Paris. On the sixth of January they drive to the city of Péronne, in the Somme, which is near the military cemetery of Herdelin, where Manech is buried. In the five months since they first visited the place with Pierre-Marie, traces of the war have faded further away, and yet the war seems even more present throughout the countryside, probably because it's wintertime.

They spend the night at the Auberge des Remparts, where Pierre-Marie had taken rooms for them in August. On the morning of the seventh – the date of the pilgrimage Mathilde has promised herself she will make every year for as long as her strength holds out, which doesn't preclude other visits at other times – the sky is overcast and sleet is falling over Péronne and the surrounding battlefields. At Herdelin, where rebuilt houses stand cheek by jowl with ruins, the road is a river of mud. In the freezing rain, the flags at the entrance to the cemetery hang limply, ingloriously. On the other side of the road, almost directly across from the front gate, the German military cemetery doesn't look any more cheerful.

Last year, in the summer sunshine glimmering through the branches of the recently planted willows, the impeccably mowed lawns, the tricolour rosettes hanging on the crosses, the gay flowers from a grateful nation in the imitation-antique bowls, all this had seemed like such pretence to Mathilde that she'd felt like screaming in disgust. Today's rain, the glacial wind blowing in from Flanders, the hopeless torpor that seems to weigh upon the entire countryside – such things seem more appropriate for these Poor Bastards at the Front. And how many of them, lying there, would disagree with her on that?

The first time she'd come here, she'd looked at once for the white cross of Jean Etchevery, nineteen years old, died for what she now refuses to pronounce because it's a lie. There'd been another lie on the next cross she'd found, in the same row: Kléber Bouquet, thirty-seven years old. And another, a few rows away, on the cross of Ange Bassignano, twenty-six years old, the pimp from Marseille, on whose grave sat a vase of flowers made of coloured beads spelling out a name, Tina, proof that for all Mathilde's efforts, she'd been a few steps behind a tart from the mean streets of Belle de Mai. In another row, knocked over on to the grave by the wind and the rain, had lain the rotting cross of Benoît Notre-Dame, thirty years old. Pierre-Marie had gone to speak with a caretaker, who had already noticed the problem and had promised him that the cross would be replaced.

Mathilde had had Sylvain push her all around the cemetery, looking for Six-Sous. They'd found him near the surrounding wall, taking advantage of the shade, no flowers, no wreath, died for the same reason, the obscenity of a war that hadn't had one, aside from the egotism, hypocrisy, and vanity of a privileged few. That's the way of the world.

Today, under a big umbrella, sitting in her wheelchair, Mathilde gazes down at Manech. The rosette on the cross is a bit discoloured; Sylvain tidies up the rest. Jean Etchevery, nineteen years old. She is now older than her lover. She has brought him, from the shore of Lake Hossegor, a sprig of mimosa, which doesn't look all that perky when she unwraps it from the piece of paper she has been carrying in her handbag, but as Sylvain says, "It's the thought that counts." Mathilde replies, "I'd like you to tuck the thought into the earth, just in front of the cross." His big hands dig a small hole over the grave of the boy who once called him "that redhead", and he lays the mimosa, tenderly, in the bottom of the hole. Before he fills it in with dirt, Mathilde gives him a pack of gold-tipped cigarettes, telling him, "Put these in, too, it'll make his mother happy. You never know. Wherever he is, even if he doesn't smoke, he can always make some new friends."

Then Sylvain goes off in the rain, walking slowly down the path, wearing a soaking-wet cap he's had since before he was married and which isn't getting any younger, either. He wants to leave Mathilde alone for a moment. He has a nice sense of discretion.

She brings Manech up-to-date. First of all, Germain Pire hasn't found either Tina Lombardi or Célestin Poux. The thread she has been following until now seems to have broken, or perhaps it's leading nowhere, but that's not important, she's not giving up. Then she tells him that his parents are fine. She has been to see them, and they both kissed and hugged her. His mother made her a scrambled egg with milk, the way she used to do, when he'd taken her home to see them in the gig with Catapult. Finally, she tells him that she has used her savings to buy the Bogey Man's property by the lake, and that her father will build her a house there. She wants it to have two terraces, one looking towards the ocean, the other toward the lake.

"Our room will give on to the lake," she says. "Every morning I'll be able to look out of the window and see our poplar." After a long silence, she adds, "I'm sticking with the idea that one of you five isn't dead. I believe what Urbain Chardolot's mother wrote to me. I'm not absolutely convinced, and for that I'll have to find one of the soldiers who was at Bingo. The only name I've got is Célestin Poux."

She's leaning forward in her wheelchair, protected by that damned wobbly umbrella; she wants Manech to hear everything.

"There's something else that bothers me. Tina Lombardi had a code with her Nino. Why shouldn't the others have had codes with their wives? I've read and reread the letters of the Eskimo and Six-Sous and That Man. I can't find any code. Even in Nino's, I haven't figured it out. Forgive me, Manech, for being only me."

When Sylvain returns, having had enough of traipsing around in the rain, he tells her, "At least they kept their promise. They gave Benoît Notre-Dame a new cross."

Mathilde would like to tour the cemetery the way she did in August, but she doesn't dare ask Sylvain.

"You know, Matti," he says, "while you were communing with Manech, I took a squint at the other graves. The beaded flowers are still on Bassignano's. There's nothing on the others. If you want to go and see for yourself, I don't mind, it's not much trouble."

She shakes her head. "Please," she says, "go back to Bassignano's grave and take a good look, see if you can find any sign that Tina has been back here."

The minutes drag by. The freezing rain is turning into snow. She's cold beneath her blanket. "You're really irritating," she tells Manech. "It's a nuisance coming here, we'd be much better off in the Landes."

In August, on their first visit, she'd asked Pierre-Marie if it would be possible to have the casket moved to the cemetery in Soorts or in Cap-Breton. He'd replied, "It might take quite a while to arrange something like that, I don't know anything about such matters, but we should be able to do it. I'll find out."

He hadn't finished speaking before Mathilde was seized with a feeling of appalling anguish that left her speechless, exactly as though Manech, deep inside her, were shouting no, no, he didn't want that at all. And when she'd finally managed to choke out a few words, she'd babbled to Pierre-Marie, "No, don't do anything. I have to think about it." And immediately, quietly, her fear had subsided. But it's back now, at the mere thought of asking Manech if he has changed his mind. "All right," she tells him, "I won't bother you with that. After all, it's a change for me, coming here. I get to see a bit of the country."

Then Sylvain returns, treading heavily, his cap awry, his hands covered with mud. He holds them up in the air so that the rain will wash them. He looks like a prisoner of war resigned to carrying out the whims of Mathilde the Nutcracker. As he comes closer, he calls out, "I didn't see anything to show she'd been back." Standing by Mathilde's wheelchair, he adds, "But I think she's been there, anyway, I don't know why. I dug a little around the cross, in case she'd had the same idea as you, but I didn't find a thing. I looked on the bottom of the basin of flowers, it's marble and weighs a ton, so it's easy to see why it hasn't been stolen. There's nothing underneath to show where it comes from, but I had another idea. I put it on someone else's grave, a bit down the line. So maybe we'll see the next time, hey?"

Germain Pire
Monday June 13, 1921

My dear child,

I've never felt so humiliated. Nevertheless, I must admit to you that my investigation has been a complete failure, and I hereby give up all claim to the hydrangeas that were to have graced my home. You see, Valentina Lombardi is as hard to find as if she had never existed. I found a few traces of her in Toulon, La Ciotat, and Marseille, but the people willing to talk about her are well-to-do bourgeois who curl their lips when they mention her name. Her own kind are the only ones who can tell me what I need to know, and they're not talking. Since you asked me particularly not to, I didn't bother Madame Conte or her friends Madame Isola and Madame Sciolla. In any case, I couldn't have learned anything useful from them.

In the course of my inquiries, I often feel very strongly as though I truly know those I'm seeking or observing. This is not at all the case with Valentina Lombardi. I sense that she is a dark creature, scarred by the torments of a wretched childhood, held completely in thrall by the only love that ever made her believe she was a worthwhile human being like everyone else, and now that this love has been murdered, she has become infinitely cruel and dangerous for anyone connected with this massacre. I sense this instinctively, and I tell you, my dear child, it would be wiser to forget about her. From now on, do not do anything that might provoke the beast.

In February of this year, she passed through Sarzeau, a village in Morbihan – where her trail disappears. I went there myself, and people still remember her gloomy demeanour and the impression she gave of barely contained violence. If I lost track of her there, perhaps it's because she's dead after all, and I for one would not mourn her.

As for my brother Ernest's search for Célestin Poux, again we've had to admit defeat, even though our quarry in this case was quite a different sort. On the Ile d'Oléron, everyone described this lad as a cheerful, clever, obliging boy, but one never knew what he was going to get up to next. After serving with the rank of corporal in the army of occupation across the Rhine, he'd come home again for three months in the autumn of 1919. He was given the post of lock-keeper at a place called Le Douhet, in the commune of Saint-Georges. He lived at his place of work. As for his family, he has only some vague cousins, also named Poux, who say simply that they never saw anything of him. In any event, he made it through the war alive. The reason he gave for leaving Oléron in January of 1920 was that he wanted to buy an automobile repair garage in the Dordogne. The Dordogne covers a rather large area, which my brother did his best to explore, but without finding our man. The last sighting we had of him was on the ferry that carried him to the mainland. He had a sailor's duffel bag slung over one shoulder and a basket of oysters over the other. The oysters, he said, were for a fool who'd wagered his motorcycle that he could eat twenty dozen of them.

I'm very sorry, my dear child, and mortified beyond words,

to have to enclose the bill for my expenses, which I have drawn up, please believe me, more to your advantage than to mine. You will find, moreover, that these expenses comprise only modest hotel rooms and third-class fares, nothing else. My sole nourishment, in this case, is the pleasure of knowing artists like yourself.

In closing, let me assure you there is always the hope that in time, or through some lucky accident, I will discover something important enough to bring to your attention, and whatever happens, I remain your friend and faithful admirer.

Germain Pire

This letter follows Mathilde to New York, where she has come – this is the life she finds the least amusing and the most wastefully time-consuming – to be operated on by a young Jewish doctor, Arno Feldmann, who has been able to restore partial mobility to three patients who have the same infirmity as she does. The operation is a boring fiasco, except that she is now rid of the chronic pain in her hips that formerly afflicted her, and she is on the verge of falling in love with the surgeon, but he is married, the father of two chubby-cheeked, freckle-faced little girls, and as we all know, apart from those faceless strangers who occasionally torment her in some regrettable daydreams, Mathilde never deceives her fiancé.

And then, there is also the fact that she is accompanied by her mother, who was wretchedly seasick during the crossing and who is tired of strolling in Central Park and browsing in the posh shops along Fifth Avenue, wilting in the oppressive heat. Mathilde doesn't wish to add to her troubles. Arno Feld-mann, therefore, becomes only a distant mirage glimpsed on the sly through her hotel window.

She returns to the Villa Poéma in October, in the final sweltering days of a summer that seems to last forever, to find everyone, people and pets alike, in fine fettle. There's a new car, a Delage, a more comfortable vehicle than the last one, with better suspension. Sylvain drives Mathilde to Hos-segor almost every day, to see how work on the new house is progressing. Bruno Marchet, Papa's architect, finds her an incredible nuisance. She argues with the construction workers over details, she's never satisfied, she assumes they all hate her. She promises her father she won't go back there until it's time for the finishing touches.

In January 1922, during her pilgrimage to the cemetery in Herdelin, the sky is blue, the temperature is brisk, the bowl of flowers, moved by Sylvain, has been replaced beneath the cross of Ange Bassignano, but this does not necessarily mean, thinks Mathilde, that Tina Lombardi has returned to the graveside. The caretaker, who is not always there, sees too many people pass through when he is on the job, and he doesn't know anything about it. In Péronne, however, where Sylvain makes the rounds, the proprietor of the Prince de Belgique does say that a young woman with a Midi accent stayed in his hotel the previous autumn, alone, drinking heavily, smoking little cigars in the dining room, and insulting the other patrons thus inconvenienced. He remembers being pleased that she stayed only that one night. She slipped out the next morning without even paying her bill. The name she used, as Sylvain can see for himself in the register, is Emilia Conte, from Toulon. She signed the register on November 15, 1921, and left the following day.

Upon her return to Paris, Mathilde passes this information on to Germain Píre, who politely refuses to pursue the investigation any further. He has aged greatly in a year and a half. He still wears the bowler, the floppy tie, and the white spats, but he hasn't the heart to take up the chase again, for he is in mourning and cannot bear even to speak of his bereavement.

During the year of 1922, Mathilde will have her own fair share of grief to bear. Manech's parents die, three weeks apart, in the sultry month of June. His mother has a heart attack and dies in her sleep, while his father is found drowned in the lake, near his oyster bed. Everyone says it was an accident, so that the priest will allow him a proper church burial, but Dr Bertrand, from Soorts, who was the first to be called to the scene by the rescue team, gives Mathilde an unopened letter addressed to her in the dead man's handwriting. It contains a few lines, almost illegible, written in purple pencil.

Dearest Matti,

I can't go on. Half my life was taken from me, now I've lost the other half. My only consolation in all this misery has been that thanks to you, my poor Isabelle and I were able to visit our son's grave last year. My affairs are in order. I have willed to you what we kept of Manech's things. I couldn't bear to kill the dog, please give him a home. He knows you, he'll be less unhappy that way.

I embrace you as my daughter.

Ambroise Etchevery

The poor man's only relative is a sister, a post office employee in Saint-Jean-de-Luz. She sells the house and the oysterage to set herself and her husband up in the hosiery business. Sylvain drives the Delage over to collect Kiki the dog and Manech's possessions, a heap of old clothes, books, school papers, the Fantomas thrillers he read before he went off to war, toys he'd made for himself, and the famous navy-blue-striped bathing suit, on which you can no longer see the place where the missing crest had once been.

In September, despite the best of care, Kiki gives up the ghost; then Tertia and Bellissima are carried off on the same night by a cough. In November, Mademoiselle Clémence, Mathilde's former tutor, is buried in Labenne. And before the year is over, Bénédicte's cat, Camembert, sets off with amorous intentions, never to return. Three days later, Sylvain finds him more than five kilometres from Cap-Breton, run over by a truck and already half-devoured by scavengers.

The year 1923 doesn't get off to a much better start. In February, a letter from Marseille informs Mathilde of the death of Madame Paolo Conte. The faithful Madame Isola writes that her heart simply wore out and she died without suffering. She had not seen her goddaughter again.

In the spring the Villa MMM in Hossegor is finished, a few months behind schedule, and Mathilde moves in with Sylvain and Bénédicte. She can see the poplar from her windows. The mimosas are in flower in the garden, along with the roses, the rhododendrons, and the camellias Sylvain has planted. Mathilde's studio is next to her bedroom. All the floors in the house are of polished marble, to accommodate her wheelchair, and the outdoor paths have been asphalted, so that she can easily go anywhere she pleases. During the summer, she paints on the terrace in front of the lake in the morning, and on the western terrace in the afternoon. She paints a great deal, to forget sad things, to forget the fact that she has nothing new to add to her mahogany box, to forget herself.

In the winter, her paintings are exhibited in Biarritz and then in Paris, at the Lettres de Mon Moulin Gallery, as before. The lady of the petits fours still has a bounce in her step and a twinkle in her eye; the comment book acquires a few prettily phrased sentiments. One woman writes, "Your flowers speak." And the next visitor adds, on the following line, "Let's just say they babble."

Mathilde takes advantage of this visit to have her advertisement printed once again in *L'Illustration*, *La Vie Parisienne*, and the veterans' monthly magazines. She removes the names of Benjamin Gordes, Chardolot, and Santini, leaving only Célestin Poux, and asks that all replies be sent to her new address in the Landes.

In the spring, a happy event takes place at MMM, which Mathilde, who can be superstitious when she feels like it, takes for a sign that the end of her ordeal is near, that 1924 has great surprises in store for her and will be a time to heal many wounds. In her ripe middle age, so to speak, Mélusine, Sylvain's cat, the once-haughty widow of Camembert, is seized with a veritable frenzy of debauchery. Unable to decide among Uno, Due, Bandit, and Master Jack, she chooses the entire quartet, either because all four of them aren't too many to satisfy her or because she's thoughtfully attempting to keep the peace in their household. And since she also steps out now and then for an afternoon on the town, or even in the woods, returning only at nightfall in a suspiciously languorous state, it would take a clever person indeed to determine the father of the five darling tiger kittens born to her on Saturday the twenty-sixth of April. That's the day on which Bénédicte and Sylvain are celebrating their fiftieth birthdays (she's two days older than he is) and their thirtieth wedding anniversary. It doesn't take long to distribute the presents. Mathilde receives D'Artagnan and Milady, Sylvain gets Porthos, Bénédicte takes Athos, which she insists on pronouncing Camembert, and Mama inherits Aramis. Mélusine, having repented her sins and renounced her flighty ways, will now devote herself entirely to the education of her offspring.

Even though Mathilde hadn't expected great results when she rebaited her hook with her amended advertisement, she is surprised to find her catch so small. Four letters in all, the most instructive of which arrives addressed to the Villa Poéma and turns out to be unrelated to her appeal. Two of the remaining three are claims to the authorship of the name Bingo Crépuscule.

A corporal in the colonial army, who had participated in the retaking of the trench from the Germans in October 1916, had searched a hastily abandoned hut and found a painting on a wooden panel, probably the work of an English or Canadian soldier whiling away a few idle hours. Since the back of the painting offered the ideal surface for a sign, the corporal ordered that the new name of the recaptured trench be inscribed there.

Eight days later, a correspondent from Château-Thierry, signing himself simply "one of General Mangin's soldiers", claims to have written in black paint with his own hands and on his own initiative the words "Bing au Crépuscule" in black letters on the back of a picture.

Both of them agree at least on the subject of the work of art in question. Pooling their descriptions, Mathilde comes up with the image of a British officer standing by the sea, admiring a brilliant sunset, while at his side, his big grey or perhaps

black horse grazes peacefully on a few meagre blades of grass.
A palm tree indicates that the scene might be set in the Orient.

The third letter is also anonymous, and surprisingly concise.

Mademoiselle,

Célestin Poux died in April of 1917 at Chemin des Dames,
so you've no need to waste any more of your money. I knew
him well.

The envelope bears the postmark of Melun. The handwriting
and the pink colour of the stationery suggest to Mathilde that
her mysterious correspondent is a middle-aged lady.

The letter that doesn't arrive in response to her advertisement
has come from far away, sent to her by Aristide Pommier, the
myopic resin tapper, the water sportsman who relished being
dunked, the man she called a lickspittle on his wedding day.

Aristide Pommier
550, Côte des Neiges
Montreal, Canada
June 18, 1924

Dear Mademoiselle Mathilde,

As you perhaps know, my father-in-law and I had a falling-
out and ended by coming to blows, so I went off to Quebec
and sent for my wife and two daughters after six months. We

have had another girl over here. I don't work with trees any more, I'm a chef in a restaurant in Sherbrooke, a very busy part of town. I'm making a good living, but I'm not writing you to brag about that.

I'm writing to tell you I spoke with a client several days ago who is from Saint John's in Newfoundland, who came to Quebec after the war. His name's Nathanael Belly, they call him Nat, he runs a heating business. He is about thirty-five years old. He was at a table with his wife and a few friends. He wanted to offer me a little *pousse café* after the meal to show his appreciation of my cuisine, and that's how I learned he was on the Somme in January '17 and knew the trench where Manech died. I surely wouldn't like to bring back terrible memories but I think that, above all, you want to know what happened. So that's how it is, I wasn't sure if I should write you this, but here goes.

According to this Nat Belly, who does like his beer but was still good and sober, he was part of a patrol of Newfoundlanders who were the first to arrive on the battlefield on the morning of January 8, 1917, because the Tommies were replacing our men in the sector just as they did all along our front out to Roye. Nat Belly says they buried five dead Frenchmen under a tarp, and they all had bandages on their hands. Their regimental numbers and other insignia had been torn off, probably by the Boches, for souvenirs. Unfortunately Nat no longer remembers their names, but they did have their dog tags and the patrol leader wrote down their names "just in case", but Nat can't remember them. What he does remember is that one of the five was very young, twenty or so, with brown hair, rather tall and thin, and I'm afraid that was our poor Manech.

There, that's what I wanted to tell you. Now, Nat told me

he thinks he can find the patrol leader again, a fellow named Dick Bonnaventure, the son of Québecois, who was born in Saint John's too, but by accident, he isn't a Newfie like they call them here, he's a trapper up by Lake Saint John who writes songs and poetry, and Nat Belly knows he comes down to Chicoutimi every autumn. If he can locate him, he'll get more details on this business, because this other man must have paid more attention and will remember more things. Nat sends his apologies, he says he didn't really take a very good look around that morning because the big shells were starting to come in thick and fast again, and although they were all quite willing to go along with Dick Bonnaventure and bury the French, all they wanted to spend doing it was a few minutes, tops. I've been there, I can understand.

In any case, and this he remembers perfectly, it was the morning of January 8 in 1917, there was thick snow that came up over their ankles, and they found these five soldiers dead and scattered all over. So they gathered the bodies in a big hole, they covered them with a tarp from the trench evacuated by the Boches, and they shovelled in the dirt at top speed.

I hope, Mlle Mathilde, that this letter won't make you any sadder than you already are. I know you're someone who prefers to be told the truth. I also hope that you are well and your parents, too. My wife and daughters join me in wishing you good health and prosperity despite your sorrow. If I have anything else to add, you can be sure I'll write you straight away.

Very truly yours in memory of the past,

Aristide Pommier

This letter does not make Mathilde any sadder than she has been since Manech's death. Pierre-Marie Rouvière had already told her almost four years ago that the five prisoners had been summarily buried by some British soldiers before getting their coffins and white crosses at Herdelin. She is troubled, nevertheless, by certain phrases: "the bodies in a big hole"; "shovelled in the dirt at top speed"; and, above all, those terrible words "dead and scattered all over". She forces herself to understand that the bodies were found in different places in no-man's-land, that Aristide writes the best he can, in other words, like the pig and lickspittle he still is but for one whole night she cannot sleep, imprisoned in a vision of carnage.

Luckily, July proceeds apace, and it's right in the middle of the summer that things get moving again.

At the end of the afternoon on Sunday, the third of August, 1924, when the kittens, already frisky and unruly, are heading gaily into their fourth month, Mathilde is on the west terrace attempting to paint their portrait, but after a minute of good behaviour, the kittens in their basket begin yawning and scrapping, and despite their mother's efforts to bring them back to the pose, they want to get on with their lives.

The sun – and Mathilde still remembers this – is just touching the top of the pines when she hears the approaching sound of a distant motorbike flying over the dirt road encircling the lake. She sits bolt upright, her paintbrush frozen in mid-air. And then, he's there, framed in the doorway, setting his cycle on its kick-stand, taking off his goggles and leather cap in one motion, revealing his blond hair, and although he's taller and more sturdy than she had imagined, she's sure it's Célestin Poux. While he speaks to Sylvain, who has come to meet him, she thinks, "Thank you, God, thank you, thank you," and she clenches her fists to keep from trembling or crying or behaving like an utter fool.

The Terror of the Armies

Please forgive me, Mademoiselle Mathilde, if I cannot remember everything. More than a few years have passed, and I've lived many a day since Bingo Crépuscule. And then, at war, everyone's off in his own little corner of worries and hopes and fears, thinking only of doing his bit and keeping his head down, getting just a hasty look now and then at the big picture. One moment erases another, the days erase each other, in the end it all seems the same. Of course I've often thought about that Sunday in January, those five prisoners in the snow, and I'm with you, I think it was a damned shame, but I don't want to lie to you: what I remember of it now isn't any clearer than an April evening at Chemin des Dames, or my mother's death when I was ten.

I didn't see your fiancé die. I know he fell as he was finishing up the snowman he was building out in the middle of no-man's-land, using just his left hand. He was wearing an overcoat without any buttons. I saw him start this snowman. It was around ten or eleven in the morning, that Sunday, and soldiers on both sides were encouraging him, without making fun of him or else it was simple teasing, because everyone had realized he'd lost his wits. The Boches even tossed him an old pipe so's he could put it in the snowman's mouth, and we'd skimmed out a tattered boater that had lost its ribbon.

I must have gone off somewhere to do I don't know what, I can't remember. I was always more or less somebody's errand boy in those days, and anyway, that was fine with me because I've never much liked staying still, so that's why everyone now says I'm married to my bike, and it's true. At least she doesn't ask anything more than to live with a man who loves the open road.

When I got back to the trench, let's say around noon, I heard that a Boche biplane had made several passes over the area, machine-gunning it for all he was worth, and that poor Cornflower had been a sitting duck out there. Afterwards, on Monday morning, when we were over in the Boche lines counting up the dead and wounded, someone who'd seen his body in the snow told me the machine gun had caught him right in the back and killed him on the spot.

I saw Six-Sous die. It was around nine o'clock Sunday morning. He stood up suddenly off to the left of Bingo, shouting that he'd had a bellyful of all this and wanted to pee like a man instead of a dog. Gangrene had been eating at him for hours, he was delirious, too, and he staggered back and forth between the trenches with his fly open, taking a piss. Then someone who spoke French over in the German trench yelled that we were pigs and cowards to abandon one of our own men like that. Over on our side, Captain Fancy Mouth yelled back, "All right, you sauerkraut-eating imbecile, if you're brave enough, let's have your name, and if I ever catch you, I'll make you eat your balls! Me, I'm Favourier!"

Then it was broad daylight, maybe an hour later. Six-Sous was still stumbling around, falling down over and over in front of the German trench, preaching about how we should all put aside our weapons and go home, that war was disgraceful, that sort of thing. Then he sang the song from the Paris Commune, "Le Temps des Cerises", just as loud as he could, singing about how those times had left a wound in his heart that would never heal. His singing was awful and he was about ready to collapse, but our hearts were aching as we listened to him. We all had our own business to attend to, and things were pretty quiet on both sides.

And then Six-Sous sat down in the snow, he was saying things that didn't make any sense, and suddenly, just like that, someone in the opposite trench shot him. He was sitting in front of them, got his bullet in the head, and fell backwards, his arms outstretched. I was there. That I saw with my own two eyes. Why one second he was simply sitting there and the next second they decided to shoot, I have no idea. Captain Favourier said, "Their major is just as much of a bastard as ours is. And their phone must have been out of commission last night or they wouldn't have had to wait so long for orders." I should mention that during the night the Boches had been lobbing grenades out haphazardly into no-man's-land and that Fancy Mouth finally got fed up and sent over a few rounds from a small trench mortar to calm them down. That was something else I had to be told about, because I'd gone off to get some grub and I didn't get back until almost dawn, loaded down like a donkey.

Now the Eskimo, him I didn't see get it, that was right after the biplane went over that killed your fiancé and blew his snowman all to hell. Before that plane, I told you, nobody was shooting any more, I think the death of Six-Sous had made even the Boches sick. I remember hearing Lieutenant Estrangin say, "If we're lucky, things will stay peaceful until tonight, then we can go out quietly and bring in those other four." You have to figure that luck just wasn't on our side that bloody Sunday.

So, it was eleven o'clock, somewhere around then. Off I go again for something or other somebody wanted me to do, taking peppermints to the lookout man in the neighbouring company, buttering up the mess sergeant, whatever. When I leave Bingo, Cornflower's busy with his snowman, doesn't seem to have a care in the world, and the Eskimo's all hunkered down in his shelter he's made overnight. There hasn't been a single sign of the farmer from the Dordogne since he climbed up that ladder and scampered off into the night with his hands tied behind his back. Now that I saw, I was there. When the flares went up over Bingo, I saw That Man crawling off to the right towards a pile of bricks sticking up out of the snow. I think he was the first one killed that Saturday night, by the machine guns or the grenades. In any case, whenever they called his name, he never answered.

So I got back to the trench around noon. Things had gone to pot, they were blazing away at each other like in the worst days of the autumn. The fellows told me, "An Albatross machine-gunned no-man's-land, went over three whole times, about fifteen metres from the ground, maybe lower. You couldn't try to bring it down without sticking at least half your body out of the trench, and then the Krauts across the way would cut you in half."

The Albatross was a 1915 Boche crate with a machine gun in the rear, because they hadn't yet figured out how to shoot through the propeller, so they were using an opening in the fuselage. And I can just imagine that dirty bastard flying low to see what the hell's going on between those two trenches and he comes back, because he's spotted Frenchies out there, so he makes another pass spraying bullets everywhere and kills your fiancé, and on his third pass he's still decorating everything with bullet holes and then, all my pals saw it and told me the same thing, all of a sudden this fellow stands up in the snow, it's the Eskimo, and he tosses something into the air with his right hand, and it's a pineapple, a grenade, that blows off the plane's entire tail unit, rudders and all, so off it goes, fluttering like a dead leaf, and crashes about a kilometre away, behind its own lines. You can bet my pals shouted bravo, but not all of them, because some had seen the Eskimo cut down by the last burst from that goddamned machine gun. They told me Favourier shouted, "Shut up, you bunch of assholes! Now get down and stay down!"

And I think it really was the Albatross that finally started the whole thing, all the butchery that went on that Sunday. Until then the Boches had believed what we'd been shouting over to them, that the five soldiers were condemned men, that they weren't armed. But there was so much stuff buried under the snow that the Eskimo had found a grenade.

From that point on, until about two o'clock, there was just random shooting at first, a few small shells came over, we took a few hits. And then the shooting stopped and we could hear the deep rumble the big guns make when they start adding their hellfire. Through all the smoke from the explosions, we could see the one from Marseille they called Common Law jump up and run across no-man's-land waving his arms in the air, covered with snow and mud, heading for the German trench. He was screaming, "I'm surrendering, don't shoot!" or something like that, because you could hardly hear anything any more, but I did catch what one of our corporals shouted up on the parapet near me: "That damn bastard, he's fucked us up enough, he's mine!" Thouvenel, that was the corporal's name. I didn't much like him, because he was cheap when it came to provisions for his men, anyway he could have snuffed out a match at sixty metres, and before anyone could stop him, he'd sent the Marseillais a bullet right in the back of the neck, a killer shot. The next day, when it was all over and Staff Sergeant Favart – who was the highest-ranking officer we had left – asked him why he'd done it, Capo Thouvenel told him, "Yesterday, before things heated up, we heard this jerk out in the snow promising the Boches that if they'd let him through their barbed wire and treat him well, then he'd tell them how many of us there were and where the phone was and where our machine guns were stashed." I don't know about that. Maybe it's true.

Anyway, that's how they all died. Afterwards, the Boche heavy artillery really pounded our front line without even caring that they were also demolishing their own, and their flares were being sent up from quite a distance away, so we realized they'd evacuated their trench some time earlier. Captain Favourier gave the order to evacuate Bingo, and we hot-footed it out of there, carrying off three dead, one of them Lieutenant Estrangin, and perhaps already a dozen wounded. I was kept busy taking care of them, and when I got back, maybe about a half-hour later, our two companies had moved about three hundred metres to the east through the trenches, and although we certainly weren't out of danger, at least it was better than Bingo. Then Captain Favourier said, "We have to get closer. Those shits won't stop dumping on us until we're close enough to bite their own asses." That's how we came to go over the top in three waves, to get a little fresh air.

We got to the first Jerry trench, which was empty, without even a scratch. In the second trench, those stubborn Boches had left behind a half-dozen poor slobs, including a *Feldwebel*, just for show. Two got themselves killed, while the *Feldwebel* and the others surrendered. I went out in the second wave, at which point Fancy Mouth had already led the first one about two hundred metres farther forward, on towards the Jerries' back-up trench, on the flank of a rise where it looked like a scar in the snow. The only shelter our men had when the Maxim guns began spitting at us were the nearby ruins of a farm.

I don't like thinking about all this again, Mademoiselle Mathilde, still less talking about it. And then, what's the use? I'll just tell you that it wasn't until a good while after nightfall that we took that rotten trench, and we left more than a hundred dead and wounded on that rise, including another lieutenant and Captain Favourier. Some friends and I were with Fancy Mouth towards the end. He asked me if I was an orphan, I didn't understand why at the time, but I answered yes, for many years now. "I thought so," he said, and added, "Whatever you do, try to stay an errand boy. You'll get in less trouble that way." He had Staff Sergeant Favart called over, to give him command of what was left of our two companies. I heard him tell Favart what he thought of our CO, Major Lavrouye, nicknamed Ol' Fraidy, then there was something about an order he'd received before the attack and a paper that Ol' Fraidy had kept under his arm, but he noticed there were several of us listening to him, so he told us to go fuck off somewhere else. He was wounded in the belly. Some stretcher-bearers carried him away, but he died before they could get him to a dressing station.

Two of my pals and I spent the night going back and forth between our former positions and that German trench, bringing in everything to eat and drink, French or Boche, that we could lay our hands on. The shelling stopped at dawn. It was snowing. Our men were clamouring for tobacco and brandy, and I gave them my usual line about how I'd kill my own parents to get them what they wanted, and that's when I suddenly understood dear old Fancy Mouth's question. The expression had become so automatic with me that I never even gave it a second thought. Now, whenever I find myself saying it, I remember the captain, it makes me feel strange all over, a bit as though I were somehow orphaned by his death.

Some Newfoundlanders joined us on the front line shortly before noon. Then some Scots in kilts and leather aprons, some English, and some Irish came up from the rear to relieve us along all our positions.

That Monday evening, back in our billet, I brought their evening meal to Staff Sergeant Favart and the corporals while they were drawing up the casualty list. I heard them say that the condemned men were being transferred to our battalion as of Saturday the sixth and that they were being counted among our battlefield losses. Corporal Chardolot found that a bit thick and even allowed as how it stank to high heaven. Favart probably thought the same thing, but he replied that orders were orders, and that Ol' Fraidy must have had his reasons and that was the way of the world.

Many years later, whenever Mathilde happens to think of Célestin Poux – which she will almost as frequently as she will think of her own youth – the first thing she'll remember about him will be his blond hair and the two big circles of clean pink skin around his blue eyes when he alighted from his cycle at the Villa MMM that Sunday in August. The rest of his face was a black mask of dirt. He'd ridden all night and nearly all day, practically without eating or sleeping, stopping only at village fountains to quench his thirst, with the single-minded purpose of reaching her as quickly as possible. The telegram that was to have announced his impending arrival was delivered to Mathilde only on the following day.

HAVE UNEARTHED SOLE ARMY TERROR OF INTEREST TO YOU. STOP. AM SENDING YOU SAME TRUSTING IN GOD AND TRIUMPH MOTORS. STOP. MY EXPENSES AS WELL OF COURSE. STOP.

GERMAIN PIRE

A few days later, the dear man will relate to Mathilde, with all due modesty, how he laid hands on at least one of his two elusive quarries.

An intrepid lady of his acquaintance – someone with whom, at one time, he'd been very intimately acquainted indeed – has a flat tyre in the forest of Compiègne while driving to Saint-Quentin to rejoin her husband. Not wishing to dirty her gloves, she waits for someone to come along. A passing farmer stops to change her tyre. She sets out again, the wind in her hair, but no sooner does she leave the forest behind than the spare tyre, no doubt improperly inflated, goes flat on her as well. Fortunately, she's in a little village. Unfortunately, the closest garage is seven kilometres farther along on the road to Noyon. The lady's motto is: "If a man can do it, so can I." And off she goes on foot to the garage, where she arrives exhausted, drooping from the heat, the neck of her blouse several buttons looser. Fortunately, the garage employee is a charming young man; he brings her a chair, a glass of water. Unfortunately, the boss isn't there and they don't sell tyres. If the boss were there to man the petrol pump, the charming young man would sacrifice his own parents to ensure her departure on four proper wheels before nightfall, and he might be able to do this without even having to become an orphan.

In short, the Amazon winds up at the petrol pump and the garage man sets off on a huge motorcycle. He returns, after numerous adventures, with the lady's car in good running order, and as she goes into raptures over his success, the young man's boss, who has turned up in the meantime, remarks with a hint of pride and a great deal of resignation, "What do you expect, after all, he's Célestin Poux. In the war we called him the Terror of the Armies." At this point, the lady can do no less than give Célestin a lift back to his motorcycle, which he left seven kilometres down the road. By now it's dark out. She doesn't like to drive at night. She prefers to stay in Noyon and rejoin her husband the following day. The more and more charming young man leads the way on his motorbike to a local inn, where the lady can do no less than invite him to dinner, which invitation he accepts, and since men don't hesitate to take someone who pleases them to bed, neither does she.

According to Germain Pire, in whom his lady friend confides a few days later in Paris, the two spent a delightful night together, but Monsieur Pire doesn't wait long enough to hear all the details, which she is about to divulge, because he is already on his way to Noyon. That very evening, having explained the situation to the garage mechanic, he sends his telegram and the Terror of the Armies (trusting in God and his motorcycle) off to the Landes, his petrol expenses as well, of course. Célestin Poux frankly welcomes the opportunity to move on at last after too long a stay in one place, and Hossegor, after all, brings him closer to his beloved Ile d'Oléron.

Standing before Mathilde – after the introductions have been made and before any other conversation can begin, Célestin would at least like to wash his face. Mathilde asks Bénédicte to show him to a bathroom. There are three in her humble home. Their guest thinks the garden pump will do handsomely, although they manage to persuade him to accept the offer of a towel. He washes his face and torso with much splashing of water, then goes to his bike for a clean shirt. His motorcycle is of a dirty red colour, and attached to the rear is a steel locker painted the same hue, not quite as begrimed as the rest of the bike. Strapped to that are a huge duffel bag, petrol cans, a camping stove, a folded tent, and a broom shrub he intends to replant on his native island. Simply unpacking these impedimenta would take anyone else the rest of the day, but he isn't just anyone, and he brings to all things a genius for organized disorder. Including his ablutions and even the short mandatory tour of inspection he conducts for Sylvain, who is naturally fascinated by the motorcycle, it takes him a mere five minutes, six at the most, before he's sitting with Mathilde on the terrace, nice and clean in a fresh pale blue shirt, ready to tell her the story of his life.

He talks for a long while, occasionally lapsing into painful silences or rising to pace in circles with his hands jammed into his pockets. He smokes enough cigarettes to fill the ashtray to overflowing. When night falls, they light the lanterns on the terrace and in the garden. Bénédicte brings an omelette, a cold joint, and some fruit, which she sets out on a big wooden table. Célestin rises to the occasion, gratefully dispatching the omelette and almost everything else on the table.

Bénédicte decides that this young man is very well-mannered indeed.

Now he's sitting across from Mathilde, pensive, blond, curly-haired. He resembles Arthur, a baby-doll she once had, with the same stocky body, robust arms, and frank countenance. And what a melting smile. But he hasn't smiled for some time now. Because of her, he's reliving his war days.

She has so many questions she'd like to ask him that she gives up. She tells him that tonight he'll sleep under her roof. She asks him if he's in any kind of hurry. He tells her no, he's here one minute, somewhere else the next, he's under no obligation to anyone, except that he should perhaps see to the broom shrub he dug up en route, which must be replanted somewhere rather soon. He'd intended to take it to the Ile d'Oléron, to the garden of a childhood friend, but he must admit that broom isn't exactly a rare plant on his island. Without a word, Mathilde points to a corner of her garden which Sylvain had left bare, uncertain as to what would go well with some purple pansies. Célestin turns around, takes a look, and without saying a word either, simply by making a tiny face and giving a tiny shrug, replies that if that's what she wants, there or wherever, it's all the same to him, he has never been stubborn about these things.

As for staying the night, he says he doesn't want to be a bother, there's no need to prepare a room for him, he has all he needs on his bike and it's a beautiful night, he'll be happy to sleep in the woods, between the lake and the ocean. Except here's the hitch: Mathilde has always been stubborn about these things.

*

The next morning, still in bed, busily writing down what Célestin told her the evening before, Mathilde feels her heart stop when she hears the roar of the departing Triumph, and she rings her bell like a madwoman. Bénédicte hurries to her side, then explains that since Sylvain was dying to try out the bike, their guest had good-naturedly unloaded all his gypsy baggage from the back of the cycle so that the two of them could go off for a spin. It's easy to tell from the backfire that this fiendish invention must go faster than a hundred kilometres an hour. What's more, they planted the broom in the garden and then were in such a hurry to be off that they left all the gardening tools lying about. "Well," says Mathilde, "this is a pretty mess."

A little later, lying on the massage table, she hears the men return, hears them loudly congratulating each other out in the garden. Apparently Sylvain drove the whole way, and the motorbike has emerged from its ordeal unscathed. Mathilde thinks they might become good friends if she were to ask Célestin to stay on for a while at the villa. On that idea, she closes her eyes.

She now has a specialist from the local sanatorium come by three times a week to give her a massage, Monsieur Michelot, a big heavy man with glasses. The lifeguard who used to come by, Georges Cornu, shaved off his moustache and decamped three years ago with the wife of a pharmacist in Dax and the wife of a fisherman in Cap-Breton, both childless, luckily, and half-sisters through their father to boot, which takes a bit of drama away from the whole affair. As Bénédicte says, "These things happen."

After Monsieur Michelot leaves, Mathilde has her breakfast out on the sunny terrace facing the lake. She asks Sylvain to bring out her mahogany box, from which she has removed only the confidential letter from Elodie Gordes. She has arranged everything else in chronological order to make things clearer for Célestin.

He's sitting across from her, as he did the previous evening, but now they are seated at a rectangular, white-enamelled table, and this time it's Mathilde who is eating, as she watches him read her notes on her first meeting with Daniel Esperanza. Although he makes no comment until he has finished, Mathilde can see from his face that he's remembering details he had forgotten, sad details.

Looking gloomily up at her, he says, "It feels strange to me, told that way, but that really is what happened. I'm sorry I didn't realize at the time what a good man that Sergeant Esperanza was."

Then he confirms for Mathilde that it was Corporal Gordes who traded his shoes and puttees for the Eskimo's German boots. They'd known each other in another regiment, and Corporal Gordes had seemed very much affected by his friend's misfortune. During the night, he'd even wanted to cut through the wire so he could go and join him, and Lieutenant Estrangin had had to yell at him to make him see reason.

He also confirms that he had himself given a left-handed glove to one of the prisoners who didn't have one on his good hand. That was Manech.

Without giving Mathilde time to grow emotional over this, he immediately adds that he was also the one ordered by Captain Favourier to deliver his letter to a post orderly, and that if Esperanza finally received it off in the Vosges, even months later, this proves that the army's postal service was not as hopeless as most of the other services were, including the general staff.

He reads the prisoners' letters. Commenting on the

Eskimo's, he says, "It was Corporal Gordes who was called Biscuit. I'm glad to hear that at least this whole business made them friends again." That Man's letter surprises him just as much as it did Mathilde. He reads it twice, goes over it a third time, holds it up in his hand, and states confidently, "This one's coded, I'd swear it on my parents' graves."

Mathilde tells him to leave his poor parents in peace for a moment, because she has always suspected that Benoît Notre-Dame and his Mariette had a private code. What she wants to know is, can he figure out which one? He replies that married couples, fiancés, lovers all had their own systems for fooling the censors. For example, certain words might be given a special meaning, one understandable only to those who were in on the secret, obviously, and even a counter-espionage expert couldn't crack those codes. There were other methods, and he knows of three that were both widely used and easy to decipher. With Flea Jump, you read the letter by skipping words in groups of two, three, four, or more. With Lovers' Lane, you read only the lines that had been agreed upon in advance. Célestin can safely say That Man used neither one of these methods, which Mathilde can see for herself, moreover. There was also the Elevator, which consisted in lining the words up on the page in such a way that one could read a secret sentence either from top to bottom or vice versa, beginning with a previously selected base word that never varied. Unfortunately, if this was the code used by That Man and his wife, then it would be legible only in the original letter, and Esperanza's copy would be useless.

Mathilde drinks the last of her *café au lait*. She asks Célestin to read the next letter, the one Common Law dictated to him in Captain Fancy Mouth's dugout. As far as he can remember, apart from the spelling, which has never been his strong point and which Esperanza had corrected, it does seem to be what the Marseillais asked him to write.

"This letter's in code, too," says Mathilde. "Tina Lombardi's godmother told me so herself, you'll see when you read her letter to me. Did you realize that?"

He shifts in his seat and sighs. "Finish your breakfast. Let me keep reading."

After going over her account of Pierre-Marie Rouvière's revelations, he stands silently in the sunshine for a long while, watching the sea-gulls that gather on the sand bars out in the lake at low tide. Then he sits down at the table again and says, "That's what the captain was talking about before he died. It was Poincaré's pardon that Major Lavrouye kept under his arm."

"Why did he do that?"

"How should I know? Because he was a bastard, that's all, or because he wanted to cause trouble for some higher-ups, or because he wanted to get Favourier in hot water. Who knows? If I were to learn one day that he hadn't felt like interrupting a good dinner to go set things right, I wouldn't be surprised."

He's puzzled by the letter from his corporal's mother, Madame Chardolot. He'd continued to run into Urbain Chardolot, now and again, for a long time after the business at Bingo. In fact, it wasn't until the spring of '18 that they were separated by the hazards of war. Chardolot had never mentioned his doubts to him, or to anyone, probably, because rumours travelled fast in the billets or the trenches, and anything like that would have quickly reached his ears.

"Did you talk much about that Sunday, among yourselves?"

"For a while, yes. We talked about the attack, about our pals who'd been killed, the wounded who'd at least been lucky enough to be sent home. And then, like I told you, it's just one piece of shit after another, the days erase each other."

"But the five prisoners – you didn't talk about them?"

He bows his head. "What for?" he says. "We didn't even like mentioning our dead friends. Better to just not talk about it."

Then he rereads the passage in the letter concerning Urbain Chardolot's confession to his parents when he was home on leave.

You're right, I must have dreamed everything, and also that I saw the five of them lying dead in the snow, except that at least one of them, if not two, was not the person I'd expected to find there.

"I can't figure out what it means," he admits. "I didn't know Chardolot went back to Bingo that Monday morning. We were in the third German trench, more than three hundred metres to the right and almost a kilometre farther forward. To go back to the rear, you'd take the shortest route."

"Who else went back to the rear on Sunday night and Monday morning?" asks Mathilde.

"I don't remember any more. Me, for example, with the wounded, or looking for some grub for the men. But it would never have occurred to me to risk making a detour with all that shelling going on." After some thought, he adds, "That Sunday night, scads of people must have gone back, at one point or another. Taking back prisoners, bringing up supplies and ammunition, helping the machine gunners to bring up their pieces. There was also lots of confusion when Sergeant Favart took over the command. Even though he wasn't the sort to lose his head in a tight spot – and we'd seen that when he was our lieutenant at Chemin des Dames – still, he needed a bit of time to get organized."

"You told me someone had seen Manech's body in the snow, Monday morning, killed by a bullet from the Albatross. So at least that person had gone back to Bingo. Who was it?"

Célestin shakes his head in despair. Too many things were happening at the same time, it had begun to snow again, he can't remember which comrade told him that, or even whether or not it was something his friend had heard from someone else.

Finally, after more reflection, he adds, "You know, perhaps that part of what Chardolot said was put into different words by his mother, and doesn't mean what you think. Maybe it meant that one of the prisoners, or perhaps even two of them, shouldn't have been there because they didn't deserve this punishment. Chardolot could have been thinking of your fiancé, who'd gone out of his mind, and also of the Eskimo, because the Eskimo claimed he was innocent."

Mathilde agrees that Chardolot's phrase might have been changed, but not to the point of acquiring a different meaning. Just read Véronique Passavant's letter and the story of her meeting with Tina Lombardi, early in March of 1917, barely two months after Bingo. He has already done so. He says that all sorts of women could be found around the billeting area seeking information that would help them locate their missing loved ones. They were often simply the dupes of soldiers or locals who told them what they wanted to believe, for money, a watch, a favour. He wouldn't like to shock Mathilde, but many called these poor women by an obscene name, and he'd heard just as many men boasting vulgarly about how they'd unbuttoned for a gullible little bourgeoise as he'd heard laughing over how they'd enjoyed someone of the likes of Tina Lombardi for free.

He rummages through the pile of papers, pulling out one of Mathilde's sheets of drawing paper. "Look," he says. "You yourself say she's mistaken, that Tina. She must have found out, I don't know how, that her Common Law had been sent to Bingo with four others, one of whom was wearing boots taken from a German. She must have found out, I don't know how, that this man was the Eskimo. She must have found out that on Monday, a wounded man from Bingo, wearing German boots, had been seen in the field hospital at Combles with a younger wounded man, so she figured it had to be the Eskimo, and perhaps the other one was her man. She was wrong. You are right. The boots were on Corporal Benjamin Gordes's feet. The younger fellow, I know who it was, a Marie-Louise from the Charentes, like me. Maybe I never even knew his real name, but we called him La Rochelle. During the night, the two of them set out to take some prisoners to the rear. On the way back, they must have had a run-in with some shells or bullets that went off course, because I heard some stretcher-bearers in our trench who had met up with them asking if this was Corporal Gordes's company. They told us he had a head wound and was pissing blood, but that he was carrying a younger fellow on his back who was even worse off, named Rochelle or La Rochelle, and that he was on his way – in his German boots – to the dressing station."

Mathilde remains silent.

A bit later Célestin reads that Benjamin Gordes was killed in the bombardment at Combles, just before he was to be evacuated. "Poor Corporal Biscuit," he sighs. "I never saw him crack a single smile, he was a real sad sack, but he was an honest man and a good soldier, and I never saw him give any grief to anyone, either." He thinks about Biscuit. He has run out of cigarettes. He crumples and uncrumples the empty pack. "Once, in our billet," he says, "I found him repairing a broken chair. We talked a bit while he worked. He told me he had a wife and five kids, he told me the kids' names. I've forgotten what they were. I remember his fingers, though. He had the hands of a jeweller. I realized that before the damned war got started he'd been at least a four-star general among cabinet-makers."

"Frédéric, Martine, Georges, Noémie, Hélène," says Mathilde. "There's a half-empty pack of Gauloises in the right-hand drawer of the sideboard, in the dining room. Sylvain left them there after he gave up smoking."

That afternoon, on the other terrace, Mathilde tries again to paint the kittens, but without her models, who have gone off to play hide-and-seek in the bushes or enjoy a refreshing siesta. Célestin reads and rereads the pages of her memoranda. Commenting on the references to himself in the letters she has received, he explains, "It's all a pack of lies. All right, I cut some corners here and there, but I never cheated anyone and I always gave favour for favour. The cauldron of soup, for example, was only a kettle that barely held enough to fill two canteens, and the cooks were telling the truth, I was in cahoots with them. As for the bigwigs' dinner that went missing at headquarters, who's to complain? Not anybody in my section, you can bet. It was a wonderful leg of mutton, nicely roasted on the outside, tender and juicy on the inside. And the peaches in syrup, simply marvellous. It was just as well off in our bellies as it would've been inside those pompous old sticklers. And I gave my source three packets of Caporal tobacco for the tip."

Later, pushing everything away from him on the wicker tabletop, he says shit, his head feels "like an overripe melon". He doesn't know anything any more and now doubts everything, even what he saw and heard for himself on that dismal Sunday, but he's certain of one thing: if one of the five men tossed into the snow that night managed to survive, it had to be That Man.

"Why?" asks Mathilde curtly, turning towards him.

He's tired. His face is flushed. He shrugs, without looking at her. He says, "Because the war they're talking about in this mess of papers, it's something I don't recognize, I'd almost believe it isn't really the same war I was in." He repeats, more loudly, "Shit!" Then he calms down, he's ashamed of himself. Mathilde is still looking at him, still holding her paintbrush poised in the air. He hangs his head. "To make it out of there," he tells her, "you had to find a good hole right away and keep your trap shut, just like Captain Favourier said. You had to stay in that hole all night, all day, unnoticed by anyone, eating snow, relieving yourself without moving even a single toe, just waiting. Now, Six-Sous belts out 'Le Temps des Cerises', Manech builds a snowman, Common Law tries to surrender, the Eskimo brings down a biplane with a grenade. There's only That Man, the steadiest and strongest of all five of them – and I know this, I saw him in the hut and afterwards – who could make it out alive. But he didn't get out of there, either, I'm telling you, there was too much stuff raining down, too much, you understand me? There was too much stuff coming down on Bingo and no-man's-land. We were in much better shelter than he was, and even we were being massacred, so we got out of there fast."

Mathilde never lets herself be affected by other people's weariness. Perhaps this is because she has been obliged, for so many years now, to do so many things "without moving even a single toe". But she's growing fond of Célestin, so she sets him free for a moment.

Off he runs, with his head like an overripe melon, to dive into the lake. She watches him swim, from a window of her bedroom. He's wearing one of Sylvain's bathing suits with shoulder straps. He's a good swimmer, but not as good as Manech. She reflects that it has been a long time since she last swam – or floated, if you prefer – with cork anklets. She'd give anything to hear Manech swim just once more, she doesn't even have to see him, she's not asking that much, she simply wants to hear the rhythmic slap of his arms and legs in the lake, on a quiet April evening.

"Brrr!" he cries, because the water is cold, and then he swims, and she hears him, she hears him.

Bénédicte comes into the room at some point, carrying the mahogany box. Through the window Mathilde sees that Sylvain has joined Célestin in the water, they're roughhousing around, trying to dunk each other. Near her, Bénédicte sighs resignedly. She says that whenever men get together, it doesn't matter if they're thirty years old or fifty, they can't help it, they behave like children.

That evening, the four of them have dinner in the dining room, with all the French windows standing open. Mathilde says it would be nice if her father hired Célestin to take care of the Delage and to help out Sylvain. There's a long silence. All three of them are looking down at their plates, and she adds automatically, just to be polite, "If it's all right with Célestin, of course."

Célestin-Arthur lifts his porcelain-blue eyes to hers and looks at her for a long time.

"Mademoiselle Mathilde," he asks, "may I address you

informally? I'd rather, because it makes me very uncomfortable to stand on ceremony with people, especially when I like them."

"I don't care how people address me as long as they tell me interesting things. I'm treating you respectfully, Célestin, because I'm afraid that I've been a great bother to you ever since you arrived here yesterday."

He smiles, the smile that melts hearts. He turns his attention to his food again. He tells Bénédicte everything's delicious. Bénédicte is pleased. There's another silence. Mathilde asks Sylvain what he thinks of her suggestion. Sylvain thinks the whole idea is catastrophic, yes, catastrophic. He and Célestin burst out laughing. Bénédicte does, too, even though she hasn't a clue what this is all about. Mathilde sits there with a long face, looking at them as though they were three simpletons.

In the end, because she hates being left out, even when it's only silly laughter, she bangs on the table so hard the dishes rattle. She says – she almost screams – to Célestin, "I want you to take me there! You understand? I want to see that damned place with my own eyes!"

Another silence. Célestin looks at her, his face all flushed, and then he says, "Where do you think we went this morning, Sylvain and I? To the railway station in Labenne. We're leaving on Wednesday, you and Sylvain on the train, me in the Delage, because we'll need it. If I get there first, I'll wait for you at the station in Péronne. If you arrive before me, I'll meet you at the hotel Sylvain mentioned, the Auberge des Remparts. You don't have to make such a fuss when you're dealing with men as bright as we are."

Mathilde rolls her wheelchair forward and stretches out her hand towards him across the table, knocking over the bottle of wine. Bénédicte has a fit, and Sylvain, well, Sylvain is deeply moved. You can tell by the way he's smoothing his red moustache with a thumb and forefinger.

The Other Side of
No-Man's-Land

The huge, freshly mown field has a lush green hill for its horizon, a little stream flowing quietly beneath a wooden bridge, and two truncated elms with leafy lower branches, their trunks ringed by suckers.

Sylvain and Célestin take Mathilde exploring in a sedan-chair, which is her old wheelchair appearing in a new guise thanks to Guess Who, with the help of some wing-nuts and two steel poles. As to how Guess Who got hold of these poles, never mind. Mathilde, borne aloft like an empress, sees everything from on high, in the pitiless August sunshine. In a lacy white dress, shaded by her parasol and a sun-bonnet trimmed with a pink silk scarf, she feels as though she were on safari in Africa, hunting sorrows.

Their guide is Monsieur Alphonse Dondut, the owner of these forty hectares, who suddenly halts and stamps the ground with his heavy shoes. "So!" he says, in his thick northern accent, "it's here, mademoiselle, Bingo was right here, across from Erlangen, the German trench." He casts a cold, vindictive eye around his domain and sighs deeply. "I left those two trees," he says, "so there'd be something to see when people visit the battlefield. For a very reasonable price, if they're interested, my wife dishes them up some tasty cabbage soup with black pepper at our house, with cheese and wine, too. If that sounds good to you, a little later, you're all three cordially invited. So! . . . The bridge, that's something I rebuilt, with my son-in-law. The Huns, can you imagine, they'd changed the course of the stream to suit themselves, far to the east, behind the hills. So! . . . I've sure seen some terrible things."

They set Mathilde down. Célestin wanders off. He doesn't recognize anything. He shouts from a distance, "There were some bricks here, a collapsed wall or something. What was it?"

Monsieur Dondut doesn't know. He bought the property in 1921, by which time the trenches had been filled, the soil already turned over. In fact, it was when he was out ploughing in his fields that the previous owner had found the grenade that blew off his right arm. "Not a week goes by," adds their host, "that we don't hear of someone exploding. So! . . . That war hasn't finished killing, you'll see, she's still got some good years ahead of her."

Mathilde tries in vain to imagine a battlefield. She asks where they might find the former owner. Monsieur Dondut tells her that with the money from the sale of his property, the man set himself up as a tavern-keeper near Montauban-de-Picardie, on the road to Fricourt.

"Ask for the Cabaret Rouge. And ask for Lefty. Hyacinthe Deprez, that's his name, but it's better if you ask for Lefty." Then he gazes out again over his fields as though it were all he can do to keep from spitting on them. He has to get back to work, so he bids Mathilde good day and leaves.

Mathilde stays there an hour, without ever being able to make the setting she'd constructed in her imagination superimpose itself on the reality before her. More than seven years have already gone by. In July, there had probably been thousands of poppies in full bloom. Fighting off discouragement, she waves her parasol at Sylvain and Célestin, two tiny silhouettes on top of the hill, signalling them to return. According to her wristwatch, it takes them less than six minutes to reach her.

"Up there," says Célestin, "we were at the Boches' third line, the one that cost us so many men."

"It isn't as far away as you said it was," she replies. "It's not hard to understand that even in the snow, even at night, even during the shelling, Benjamin Gordes had to come back to see what he could still do for his friend the Eskimo." Since Célestin doesn't look all that convinced, she adds, in Monsieur Dondut's drawling accent, "So! . . ."

They eat lunch at the Cabaret Rouge, where they are the only customers. The walls are covered with war souvenirs. Lefty is fifty-five years old, as strong as an ox, dressed in dingy grey, with a rugged face and a huge droopy moustache. In the neighbouring building, where he lives with his wife, he has set up a kind of museum. The entrance fee is posted over the counter: a hundred sous general admission, fifty for children and old folks, gratis for the brave men who lived through the butchery.

Lefty roars with laughter when he meets Célestin.

"So you're the one they still talk about! Justa Bit More, Toto the Soldier, the boy wonder who served the officers' leg of mutton to his platoon! Ah, put 'er there, my lad – how proud I am to meet you!"

And a kiss on one cheek, and a kiss on the other. When

men get sentimental, thinks Mathilde, they're even more nauseating than painted old biddies.

Nevertheless, she tackles her lunch with a good appetite, and somewhere in her amorphous little brain, a dream is born. Towards the end of that snowy Sunday, in the dark, Benjamin Gordes and young La Rochelle, having taken in their German prisoners, are returning to their lines. "Follow me," the corporal tells the Marie-Louise. "I want to see about my friend. It will take us only about a half-kilometre out of our way, and if he's still alive, I'll rescue him." And off they go, the two of them, through the great bursts of fire, the exploding shells, and the hellish din of that night, a night on which Manech was perhaps breathing his last.

"I came back to my fields and the ruins of my farm in April of '17," Lefty tells her, "after the Boches had tightened up their front by falling back about forty or fifty kilometres to their Siegfried Line. The countryside was swarming with Britishers from everywhere, English, Scots, Irish, Australians, New Zealanders, even natives from India with their turbans. In all my life I never heard so much English jabbering as I did in '17 and '18, and it's not half tiresome, but they're the bravest soldiers you'll ever want to see, apart from my pal here Célestin Poux, and General Fayolle. Because I've read loads of books about the war and my considered opinion is, if anyone got close to a breakthrough, it was definitely Fayolle in the Somme, during the summer and autumn of 1916."

Célestin announces his complete agreement. Emile Fayolle is by far his favourite general. He has seen him with his own eyes, and once, in Cléry, not far from where they now sit, Fayolle actually spoke to him, saying a few unforgettable words he can't recall at the moment. Yes, Fayolle was a great-hearted man. Then they review the generals. Mangin was a savage. Pétain is the victor of Verdun but a hard man, full of his own importance. "Definitely a hypocrite," adds Lefty. Foch was a tough nut, too. Joffre was getting old. Nivelle blew it for good at Chemin des Dames. Sylvain, who did his bit during the war like everyone else, lets it be known that he has read some books, too, and they shouldn't be too hard on Nivelle, who just didn't have any luck and was that close to victory. Then he adds immediately, because he's no fool, after all, "I don't give a damn about victory. The whole lot of them, they all massacred too many people." To which Lefty replies, That's so true.

Célestin, who always wants to have the last word, concludes, "Still, Fayolle was the best of a bad bunch. And I'm glad all those crummy politicians gave him his field-marshal's baton."

Before this orgy of nonsense, Mathilde manages to learn a few interesting things. The remains of the brick wall out in front of Bingo were all that was left of a long-abandoned chapel that Hyacinthe Deprez had used as a tool shed. Beneath it was a small cellar. Monsieur Deprez and his wife had taken refuge with her younger brother, a real-estate agent in Compiègne, so they weren't around when the bodies of the five French soldiers buried by the British were found in their field. Monsieur Deprez had heard that it was the mischievous little daughter of his neighbours, the Rouquiers, who had discovered the grave one day when she was roaming around the devastated trenches looking for souvenirs. The girl had told some soldiers of her find and then received a stinging smack on the face from her mother as a reward for her good intentions. As far as he can remember, the girl was named Jeannette, and ought to be getting on towards seventeen or eighteen years old by now.

"It's a miracle she didn't get herself blown sky high that day," adds their host. "The mine-clearance experts had only just started work on that area, and by the time they were finished, they'd turned up enough stuff to blow an entire village to matchsticks."

After lunch, Mathilde is carried in her sedan chair to the museum next door, when what she really wants to do is hurry back to Bingo and locate the Rouquiers. The museum is a large room lined with niches in the masonry, illuminated by nightmarish electric lights, where life-sized mannequins stand waiting in a terrible stillness: French, British, and German soldiers arrayed in all their horror, with full kit and weapons, their empty eyes staring out into nothingness. Lefty is quite proud of his creation, and has invested all his savings in it, not to mention the heritage of his descendants down to about the fifteenth generation. He shows Mathilde a red metal box of Pall Mall tobacco or cigarettes on a big trestle table in the middle of the room covered with uniform buttons, shoulder tabs, insignia, knives, sabres, all neatly arranged, and he tells her, "It was one like this that scamp found in my field, buried in the soldiers' grave. Inside, her mother told me, was a note one of the Canadians who buried them had kindly written, so they wouldn't cross over without an epitaph."

Next, the air of the open road. Mathilde, who disturbs Him only when she absolutely must, asks the Good Lord never to make her dream at night about that museum, even if she has been bad, even if she finds herself imagining once more that she's having a certain sergeant from the Aveyron named Garenne pulled to pieces by the horses of death's-head-sporting uhlans.

Without needing to become an orphan, Célestin quickly finds the Rouquiers' farm, a ramshackle affair of stone, brick, cement, and various odds and ends held upright by some big posts, between which run lines festooned with laundry. Madame Rouquier informs them that her daughter left with a big belly and a Norman tramp from Lens, that she received a postcard from Trouville telling her Jeannette was in good health, working as a charwoman, and due to have her baby in October. Sylvain and Célestin go out into the courtyard to play with the dogs. Mathilde drinks a glass of lemonade in a spic-and-span kitchen perfumed by the rope of garlic bulbs hanging from the ceiling, a thing one often sees in the Midi. Garlic's good for the heart and keeps the devil away.

Yes, little Jeannette dug up the Pall Mall tin. She was ten years old, and she could read. She ran out on the road and found some soldiers. She came back to the farm and received the proper box on the ears she so richly deserved for gallivanting off like that with all those nasty explosives lying around. Madame Rouquier claims to have been right at the scene from then on. She went to watch the soldiers digging up the grave in Hyacinthe Deprez's field. They had five pine coffins brought up immediately to transport the bodies.

"Obviously," she tells Mathilde, "they weren't a pretty sight."

"That figures," replies Mathilde coldly. In any case, the five of them were under a big brown tarp, and they all had bandages on one hand, some on the right one, some on the left. Madame Rouquier couldn't get too close, especially since other people from the neighbourhood were crowding around and the soldiers were beginning to get browned off, but she heard everything, absolutely everything. She knows, for example, that one of the unfortunate soldiers was named Notre-Dame, and another, Bouquet, like a bouquet of roses, and still another had an Italian name. The one in command of the detail, a corporal or a sergeant – she never could tell the ranks apart – read aloud the names and military class years from the dead men's identity discs before they were wrapped in their shrouds, and she remembers that the youngest one must have been just barely twenty years old.

They carted the coffins away in a horse-drawn wagon. It was cold. The wheels and the horses' hoofs were slipping in the frozen ruts. That's when one of the soldiers, a surly Parisian, turned around to scream at the watching crowd, "Get away, you flock of vultures! Haven't you anything better to do than stand around gawking at death?" Some people were so outraged at such treatment that they protested to the mayor, who'd returned to the community not long before, but the mayor received an even worse reception from the officer to whom he protested in turn, for the officer told him to go find a violin to piss in, can you imagine that, to piss in, because as far as the officer was concerned, the mayor might as well waste his own time that way rather than waste both their times with this idiotic complaint. Those troops left in April, finally. The English soldiers were more polite. Or perhaps it was simply that no one could understand what they were saying.

Shortly afterwards, the leaves of the two elms at Bingo flutter in the breeze. Mathilde had wanted to see the place one last time.

"You're making yourself unhappy," Célestin tells her. "What for?"

She doesn't know. She watches the blazing sunset light up the hillside. Sylvain has gone off in the car to get some petrol. "That glove you gave Manech," she asks, "what did it look like?"

Célestin tells her red, with white stripes on the wrist. One of his childhood friends had knitted it for him, a girl in Oléron.

Since he hadn't wanted to part with this gift, he'd worn the remaining glove on his right hand for the rest of the winter, matched with an officer's glove of pale yellow kid, from a pair he'd found lying around somewhere.

She can easily imagine him with one glove of red wool and another of pale yellow leather, with his helmet, his knapsack, his canteen, and his ration loaves of bread. She thinks he makes a touching picture.

"Why do you want to know what my glove looked like? Did Madame Rouquier tell you one of the five bodies was wearing it?"

"No, that's just the point," observes Mathilde.

He thinks this over. "Maybe she didn't notice it. Maybe she forgot. Or maybe Manech wasn't wearing it any more." Mathilde thinks that for such a gaudy glove, that makes a lot of maybes. He stands next to her for another moment in silence. "It's true," he says, "Manech did have it on when he was building his snowman. So Madame Rouquier didn't see things from as close up as she said, that's all."

He walks off through the field. She has the impression he's trying to take his bearings from the trees and the stream bed to locate the spot where the snowman stood. He's about fifty or sixty metres away from her. "Cornflower was here when my pals saw him fall!" he shouts. "After all, they wouldn't make up something like that!"

Mathilde has grown fond of Toto the Soldier. He's understanding with her, and generous with his time. Besides, he wore mismatched gloves all winter to help out Manech. Otherwise, she'd be perfectly willing to tell him to go find himself a violin.

*

That evening, on Friday the eighth of August, 1924, at the Auberge des Remparts in Péronne, three events occur within less than one hour, events so upsetting to Mathilde that she will always find it difficult to separate them in her memory. They will be like a single lightning bolt in a storm.

First, when she takes her seat in the dining room, a young woman her own age comes over and introduces herself. She speaks French almost without an accent. She is wearing a black-and-beige dress, a cloche hat. She is thin, not very tall, a brunette with blue eyes, neither plain nor pretty, an Austrian. She's travelling with her husband, whom she has left finishing his crayfish dinner at the other end of the room. He is Prussian, a customs official. When Mathilde looks over in his direction, he stands up immediately, bowing to her with a brusque snap of his head. The woman's name is Heidi Weiss. She has learned from the maître d' that Mathilde lost her fiancé in January 1917 in a trench named Bingo Crépuscule, or Bing au Crépuscule, or, more likely, Byng au Crépuscule, because there was a formidable English general of that name. She has come here to pray at the grave of her brother Gunther, who was also killed in front of Bingo, at the age of twenty-three, on the first Sunday of that same January.

Mathilde signals Sylvain to bring up a chair for the young Austrian woman. Heidi Weiss sits down and asks the two men if they were in the war. They say yes. She asks them not to take offence if she cannot shake their hands as she does with Mathilde, because her brother is dead, it wouldn't be proper, and her husband, whose family was traumatized by Germany's defeat, would be angry with her for weeks.

Sylvain and Célestin say they understand, they're not the least bit offended. She's happy to learn, however, that Sylvain was busy with navy ordnance in Bordeaux, fighting the enemy with the sweat of his brow, and that he never saw any Germans face to face except prisoners of war. Célestin sits there quietly. But she insists, greatly distressed, tears already welling into her eyes.

"And you, were you there too, that day?"

He replies softly, looking her straight in the face, that he was there, yes, and that he considers himself a good soldier who did what he could, but that during the entire war, as far as he knows, he killed two enemy soldiers, one at Douaumont, before Verdun, in 1916, and the other in the debacle of the spring of 1918. But please continue, he says, because he may have seen her brother.

If she correctly understood the *Feldwebel* who told her about Bingo after the war, Gunther was killed by the French at the end of the day, on Sunday, in a second-line trench where he was a machine gunner's mate.

"That's true," says Célestin. "There were two dead, and the others surrendered, they had no more ammunition. The *Feldwebel*, I can still see him, he was a big fellow with blond hair. He'd lost his helmet, his hair was falling down over his eyes. It was the grenadiers who killed your brother, when they took out the machine gun, but no one can blame anyone for anything any more in that damned mess."

Heidi Weiss understands those last two words. She nods, her eyes closed, her lips white with strain.

She recovers her composure, tells Mathilde the name of the *Feldwebel* who was her brother's commanding officer and who came to see her in 1919, to tell her how he died: Heinz Gerstacker. He told her that the French had tossed five of their own men, all wounded in one hand, without weapons, into the snow. He told her that early that Sunday, they'd had to send dispatch riders to the rear to receive orders, because the telephone had been destroyed by a trench mortar during the night. He told her some other things she has forgotten, but she clearly remembers one detail that struck her: as he was being led away a prisoner behind the French lines, Heinz Gerstacker saw one of the five dead men – for all five of them had been killed – kneeling in a hole, as though he were praying.

Mathilde feels a sudden chill come over her and turns towards Célestin, who asks Heidi Weiss, "Your officer – just when did we take him behind our lines? Was it late on Sunday or on Monday morning?"

"He only talked to us about Sunday and Sunday night. But I know where to find him, in Germany. I will write to him or go and see him to let him know that I have met you."

"Didn't he mention the youngest of the five men, my fiancé?" asks Mathilde. "The one who built a snowman out between the trenches? With one hand? Surely you must remember that?"

Heidi Weiss closes her eyes, sets her mouth in a grim line, nods her head slowly, yes. After a few seconds, without looking at Mathilde, looking at the corner of the tablecloth or a glass or anything else at all, she says, "It was one of our planes that killed your fiancé, but I swear that no one in our trench wanted that to happen. You must know, he was no longer in his right mind. And then suddenly the one who had the best hiding place threw a grenade at that plane and brought it down, Heinz Gerstacker told us about that, and then the orders came to evacuate our trenches to give a free hand to the artillery."

No one is eating. Heidi Weiss asks for a piece of paper, a pencil, to write down Mathilde's address. She repeats that her husband will be angry with her for weeks. Mathilde touches her hand resting on the table and tells her, "You'd better go now, but do persuade that *Feldwebel* to write to me." Mathilde is beginning to think that Heidi Weiss has beautiful, sad eyes. She swivels her wheelchair around to watch her rejoin her husband. The Austrian has the slender carriage of a doe in her native mountains, and the cloche hat of a saucy girl from Montparnasse. The husband rises again to give a curt bow.

Taking a second helping of the now cold sautéed potatoes, Sylvain remarks, "It really was an incredibly stupid fuck-up, that war. Maybe one day we'll be right back where we started, and we'll have to get along with our neighbours no matter what."

In the next few minutes, the waiter for their table – whom Mathilde has taken to calling Fantomas, because he's always whispering in people's ears with a conspiratorial air – whispers to Sylvain that he's wanted on the telephone.

When Sylvain returns, he has no eyes. Mathilde means that his eyes are empty, vacant, that he has retreated inside himself in response to something that is completely beyond him. He holds a folded newspaper. He sits down. He hands the paper to Célestin.

The phone call was from Germain Pire, who told him to get a morning paper and break the news gently to Mathilde. Célestin scans the front page, reads briefly, puts the paper down in his lap, and says, "Shit!" Mathilde rolls her wheelchair towards him and tries to grab the paper. "Please, Matti," he says, "just a minute, please." Then he says, "That Tina Lombardi was guillotined yesterday morning. They called her the Officer Killer."

The third event occurs when Mathilde is in the hotel room with Sylvain, who stays with her whenever she travels. She has read and reread the article of some twenty lines on the execution, in a courtyard of the prison at Haguenau, in Alsace, of a twenty-three-year-old woman from Marseille named Valentina Emilia Maria Lombardi, alias Emilia Conte, alias Tina Bassignano, sentenced to death for the murder of an infantry colonel named François Lavrouye, a hero of the Great War, in Bonnieux, in the Vaucluse. She has also been a suspect in the murders of four other officers, about which she had remained silent to the end. She died, according to the anonymous author of the article, "refusing the sacraments of the Church, but showing remarkable dignity in the face of death." The public had not been permitted to attend either her trial or her execution, "for obvious reasons".

It is almost ten o'clock. Sylvain is sitting in his shirtsleeves near Mathilde, who is lying on her bed. There's a knock on the door. This time it's Pierre-Marie Rouvière on the telephone. Sylvain slips on his jacket and goes downstairs to the reception desk. Mathilde continues to think about Madame Paolo Conte, née Di Bocca, about her husband who died from having worked too many years in the mines, about Ange Bassignano, who tried to surrender to the enemy and got a bullet in the neck from his own side, about the pathetic wanderings of Tina Lombardi, about her beaver bonnet and collar, about her crazy promise to "blow out the brains" of anybody who had hurt her Nino, about the horror of a prison courtyard in the pale light of an August dawn.

When Sylvain returns, she's lying on her back, crying, she can't bear it any more, she's choking on her own tears.

Sylvain is a second father to her; he comforts her gently and says, "Be good, Matti, be good. You haven't given up, you're almost there."

Pierre-Marie has received a visit that afternoon from Tina

Lombardi's lawyer, who knows that he is Mathieu Donnay's legal adviser. The lawyer wishes to see Mathilde. He has a sealed letter he has sworn to deliver safely into her own hands.

Mathilde snuffles loudly and puts on a brave front. He'd better deliver it into her hands, she says, because her feet are on vacation.

The Lovers of Belle de Mai

Mademoiselle Donnay,

· I never learned to write like you so maybe you won't understand what I'm telling you, especially because I write this waiting for them to come and wake me in my cell one morning saying it's time. I'm not afraid, never have been for myself. First they'll cut off my hair then they'll cut off my head but I try not to think about it, like I always do when I'm uneasy. It's just that what I know is coming makes it hard for me to find the words I need, you understand?

I'm not looking to tell you of what they call my crimes. When they asked me all those questions hoping to trip me up I kept my mouth shut, I mean shut, my lawyer will tell you that when he gives you this letter. They got me when I was fool enough to stay around Carpentras after I took care of that Lavrouye. I should've got on the first train out of there, then I wouldn't be here now because they'd never have caught up with me. But I still had the gun in my travel bag and that's what did me in. And I'd have been perfectly willing to spill the whole thing if there'd been anyone at my trial. I'd have yelled out the truth about this Lavrouye and the pardon from Poincaré he kept secret for more than twenty hours, but they wasn't going to let me say none of that to no one, believe me. They murdered my Nino, all of them. The rat-faced bastards they wanted me to say I killed deserved worse than death. That Thouvenel, what was made a lieutenant, the one as fired that damn bullet in the trench, that Captain Romain at the trial in Dandrechain and the other two officer-judges what made it through the war, the one on the Rue de la Faisanderie and the one on the Rue de Grenelle, all of them, they just got back what they gave and I'm glad of it. As for them claiming I did it to them and with premeditation because they found those stiffs in some shady places and brothels, well who says so? Not me, you bet.

But I've better things to tell you about than those worms. If I didn't before it's because you wanted like me to discover the truth about the trench nicknamed Bingo, and I felt you might cross me unknowing in my plan or get me arrested by finding out too much. Now my hour is come and it don't matter, when you read this I will be dead and at rest and happy to be delivered from all this. And also I know you are like me somehow to be still looking for this truth after so many years, like me you're faithful to your one true love, and so what if I peddled my ass, I never loved anyone else except for my Nino, and also I remember my poor godmother, she took it so to heart when I wouldn't answer you, I owe it to her and she knows now I did the right thing, she's where I'm going to join her soon, but she'll be that happy I wrote you, you understand?

She must have told you me and Ange Bassignano go back

together since forever, both of us come into this world in Belle de Mai, that's our neighbourhood in Marseille. He was on his own quick, as for me my father was drunk every night, but don't waste tears on me as it wasn't so bad, kids don't ever get that unhappy and we played in the streets with the others, under the plane trees, and Nino he was already the handsomest and sharpest and talked the sweetest to me. We quit school by twelve or thirteen, we spent our days in vacant lots and our nights in doorways, the ones on those streets that cut down to the Chûtes-Lavie where no one ever goes late. We made love standing up, we had our dreams together. I was a few months younger but until I was seventeen or eighteen it was me took care of things. Some idiots said later Nino put me on the street. I did it myself, or it's just fate, because it's a lie Nino pushed me, he had to eat and me too, we had to have clothes and go dancing and make love in a real bed like everyone else. Maybe I'm not saying too good what I want you to see because you're different than us, your family's rich, but I don't know you and my mouthpiece said you had an accident when you were only little, a big tragedy, so who knows? What I want to say to you is how I got the money don't matter so long as we could be together and happy, so after all it was the same as with you and your fiancé because it's the same everywhere, love is the same for everyone and brings the same joy and the same pain.

We had our happiness, Nino and me, until '14. We rented a small flat on the Boulevard National on the corner of the Rue Loubon, we bought cherry-wood furniture, the bed, the wardrobe, the chest of drawers had carved seashells on them, I had an ice-box in the kitchen, a chandelier with glass pearls, Limoges china ornaments on the mantel. For work I rented a room across from the station, the Gare d'Arenc. I did the men at Customs, sailors, well-to-do folks from the Rue de la République. Nino had his own rackets, he was respected in the bars around town, everything was fine until that April night he got into a fight over me with that son of a bitch Josso, that slime-eel, he had his eye on me for a second-stringer to his fat hag of a whore. There's no point in me explaining all this stuff to you, but anyways Nino pulled out his knife what he used just to clip his cigars and wound up inside for five years. I went to see him in Saint-Pierre of course, I saw to it he had everything, but the days still dragged for him. In '16 when they had him choose he went off to join them dying for their country. So that's how he went from one Verdun to another and finished in the snow and mud in front of that trench called Byng's Man.

The night before they killed him he got someone to write me about his love and his regrets. My godmother told you, and I chewed her head off over it, that I had a code with my Nino to always know where he was so I could find him in the billeting areas, I had the run of those places like all camp followers, just the bourgeoises were kept out, and even then I knew some to pretend to be whores just to see their men.

The code we had wasn't complicated, we used the same one to cheat at cards before the war when Nino played for money, the trick being what we called each other, my Angelface, my Beauty, my Cream Puff, and so on. In his letter my Cream Puff was repeated three times, this meant he was still on the same front, the Somme, but was more to the east, the name of the closest town began with C, so I had my choice of Cléry or Combles on my map. He signed your Angel from Hell and that meant he was at the front line. There were other nice names in that letter to say big trouble was coming and things looked black for him. If like I think you got a copy from that Sergeant Esperanza or that Célestin Poux you asked about in the newspapers but I never could find, you'll quickly guess yourself how Nino told me that. By misfortune when the letter my godmother sent on got to me in Albert where I was doing the English, already a month too late, they had shot him like a mangy dog.

I mostly figured out the trail you followed looking for your fiancé, it's not exactly the same as what I did but many times I'm sure our paths have crossed. Mine begins in Combles in early February '17, no longer nothing but Tommies there, but I snooped around and found out about a field hospital they'd moved to Rozières. There I met a medical orderly, Julien Phillipot, he had worked with Lieutenant Santini. He's the one told me about the five men sentenced to death and one of them he saw again in Combles on Monday, January 8, with a head wound, but Santini told him to keep his mouth shut it wasn't no business of theirs, they should evacuate him like the others. Then the hospital was shelled, Santini was killed, Phillipot didn't know what happened to the condemned man. I asked him to describe the man and he wasn't nothing like my Nino but later he learned the wounded man came to the hospital with a dying soldier, younger and thinner, and he was evacuated too, maybe it was a false hope but it was still a hope. Anyway Phillipot told me one thing about the older fellow and that was he had German boots on.

Next I went to Belloy-en-Santerre to find the territorial troops he said had brought the five prisoners on Saturday night. Gone, they were. A tart there told me a man named Prussien was in the escort and he was now in Cappy. I went there and talked to him in a soldiers' bar by a canal and he gave me lots more information than Phillipot on the prisoners. He knew them better because of bringing them up to the trench called Byng's Man. He didn't call it Bingo because a soldier in the trench had explained that night where the name came from. All I remember is it had something to do with a picture painted by a Canadian. He told me the prisoner wearing the German boots was a Parisian name of Bouquet, but the Eskimo's what they called him. Prussien couldn't tell me the others' names, as this fellow was the only one he'd got to talk to in that trench waiting for nightfall, and he asked Prussien if he ever one day got to Paris to go look up Véronique at Little Louis's Bar on the Rue Amelot.

He told me bags of other stuff, they hadn't shot the prisoners, they'd thrown them to the Boches with their arms tied, but that he didn't see, that his sergeant told him. This sergeant, Daniel Esperanza, he took Nino's letter and the letters of the other four and Prussien saw him back at the billet copying them before he sent them off. He said: "When I can I must check and see they arrived safely." I wanted to find this Esperanza right away but he was off in the Vosges, Prussien didn't know exactly where he was, so I decided to go on to Paris.

At Little Louis's Bar, Rue Amelot, I asked for the Eskimo's friend Véronique, but the owner, he used to be a boxer, didn't have her address. Anyways I learned her name, Passavant, he said she worked in some ladies' shop in Ménilmontant, it took me two days to ferret her out. By then it was already March. I still had hope but not much, and that Véronique wouldn't open up at all, so I left as I came. Now I see she had nothing to hide from me, I got that wrong.

So now this bloke I know writes me, he works in headquarters, a customer of mine. I'd asked him to find the battalion what was stationed in that damned trench. All I knew was the regiment number Prussien told me and a captain's name, Favourier, but my bloke found that company I was looking for anyway. It was in reserve off in the Aisne, at Fismes. I went back into a zone of operations in great uproar from the German withdrawal, and three days it took me to get to Fismes through all the devastation, but I met someone there who put an end to all my illusions and broke my heart. After that it was only my desire to avenge my Nino kept me going.

His name was Staff Sergeant Favart. He told me the whole story. First off that Nino was dead and it was that bastard Corporal Thouvenel shot him in cold blood because of how he wanted to surrender to the Boches. Then he told me that on Saturday, January 7, a pardon arrived for the prisoners when there was still time to stop the whole thing, but the battalion commander Lavrouye he kept the pardon a secret until Sunday night because of some officers' scheming and jealousy. Later, in the summer, I went to Dandrechain near Suzanne where the court-martial was at and one by one I found out the names of the judges and that cockroach of a prosecutor, but I told you I don't want to talk no more about those sons of bitches, and anyway it's all over now for them and me both. And for that peasant from the Dordogne too, the one as kicked my Nino in the head, but all I could do to pay him back was kick his wooden cross to pieces with my own feet in the cemetery in Herdelin, you understand?

You can't possibly know the things Favart told me because he died in May at Chemin des Dames, and him, he didn't deserve that, no more than Captain Favourier, he died cursing that stinking major of his. Well in all the frenzy of the fighting he told me about there's two pieces of news I want to give you as maybe they have to do with your fiancé. First there's this corporal, Benjamin Gordes, he was in the field hospital in Combles on Monday, January 8, and he had changed his shoes for the Eskimo's German boots so's he wouldn't be shot straight off like a rabbit out in no-man's-land. Then there was some business with a red woollen glove the soldier Célestin Poux gave your fiancé. Two or three days after it happened, Favart questioned a stretcher-bearer what had seen Benjamin Gordes wounded out on the battlefield helping along another soldier from the company named Jean Desrochelles, and he found their comrades later to tell them this. As they talked, this stretcher-bearer remembered one detail, and that's the soldier Gordes was helping wore a red glove on his left hand. Favart was so caught on this he questioned another corporal, Urbain Chardolot, what crossed over the area in front of Bingo in the early dawn on Monday and came back saying he saw the five prisoners all dead. Now this Favart got the definite idea the corporal didn't much like being asked all these questions but the other answered he hadn't noticed if the Cornflower, that's how they called your fiancé, still had his glove or no, because it was snowing again so he couldn't see too well, or maybe Gordes and Desrochelles took the glove when they passed by so as to give it back to Célestin Poux. Well Favart had to say he believed all this but to me he said: "If Chardolot hid something from me before, then he couldn't admit it now, and anyway, just to get the major in trouble, if one of those poor souls managed to get out, I was glad of it."

I hope you find what I say useful, as for me, what with Nino dead, I turned my thoughts from the victims and set my mind on the murderers. But I didn't want to go without telling you because now your nosing around cannot bother me and also if there is another world and I meet my godmother there again, she won't be happy if I keep what I know from you. As to all the rest, what my judges call my crimes, they'll never know what really happened, I'll screw them to the end. So I ask you, copy what I have written if you want, that way you can fix my mistakes too, but burn this letter, for if it falls into other hands I don't want it claimed for a confession.

Today is August 3. I will put my story in an envelope my mouthpiece, Maître Pallestro, will give you, but only the day after I meet my fate in case you're like him wanting to beg President Doumergue for a pardon. I don't want their pardon. I want to share everything up to the end with my Nino. They condemned him to death, they condemned me too. They executed him, let them execute me. At least nothing will ever have separated us since our childhood when we kissed for the first time under a plane tree in Belle de Mai.

Adieu. Don't feel sorry for me. Adieu.

Tina Lombardi

Mathilde reads this letter over and over, up in her room at home on the Rue La Fontaine. After copying it, she burns the original, page by page, in a blue and white faience fruit bowl that has never served any other purpose but that one. The smoke stagnates in the air, in spite of the open windows, and Mathilde feels as though the odour will permeate all the rooms of her life.

She sits motionless for a long while, her head resting against the back of her chair. She thinks about two elms, truncated but still alive, surrounded by new growth. Her mahogany box is at Hossegor, and she misses it. She thinks she has understood what really happened at Bingo. However, to be sure of it, she must verify everything, the notes she took, the letters she received, everything, because the story of those three snowy days is interwoven with too many voices and too many lies for her to be certain she has not missed the most revealing whisper of truth. She's only human, she's only one person, she's only herself.

Nevertheless, if simply to gain time, she trusts her memory and writes to Anselme Boileroux, the priest at Cabignac, in the Dordogne.

Nevertheless, she trusts her intuition and calls Germain Pire from the telephone near her bed, which Mama has decorated in virginal white – wishful thinking. She asks Monsieur Pire to come and see her as soon as he can, that very evening in fact, and within the hour would be perfect.

Nevertheless, she trusts her heart and rolls out of her bedroom and over to the top of the stairs, where she can hear the voices of those playing cards in the living room below. She shouts down to Célestin that she's sorry to ruin his life but would he come upstairs please, she needs him.

When he enters the room, he has the pinkest cheeks and the bluest, most candid eyes that ever there were.

"That soldier you called La Rochelle," she asks, "Jean Desrochelles, actually – did you know him well?"

He brings over the chair from beside the fireplace and sits down. "Sort of," he replies.

"You told me he came from your area, from Charentes. From where, exactly?"

Either the question surprises him or he needs a moment to remember.

"From Saintes. It's not far from Oléron. His mother had a bookshop in Saintes."

"After Bingo, did he come back to the regiment?"

He shakes his head.

"You never heard anything else about him?"

266

He shakes his head again. He says that doesn't mean much, that if the wounded man was still fit for service after his recovery, he was probably transferred to the army pay corps, the artillery, or somewhere else, because the terrible losses in 1916 meant that everyone was needed. It's also possible that he received a serious wound and was sent home.

"Tell me about him."

Célestin sighs. He's been playing cards downstairs with Mama, Sylvain, and Paul. If he's playing against Mama, he must be about fit to be tied, despite his easy-going disposition, and on the verge of being roundly trounced. At bridge, manille, bezique, Mama is a dirty rotten swine. Not only is she an ace with the pasteboards, but she throws her opponents off their mettle by insulting or making fun of them.

"We called him Jeannot," says Célestin. "He wasn't any more pleased than the rest of us to be in the trenches, but he did his job. He read a lot. He wrote a lot. Everyone wrote a lot, by the way. Except me. If there's one thing that wears me out, that's it. Once I asked him to make up a letter for me to Bibi, that friend in Oléron, who knitted me those gloves. It was such a marvellous letter I fell in love with her, until I actually saw her again. Other than that, I can't think of anything special to say about him, there were so many fellows everywhere, in that war."

Mathilde knows this. But what else can he remember?

He makes an effort. "Another time, back at our quarters, he told me about his mother. He'd lost his father when he was just a little boy, so it was his mother he wrote to. He didn't have any girlfriends, he didn't have any other pals besides us, he told me his mother was all he had. A mama's boy, you know. He showed me a photo. To me she looked like an old woman, not very pretty, in dowdy clothes, but he was so proud of her, he got all sentimental and said she was the most wonderful mother in the world and he missed her, so I told him I had work to do and got out of there, because I know what I'm like, I get sentimental, too."

Mathilde almost hears the voice of Tina Lombardi, whom she has never met: "You understand?" She tells Célestin he's the Disgrace of the Armies. She wheels herself over to her table, hands him her letter for the priest in Cabignac, and asks him to mail it when he's finished playing cards. He replies that he'll go and do it right away, he's only playing because the others want him to, he hates arguing over every measly point, he doesn't appreciate being teased for holding on to his king of diamonds too long, and they're robbing him blind. In short, at cards, Mama is a dirty rotten swine.

After he leaves, Mathilde telephones Pierre-Marie Rouvière. He is the one who made inquiries in 1919, five years ago, about the mental patients in military hospitals, just on the off chance. She asks him if it would be difficult to find out what has happened to a soldier from a company he knows all too well, evacuated from a front with which he's quite familiar, on a date he can easily guess.

"What's the name?" asks Pierre-Marie.

"Jean Desrochelles, from Saintes, in the Charentes."

As he writes down the information, he sighs. "I must love you a great deal, Matti. A great deal." And he hangs up.

When Germain Pire enters her room to find her waiting for him, sitting stern and stiff-backed in her wheelchair, facing the door, she gets right to the point.

"When you abandoned your investigation and sent me that letter I received in New York, did you suspect that Tina Lombardi was a murderess?"

Before replying he kisses her hand, although she's supposed

to be a young lady, not a middle-aged matron, and he compliments her on how well she's looking, even though the trip to Bingo has left her exhausted, completely worn out, and looking, she knows, like something the cats dragged in. Finally he says, "It's my business to figure out these things. At Sarzeau, in the Morbihan, a Lieutenant Gaston Thouvenel had recently been murdered just when that madwoman was in the area. Such a coincidence didn't mean anything to anyone else, but to me it spoke volumes." He takes the same chair Célestin chose. "Matti dear," he says, "you should be congratulating me for having called off that chase. Especially since it cost me your hydrangeas."

Mathilde tells him that the painting is now his. The item in question is downstairs, hanging on a wall in the morning room. As he leaves, he has only to take it down and carry it away. If Mama expresses her astonishment, he should explain that he is a burglar, for she is almost as afraid of burglars as she is of mice.

He doesn't know how to thank her.

"Then don't," replies Mathilde. "Do you remember those mimosas you had originally chosen? They'll be yours, too, as soon as you've found someone else I'm looking for. Your expenses as well, of course. There's one condition to this bargain, unfortunately, which is that I can't propose it to you unless this person is still alive. If you'd be good enough to wait just a little while, I'll soon know."

He replies that he's never in a hurry when the stakes are so high. He has placed his bowler on a corner of Mathilde's desk. He's wearing a black tie. His spats are impossibly white. "By the way," he asks, "what do those three Ms carved on the tree trunk mean, in your delightful painting?"

"Mathilde's Marrying Manech, or Manech's Marrying

Mathilde, as you like. But enough of that. I want to have a serious conversation with you."

"About what?"

"About boots," replies Mathilde nonchalantly. "When you investigated the disappearance of Benjamin Gordes, in Combles, three witnesses claimed to have seen him just before the bombardment and remembered that he was wearing German boots. Does that mean one of the bodies found in the ruins was wearing these boots?"

Beneath his little circumflex of a moustache, Germain Pire's lips curve into a smile, and his eyes twinkle.

"Come now, Mathilde, don't make me think you really need an answer to that question!"

She replies that it's true, she doesn't really. If on January 8, 1917, they'd found a body wearing German boots amid the ruins, Benjamin Gordes would have been identified right away, instead of listed as missing until 1919, and there would have been no need for an investigation.

"The object of my inquiry," says the detective, "was to establish the death of this poor soul in the interest of his wife, my client. How could I, in all decency, start such a hare? It has bothered me quite enough, you know."

Mathilde is glad to hear him say so. When he wrote to her that this detail had slipped his mind, he was therefore lying. Holding up a thumb and forefinger, he indicates that it was just a tiny little lie.

At the same moment the phone by her bed rings. Mathilde rolls her chair over to answer it. Pierre-Marie is on the line.

"You've made a shambles of my evening, Matti. Jean Desrochelles, military class of 1915, from Saintes, was in fact evacuated from the front in the Somme on January 8, 1917. Gravely ill from pneumonia, suffering from multiple wounds, he was cared for first at Val-de-Grâce, then at the military hospital in Châteaudun, and finally at a hospital at Cambo-les-Bains, in the Pyrenees. On April 12, 1918, he was invalided out of the army and returned to his family, in the person of his widowed mother, Madame Paul Desrochelles, bookseller, living at 17, Rue de la Gare, in Saintes. I repeat, I must truly love you a great deal, Matti, a great deal."

She tells him she loves him, too.

As soon as she has hung up, she swivels her chair around and asks her guest to get out his little notebook. The one he produces from the inside breast pocket of his frock coat cannot possibly be the same one he was using in 1920, it couldn't have lasted that long, but it is equally worn-looking and held together by a rubber band.

Mathilde dictates: "Jean Desrochelles, twenty-nine years old, widowed mother, Madame Paul Desrochelles, bookseller, 17, Rue de la Gare, Saintes."

"If you have the address," remarks Monsieur Pire, closing his notebook, "what am I to do to earn your mimosas? Must I really steal them?"

"Wait," says Mathilde, "I have to think of a satisfactory reply." She crosses the room towards him. "I could get away with a little white lie, but I always prefer a disguised truth to a lie. So I will confess to you that I hope with all my heart, as I have probably never hoped before in my life, that at Saintes, at least, you will draw a blank."

He looks at her without saying anything, gimlet-eyed, his brow slightly furrowed. She hands him his bowler.

That evening, at dinner, Mama tells everyone about the quite pleasant and apparently well-brought-up man who nevertheless walked right into the morning room, removed a painting from the wall, and carried it off without any other explanation save this: Mademoiselle Mathilde herself had just told him that he should take the picture home to keep it safe from mice. And so the dear lady has had mousetraps placed everywhere. Which means there will be no cheese course tonight.

The Sunflowers at the End
of the World

Hossegor lies prostrate in the heat of August. Even the cats are suffering from the oppressive weather. Every evening there are storms that pelt trees, tear off leaves, massacre flowers. Bénédicte is frightened of the thunder-claps.

Célestin stays on a few more days at the Villa MMM. He spruces up the Delage, helps Sylvain in the garden, and saws wood with him for the winter. He swims in the lake. Mathilde teaches him how to play Snap. He displays a hearty appetite, which utterly delights Bénédicte. He is bored. Sometimes Mathilde sees him pensively watching the rain fall outside the French windows. She rolls over towards him, and he taps her hand gently with the pleasant, distracted smile of someone who is already elsewhere. One evening he tells her he'll be leaving the next day, that he'll frequently send them news of his doings, that she will always know where to find him if she needs him. She says she understands.

The next day is August 15. Cap-Breton must be celebrating a feast day, for the street is crowded with people following the procession. Célestin re-attaches the baggage carrier to the rear of his motorcycle. Sylvain pretends to be busy at his duties. Bénédicte stays out on the terrace with Mathilde, saddened by the prospect of waving good-bye to such a fine lad. On a Sunday twelve days ago, when the setting sun was already sinking behind the pines, he had arrived to help Mathilde pick up a thread. Somehow it doesn't seem like only twelve days ago to Mathilde. He comes over to her, carrying his motorcycle helmet and goggles, to say farewell. She asks him where he's going and immediately wishes she hadn't. He smiles, once again, that melting smile. He doesn't know. Perhaps he'll pay a visit to Oléron. He doesn't know. He kisses Mathilde and Bénédicte. He goes off to embrace Sylvain. He leaves as he arrived, at about the same time, in the throaty roar of a motor going all out, and, wherever he's heading, when he arrives he'll have two big circles of nice white skin around his blue eyes. Mathilde suddenly wonders wherever did she leave her dolly Arthur, back when she was a child beginning to outgrow such things.

A few days later, she receives a letter from Leipzig, in Germany. As soon as she returned from her trip, Heidi Weiss went to see the former *Feldwebel*, Heinz Gerstacker, who told her again what happened that Sunday at Bingo. It's more or less what she told Mathilde at the Auberge des Remparts, but she does have a few additional details, the last of which would have astounded Célestin if he were still there but which confirms Mathilde's belief, as though she didn't already know, that in spite of her unruly imagination, her parents, during their amorous transports in Toledo, didn't make too bad a job of her.

Gerstacker, along with three of his comrades, was captured and taken behind the French lines shortly before dawn on Monday. They were led by two soldiers who made a detour to go by Bingo, where the bodies of the five condemned men lay scattered in the snow. The two soldiers separated to explore the area with torches. Gerstacker, who followed one of them, first saw a man frozen by death in a kneeling position, with his arms on his thighs, his head falling forward on to his chest. This was the man who had brought down the Albatross with the grenade. Another man was in a hole, which appeared to be a collapsed cellar, because some steps were still visible. Gerstacker distinctly saw, in the torch beam, that this man lying on his back across the stairs was wearing German boots. The French soldier had whispered, "Shit!" – one of the few foreign words the *Feldwebel* understood perfectly. Afterwards, when they were continuing on their way, the French soldier had argued with his companion, who had told him, "So, well, just shut up about it!" And Gerstacker hadn't had any problem understanding that, either.

Mathilde is not surprised by this news, still less astonished, as Célestin would have been; her heart beats a trifle faster, that's all. After rereading Tina Lombardi's letter and reviewing the contents of her mahogany box, she has imagined a sequence of events that makes sense only if Benjamin Gordes returned at some point to Bingo during that night of heavy fighting. Gerstacker confirms that he did.

Poor, poor Benjamin Gordes. You had to die there, she thinks, for me to go on believing that one of the five, who took your boots, remained alive at least until reaching Combles. It couldn't have been your friend the Eskimo, or Six-Sous, or Ange Bassignano. In the state in which everyone describes him, Manech would never have thought of it. That leaves the uncouth farmer from the Dordogne who was found as an infant on the steps of a chapel, and who went to ground on his last day, through a quirk of fate, in the ruins of another.

That leaves what Urbain Chardolot said, when he came back in the morning to no-man's-land, when snow had begun falling again, long after you returned, long after the German prisoner and the nameless soldier saw you in that hole: "At least one of them, if not two."

Yes, Chardolot was certain of one thing and suspected another. He mentioned the certainty to Esperanza in July 1918, on the platform at that station where they were evacuating the wounded: "I'd gladly bet two louis with you on Cornflower, if I had them, but I'm broke – the girls cleaned me out." The suspicion was That Man, simply because the nameless soldier hadn't, in the end, followed orders to just shut up about it.

The letter Mathilde has been awaiting with the most impatience, the one from the priest in Cabignac, arrives two days later.

Saturday, August 16, 1924

My dear child,

I must confess that I am somewhat confused by your question. I really cannot imagine how Benoît Notre-Dame's last letter, or a copy of it, came to be in your hands. I must conclude that you have seen Mariette, and that your silence on this point is due only to her express wish, which saddens me deeply.

Nevertheless, I will answer you as best I can, through my faith in Our Lord and the confidence I have in you.

I read the letter several times. First of all, I can tell you that although the Benoît I knew as a child, youngster, and

276

man was always blunt and close-mouthed, he was never that abrupt. It's true that men and their feelings may be changed by the horrors of war, but my strongest impression is that his message to Mariette, on the eve of his death, meant something else besides what he wrote.

Following your instructions, I endeavoured to understand what there was in his letter that might be called "inappropriate", as you put it. I made inquiries in the surrounding villages, as far away as Montignac. The time these efforts have taken explains the delay in my reply. I spoke to many people who knew the Notre-Dame family: They all assured me that Benoît never needed to buy manure to fertilize his fields, which were not extensive, since he was for the most part a stock farmer. I met no one in the area who had ever heard of a Monsieur Bernay, or Bernet. The name I heard that came closest to that is Bernotton; Monsieur Bernotton is a scrap merchant and does not sell manure. What is inexplicable in that letter (and not, begging your pardon, inappropriate, a term you use improperly, for what is inappropriate merely offends propriety, not reason) is this Monsieur Bernay, who seems not to exist.

My dear child, I am an old man. Even if Mariette has made a new life for herself outside the pious bonds of the Church, I should like to know, before God calls me home, what has become of her and her son Baptistin, whom I baptized, and whose parents I joined in holy matrimony. Tonight I shall pray for Benoît Notre-Dame. I shall pray for you with all my soul, even though I do not understand this path you have chosen, for the ways of the Lord may be unfathomable.

Au revoir, my dear child. If I might receive a few lines of reassurance from you, I would willingly forgive you that "inappropriate", even though I can surmise simply from reading your letter that you have studied Latin and should have known better.

Your obedient servant in Our Lord,

Anselme Boileroux
Curé de Cabignac

It's midday. The first thing Mathilde does is to consult the Littré dictionary in her room. He's right, she's wrong. Still, she sticks out her tongue and sends the good priest what might be called an incongruous salute. She then takes a pair of scissors and some drawing paper from her desk drawer. She cuts as many small pieces of paper as she needs to copy out, one word per piece, the letter That Man wrote on the evening of January 6, 1917.

She clears everything else off the table. She lines up all the tiny scraps of paper in order. She moves them here and there, attempting to recreate the Elevator, the code Célestin explained to her. She doesn't know the base word chosen by That Man and his Mariette, so she pins her hopes on "Bernay", the name no one in Cabignac had recognized.

At one o'clock, Bénédicte and Sylvain are ready for lunch. Mathilde tells them to go ahead and eat without her, she isn't hungry. She drinks directly from her bottle of mineral water. At two, Bénédicte comes to her room, but Mathilde insists that she's not hungry and wants to be left alone. At three, Mathilde is still fiddling and the cats are becoming obstreperous, so their mistress shoos them out of the room. At four o'clock, the words are lined up on her table in the following arrangement:

Dear wife,

	Come	spring, the work in the fields won't wait, so
tell	Bernay	the deal is off unless it's all settled by
early	March.	I have thought over his price. He's try-ing
to	sell	us his manure too dearly. I think in spite
of	everything	he will come around.
	Say	to my Titou I send him a big hug and tell him
that	nothing	bad can happen to him as long as he pays
close	heed	to his dear mama. As for me, I know there can
be	nobody	better in the whole world. I love you,
	Benoît	

Going from top to bottom, in the column in which the word "Bernay" appears, one reads:

Come Bernay March. Sell everything. Say nothing. Heed nobody. Benoît.

Mathilde sits absolutely still for a moment, feeling something that must be akin to the pride of having brought off a painting all by herself, like a grown-up, a painting or anything else at all that would easily make the tears come if she weren't trying so hard to avoid giving in to self-pity. She reminds herself that her troubles are not yet over and that she's now quite hungry. She rings her bell.

When Bénédicte arrives all smiles, probably because her quartermaster just gave her an affectionate pat on the derrière, Mathilde apologizes for her impatience a short while ago and asks for a sandwich of Bayonne ham with lots of butter and Sylvain instead of mustard. Bénédicte replies that if Matti knew the unspoken names she sometimes calls her, Matti wouldn't bother apologizing.

By the time Sylvain arrives with a fearsomely big sandwich and a glass of Saint-Emilion, Mathilde has put aside the slips of paper and selected from the mahogany box the notes she took in 1919 that concern Sylvain directly. As usual, he lies down on the bed, clasps his hands behind his neck, and kicks off both his sandals.

"When you went to the house on the Rue Gay-Lussac to find out about Mariette Notre-Dame," asks Mathilde, speaking with her mouth full, "the owners did tell you that when she left so mysteriously with her baby and belongings she took a taxi for the Gare de l'Est? That was the station, right? Not the Gare du Nord, the Gare d'Orléans, or the Gare Whatchamacallit?"

He replies that if she wrote down what he told her when he told her what he told her, then she can be sure of it, but that anyway, even after five years, he remembers it quite well.

Mathilde swallows a great bite of her sandwich. "I also wrote down that both times Mariette left with her baby to visit friends, it was only for the day, so she couldn't have gone very far from Paris."

"So?"

"So would it be difficult for you to find a village named Bernay that isn't far from Paris and that may be reached from the Gare de l'Est?"

"Right now?"

She doesn't answer. She's locked in a ferocious struggle with her slice of Bayonne ham. Sylvain rises, slips on his sandals, and goes to fetch his railway timetable. He adores trains. He once told Mathilde that if he weren't married, his dream would be to take a train to anywhere, to visit cities he didn't know and didn't even want to know, to stay alone overnight in the Hotel Terminus that's always across the street from the station, and to leave the next morning for somewhere else. He claims that trains are magical, bewitching, and that only a very few superior souls understand this.

He returns and sits on the bed, looking over at Mathilde with fond eyes, her second father. "It's Bernay near Rozay-en-Brie, in Seine-et-Marne," he announces.

Mathilde leaves the rest of her sandwich, downs her wine in three gulps. "I know it's a bother for you, we just got back. But I have to go there."

He barely sighs, he shrugs one shoulder. "It's not me that's going to squawk. Didi's the one who won't be pleased."

Leaning forward in her chair, Mathilde murmurs insidiously and ardently, "Give her a good workout tonight. Let's hear the rafters ring. She always adores you afterwards, she'll be putty in our hands."

He laughs, bent double on the edge of the bed, his forehead almost touching his knees, both proud and embarrassed. No one, at the moment when Mathilde writes these lines, can imagine how much she loved Sylvain.

The next day, off they go.

Beneath a blazing sun, Bernay is no farther from Rozay-en-Brie than Mathilde is from her destiny. Her back aches. Actually, she aches all over. Sylvain stops the car in front of the school. He brings back to the Delage a little man with wildly unkempt hair, carrying an open book in his hand. He lives there, he is the teacher, Monsieur Ponsot. Mathilde notices that the book is Edgar Allan Poe's *Narrative of Arthur Gordon Pym*. She can recognize this book at ten paces in anyone's hands, although it's clear that the man coming towards her cannot possibly be just anyone, since he's devoting his precious Sunday to reading it. *"I have graven it within the hills, and my vengeance upon the dust within the rock."* A fitting epitaph for Tina Lombardi, written more than a century ago, in the diary of a madman.

Mathilde asks the teacher if he has in his class a boy of about eight or nine years old named Baptistin.

"You mean Titou Notre-Dame?" replies Monsieur Ponsot. "Of course he's in my class. He's a very good student, I'd even say the best I've ever had. He can knock off compositions that are simply amazing for his age, and one of them, just before Christmas – on vipers, it was – well, it showed me that one day he'll be a scientist or an artist. He's bursting to learn things."

Mathilde says she simply wants to know where he lives.

"In that direction," says the teacher, pointing up the road. "You get to Vilbert, you turn left on to the road to Chaumes, and perhaps a hundred or two hundred metres along, you take the dirt road, still on your left, that goes down along the river. You pass the Mesnils' farm and La Petite Fortelle, you keep going, keep going, you can't miss it, at the end of the valley you come to some fields, and out in the middle of them is a farm we call the End of the World, and that's where Titou lives."

The dirt road is flanked on one side by a thick forest, on the other by a line of trees that hides the river. The road is shady and cool, so the shock of sunlight is all the more brutal when the car suddenly comes upon the End of the World: vast, endless fields of yellow sunflowers so high that all one can see of the farm set in their midst are the roofs of ochre tile.

Mathilde asks Sylvain to stop the car. When he turns off the motor, the only sounds are the murmur of the river, and the birds far off in the woods. No fences anywhere. All around them, covering the slopes encircling the valley, the fields are marked simply by their colours of gold or lingering green. Sylvain unfolds the "scooter". He finds the place very beautiful but somewhat oppressive, although he doesn't know why. The truth is, Mathilde has told him to make himself and the Delage scarce for about two hours. He is to leave her sitting in her chair beneath her parasol, near the trunk of an oak tree lying alongside the road.

He's worried. "You're not being reasonable," he says. "You never know what might happen. At least let me drive you up to the house."

She says no, she has to wait alone for her quarry to come to her.

"What if he doesn't?"

"He will," replies Mathilde. "Perhaps not right away, since he's more afraid of me than I am of him. He'll keep an eye on me at a distance for a while, and then he'll come. So go on back to the village, drink your beer in peace."

The car drives away. These endless sunflowers give Mathilde a strange feeling of *déjà vu*, but she thinks it must be from a dream she once had, years before, and has forgotten.

A minute or two later, a dog barks briefly, and she guesses that it has been quickly hushed. Then she hears someone running on the path leading down from the house. From the lightness of the footstep, she can tell that it is a child. He appears at the end of the path, about twenty paces from her, and stops short. He is blond, with big dark eyes. She thinks he must be eight and a half by now. He's wearing grey shorts, a blue short-sleeved shirt, and a bandage on one knee to cover a graze that can't be very serious or else he wouldn't have been running so fast.

"You're Titou?" asks Mathilde.

He doesn't answer. He's off again at a gallop, disappearing between two fields of sunflowers. A moment later Mathilde hears That Man coming down the path with a calm, measured tread. The closer he comes, the faster Mathilde's heart beats.

He stops in the same place his son did. He stares at her for a few seconds, motionless, expressionless, a robust man as tall as everyone said he was, perhaps even taller than Mathilde's father. He's wearing a white collarless shirt with rolled-up sleeves and beige linen trousers with braces. As far as Mathilde knows, he just turned thirty-eight in July. He's bareheaded. His hair is brown, and he has the same large, dark eyes as his son.

Finally, slowly, he comes over to her.

"I knew that you would find me one day," he says. "I've been waiting for you ever since someone showed me that notice in the newspaper." He sits down on the trunk of the oak, resting one foot on the tree, the other on the ground. He's wearing dust-coloured espadrilles with their backs under heel, like slippers. His voice is slightly resonant, a quiet voice, surprisingly soft given his height.

"In 1920, in April," he tells her, "I even went to Cap-Breton, I saw you painting in the garden of a house. I don't know any more what I was thinking of. You were a terrible danger to me, and you understand that, when I say to me, it's my wife and son I'm thinking of. Perhaps it was seeing you in that wheelchair ... and maybe it's because I haven't the heart any more to kill even a chicken, since the war. I do it because I have to, I try to spare the poor creature as much suffering as I can, but it distresses me. I decided, so what if she finds me one day and denounces me, let the future take its course. And I went home."

Mathilde replies that she has never told on anyone, not even when she was little, and is not about to start now.

"What became of you after Bingo is your own affair. I'm glad you were able to escape all that, but you should understand that the one who concerns me is the boy they called Cornflower."

He picks up a small dead branch, breaks it in two, in four, then drops the pieces.

"The last time I saw Cornflower," he tells her, "he was in bad shape, but not as bad as you'd think. He was tough, for a fellow skinny as a rail. I had to work hard that day, carrying him on my back. If they took good care of him, he came out of it all right. I can guess why you haven't found him yet. He'd already lost complete hold of who he was."

Mathilde wheels her chair across the dry dirt of the road to get closer to him. That Man had shaved off his moustache a long time ago. He has the tanned face, neck, and forearms of someone who works out in the open air, like Sylvain. His right hand is resting on one knee, and now she sees the neat, impeccable hole in the middle of it, about as big as a one-sou piece. A ghost of a smile plays about his lips when he notices Mathilde looking at his hand.

"I sharpened the bullet for hours, I did everything right. I can still use the thumb, the forefinger, and with the little finger I can clean my ear." He wiggles those fingers against his knee to show her it's true. Mathilde places her right hand, gently, on his.

*

I waited and I walked. And in the end, that's all I remember. I found the caved-in cellar almost immediately, because I spotted that pile of bricks sticking out of the snow when the first flares went up. I was with the Eskimo and Cornflower in a shell hole too shallow for us to stay there. It was Cornflower untied us, really quick – even though he had only one hand, and his left one at that – I could tell he knew his way around knots. I told the Eskimo we'd better not all stay together, and he was an experienced soldier, he agreed with me. I started crawling through the snow towards those bricks, while they went off towards the middle of no-man's-land looking for a deeper shell hole. The one you call Six-Sous, I didn't know what had happened to him, or that lousy Marseillais just dumb enough to get us all killed, the one I gave a swift kick in the head, to settle him down.

The German trench threw out grenades, sent up more flares, I could hear the machine guns. I waited by the brick pile, flat on my stomach. Later, when everything was quiet, I felt around me in the dark and found a big wooden panel under the snow, a door it was, and underneath was nothing. When the next flare went up I quickly stuck my head in the hole and saw what was left of a cellar. There were five or six steps going down, the rest was flooded. When I pulled the door to one side, some rats ran away, I didn't see them, just felt them running over me. I slid down into that cellar, step by step, on my back. I felt around and discovered a fallen beam at the base of a wall. It wasn't in the putrid water, so I sat on it, then lay down there.

I waited. I didn't feel the cold yet, I wasn't hungry. I knew if I got thirsty, all I had to do was stretch out my hand to gather snow right outside. I hoped for the best.

Later I fell asleep. Maybe the two trenches went at each

other again that night, but I couldn't tell you, the noise didn't wake a soul any more. In the war, when you had a chance to sleep, you took it, and didn't worry about whatever was going to happen anyway.

It was still dark outside, that Sunday, when I woke up in that cellar you say was part of a chapel. Then I was cold. I walked in the water, bent double, because what was left of the room wasn't more than about a metre and a half from the ground. I looked in the darkness for something I could use. I found a shelf on a wall, I felt old tools under my hands, and rags stiff with frost, but nothing to give me a light.

I waited for dawn. Day broke, little by little, overcast, as white as the snow. Enough light came down the stairs to show me where I was holed up. There was even a drain over in a corner, beneath some rubble, and I pulled on a rusty chain that broke, but then I was able to claw up a metal plate with my fingers, and all the stinking water went down the drain.

I waited. And waited. Someone called out to us from our trench to see whether we'd got killed or not: Bouquet, Etchevery, Bassignano, Gaignard, and then Notre-Dame. They repeated my name, because I never answered. And of course right after that, the Boches threw out grenades, and then I heard trench mortars, so obviously the world was still as stupid as ever. Later on, the one they called Six-Sous started singing. There was a gunshot, and he stopped.

When a Boche crate flew over and then made another pass, machine-gunning the area, I made my first mistake. I wanted to see what was happening. I crawled up to the top of the stairs and stuck my head out. I saw Cornflower standing in front of a snowman that was wearing a straw hat. The plane swung in a wide turn over its own lines and came straight back at us, no more than fifteen metres from the ground. It was an Albatross, they have the gun mounted at the rear. When it was almost directly overhead, I saw the snowman explode and the boy go down with it, and the two trenches blazing away at each other like in the worst days of the war.

My second mistake was that I didn't go right back down into the deepest part of my hiding place. The biplane went over again, a third time. I saw the black crosses on its wings, and then I saw the Eskimo, maybe thirty metres away, stand up bang out of the snow and throw something in the air with his good hand just when that plane went over him, and almost at the same time as the back of the plane blew up, I saw him hit square in the chest by the gun, and my head exploded.

When I came to again, I was sprawled on the bottom of the cellar. It was still light out, but I guessed that it was going on towards sundown, and big shells were falling all over, shaking the ground, some 220s sent from a good way off. I crawled along against a wall to get to the very back of the cellar, and that's when I felt dried blood on my face. Some of it was sticky, so I was still bleeding.

Wasn't a bullet that hit me in the head but a brick, probably, hit by the gunfire and sent spinning, or a piece of the plane fuselage. I don't know. I felt the blood trickling down my face, I felt through my gummy hair until I found the wound, and then I decided I'd live.

I waited. I was hungry. I was cold. The shells were coming down so thick and fast I could tell right off the Boches had evacuated their front-line trenches, and we'd done the same, because that captain at Bingo, I'd seen he wasn't the sort to let his men get mowed down.

Then I heard that rumbling noise the big guns make moving off to the east, while to the west the English linked up with us must have been having the same hard time of it. When a front goes up, it either gets really hot only in one place or else the action spreads for miles along the line. I started to feel more confident again. I told myself I had to keep waiting, stay right where I was, and in the confusion there'd be the next day along such a wide front, I'd get my chance to clear out of our lines. Then, as long as I could still walk, that would be all I'd have to do.

I fell asleep again. Once in a while a shell would land and shake the cellar so that dirt fell on me, but I was far away, I'd go straight back to sleep.

Then something startled me awake. I do believe it was the silence. Or maybe the voices in the silence, uneasy, muffled, they were, and the footsteps in the snow, yes – the snow was squeaking underfoot. I heard someone say, "Cornflower's still breathing!" Someone else answered, "Bring your light over here, quick!" Almost at that moment a couple of shells came in, I heard the shrill whistle they make, and the earth quaked under my feet. Explosions lit up the cave and I could see that the door partly covering my entrance hole was burning. Then one of the soldiers I'd heard came down the stairs all bent over. What I saw first was his German boots. Then the beam from a torch swept over the walls and he fell headfirst near me, all over the place, like a puppet with its strings snapped.

I picked up the torch and recognized one of the corporals at Bingo, the one the Eskimo'd called Biscuit. He moaned, he was hurt. I pulled him the best I could back into the cellar, I sat him up against a wall. He'd lost his helmet. The front of his coat was soaked in blood and he was holding his belly. He opened his eyes. He told me, "Kléber's really dead. I didn't want to believe it." After that he coughed and gasped out, "And I'm done for, too." He never said another word. He groaned softly. I tried to see where he was hit but he pushed away my hand. I turned off the light. Outside, the cannonade had shifted again, but both sides were still hard at it.

A bit later, the corporal stopped moaning. I switched on the torch. He'd passed out. He was still breathing. I took off his haversacks. He had grenades in one, papers and personal things in another. I saw his name, Benjamin Gordes. I found a bite of bread and cheese and a bar of dark chocolate in a third bag. I ate. I checked his canteen. It was wine. I took two swallows and switched off the light. Outside, over my head, the door had stopped burning. The sky was constantly lit up by flashes from the fighting. I went back to sleep.

When I opened my eyes, just before dawn, the corporal wasn't near me any more but lying in a heap across the steps. I think he'd come to from his faint and tried to crawl outside. He was dead, I could see that, and most likely for a good hour at least, his face being so cold and pale. Just then I heard more footsteps in the snow, and voices. I went to huddle at the very back of the cellar and didn't move a muscle. A few seconds later, a torch beam lit up Benjamin Gordes's body. I heard a voice say "Shit!" and another say something in German I didn't understand. Then, from the noise of their steps in the snow, I think they moved off, but I stayed on in my corner for quite a while.

It was daylight outside, and now there was this huge silence everywhere, the way there almost always is after a night of heavy artillery fire. I decided it was time for me to get out of there. I shucked off my overcoat, jacket, and shoes. I pulled the corporal's body over to me and took off some of his clothes, so that I could put mine on him, and my shoes. That was the hardest part. I gave up trying to lace my shoes up on him, my fingers were that numb, but I didn't feel the cold. I rolled my puttees around his legs any old way. I put on his torn jacket and coat, all stiff with dried blood, and the German boots, and I took Benjamin Gordes's gloves and the haversack with his personal things in it. Just in case, I took the bandage that had fallen off my hand ages ago and tied it around his fingers. That's when I saw his identification bracelet and remembered the most important part. Before I left him there, I looked at the poor soul one last time, but you don't beg pardon of a dead man.

Outside was another white day, no sun in the sky. I found the corporal's helmet and gun in the snow, near the partly charred wooden door. I threw them into the Bingo trench. I walked across no-man's-land. Halfway between the cellar and the ruined snowman, I found the body of the soldier who'd been with Gordes. He was on his back, his head hanging over the edge of a shell hole, his chest all stove in. It was when I stood there in front of this poor fellow not more than twenty-five years old that I saw something moving in the snow not far from me. I saw Cornflower heave himself up and try to crawl, all covered with mud, his eyes closed.

I went over to him, sat him down. He looked at me and smiled. It was his same smile I'd always known, gone clean out of time and this world. He leaned on my shoulder and my arms, trying with all the little strength he still had to stand up. "Wait, wait," I told him, "I won't leave you. Stay quiet now."

I looked to see where he was wounded. It was on the left side, just over the hip. His shirt and jacket were stained black with blood there, but I saw straight off he'd not die from that wound. His face and neck were burning up, though. It was being out so long in the snow that would kill him. He clutched at me, shaking with fever and cold. For a moment I was tempted to go back to being the same man I'd always been in that war, thinking only of myself, and leave him there. I didn't do it. What I did do was take his identification tag off his wrist as well. It was snowing again, just light flakes at first. When I took the tag from Benjamin Gordes's companion and made the switch, the flakes were heavier, thicker, they began covering that whole gutted battlefield. The young soldier's name was Jean Desrochelles. I still had lots to do if I was to get scot-free out of the combat zone but there I was, squatting by the corpse, completely exhausted. Then I looked over at Cornflower, sitting so still, with the snow falling on him, and I got up again. The only other thing I did was pitch Desrochelles's gun as far as I could towards the German trench. I decided to forget about the rest, his helmet and puttees. I went over to the boy and said, "Cornflower, help me, try to stand up." I swear to you, I was that worn out.

He hung on to me, one arm around my neck. We went step by step to that dry river bed. He didn't complain. He staggered along. We fell. He was so hot I could feel the heat through his clothes, I'd never felt anything like it. He shivered. His breath came short, wheezing, his eyes were wide open but staring at nothing. I told him, "Hang on, Cornflower, try to hang on. I'll carry you on my back."

So that's what I did, holding him by the legs, and the snow kept falling on us and I just kept walking.

Farther on, through this curtain of white flakes, I caught sight of some stretcher-bearers heading towards the front lines. I shouted. I told them if they found Captain Favourier's company to let them know Corporal Gordes was on his way to a first-aid station. One of them shouted back, "Don't worry, Corporal, we'll tell them. And who's that you're carrying?" "Private Jean Desrochelles," I answered. I heard, "Long live anarchy! But we'll tell them, pal, and see if you can get evacuated!"

Next I had to drag Cornflower through the trenches. I was pulling him up the slopes by the arms. The snow stopped, I rested a while. Some English went by. One of them gave me something to drink from his canteen, something strong. He told me in broken French, "Keep on, Corporal, keep on. Over there, is Combles. After, you don't die, and your soldier neither."

I did some more walking. On my back, Cornflower was in pain, but not a whisper of complaint. I could feel his feverish breath on my neck. And then finally there was a road full of wounded Australians and we both got loaded into a truck.

Combles had been wrecked long before. That half-French, half-English field hospital was in an uproar, what with everyone shouting, nurses and nuns in their coifs running along the corridors, and you could hear a locomotive getting up steam to evacuate some wounded.

That's where I lost track of Cornflower. Later, I was up on the second floor having a bowl of soup and this doctor, Lieutenant Jean-Baptiste Santini, he came to see me. He told me, "I evacuated your companion. That wound in his side is nothing, but I've done what was needed to his wrist, they'll think it was a battle injury. What's serious is that he's caught himself a fine bout of pneumonia. How long was he out in the snow?" I said, "All night, and all day, and all night again." He told me, "You're a good and brave man to have brought him in. I don't want to know that I've seen you before, I don't want to know your real name, I'm going to evacuate you, too. And as soon as you can, save yourself, get as far away as possible from all this. The war will end someday. I hope you make it."

Dr Santini was sick at heart over the war, but all the doctors must have felt that way, even more than the rest of us. I saw his body an hour later, lying under a tipped-over camp bed. His head had been blown off.

Mademoiselle, you know how tired I am of talking about these things. When the bombardment began, Cornflower was on a train, long gone on his way to the rear. I never saw him again. The worst of his condition came of lying for so long in the snow, thanks to the cruelty of horrible men, but if in Paris or somewhere else they did pull him through and you still haven't seen him again, then that means he was at least lucky enough to forget everything.

As for me, when the hospital collapsed at Combles, I was able to get down the stairs and across a courtyard where soldiers were lying, calling for help, with others dashing in every direction as the shells came down. I walked right ahead, my evacuation ticket looped around a button of Gordes's overcoat, and I didn't look back until I reached the country-side.

After that I walked at night and slept during the day, hidden in a ditch, a thicket, some ruins. All the trucks, guns, and soldiers heading up the line were English. I began seeing fields that hadn't been completely destroyed, and I saw birds fluttering in treetops. One morning I saw a boy on a road, he was singing "Auprès de Ma Blonde," and I knew I'd come out of the war. That child – as old as mine is today, he was – he took me to his parents, country people like me. They surely suspected I was on the run, but they never asked me a single question I couldn't answer straight. I helped them out for a week, maybe more, repairing their barn and mending their fences. They gave me some clothes – shirt, jacket, trousers – so I wouldn't look like a soldier, and because they'd shaved my head in Combles to treat my wound, they gave me a straw hat like the one Cornflower's snowman wore.

I walked some more. I headed towards the sunset, to go around Paris, where I'd have been likely to be picked up; then I turned south, night after night, sleeping by day, eating when I could, depending on the charity of others, making my way to these beautiful fields you see here, where things will always grow in spite of man's stupidity.

Why the Brie country? I'll tell you. I came home when I was twelve. Child Welfare had placed me for six months in the home of a farmer in Bernay. He's dead now, and his sons don't recognize me. Whenever I talked to Mariette, I always told her how happy I was in Bernay, how I wanted to come back to these fields where the grain grows better than anywhere else and the sunflowers are so high the children get lost in them. Just look at my sunflowers! I should have cut them a week ago. Now I understand why I didn't do it. I'll start cutting them tomorrow. Once, long after those terrible times I told you about, I dreamed of you at night. I didn't know you, but you were coming towards me through this field and I woke up with a start, soaked in sweat. I looked at Mariette sleeping beside me, I got out of bed to go and listen to my son's breathing. It was a nightmare, and I was afraid.

Now I'm glad that you can see my sunflowers. In '17, the way I told her to in my letter, Mariette sold our farm in the Dordogne and came to Bernay with our boy. I had been waiting for her for several days, sitting on a stone bench across from the inn where I was staying, on the town square. Once, some policemen asked me who I was. I showed them my head and my hand. They said, "Sorry about that. There are so many deserters, you see." Mariette arrived one morning in March, on the bus from Tournan. Titou was all nestled in a blue woollen shawl.

A few months earlier, during that wretched autumn of 1916, I wrote to Mariette in our way that I'd be at the Gare de l'Est. I decided to go off on leave, without telling the army. She understood, she was there. I didn't even try to slip out of the station, there were too many checkpoints at the gates. We kissed through the bars. I could feel her warmth, and then, I'd never cried in my life, even when I was only a kid, even when they'd beaten me in the shelters, but suddenly I just couldn't help it. That was the day I decided to get myself out of the war on my own.

I won't ever cry again, mademoiselle. Since the day I carried your fiancé on my back, my name is Benjamin Gordes, the farm manager for the Widow Notre-Dame, and everyone here calls me Benoît, because that's the way I want it. Titou knows in every fibre of his being that he is my son. I can wait. I'll keep waiting, for as long as it takes, for this war to be seen in everyone's eyes for what it always was, the most filthy, savage, useless obscenity that ever there was; I'll wait until the flags stop flying in November in front of the monuments to the dead, I'll wait until the Poor Bastards at the Front stop gathering, wearing their damned berets and missing an arm or a leg, to celebrate what? In the corporal's haversack, along with his service booklet, his identification papers, and a bit of money, I found some photographs. They were of no use to me, but they made me feel even sorrier for him. One especially, a picture of his five children, his boys and girls. And then I told myself that time passes, that life is strong enough to carry them on its back.

I hear your car returning. I'm going to leave you and go on home. I know I've nothing to fear from you, I know you won't turn me in. If ever you see Cornflower alive again, and he's forgotten those evil times, don't remind him of them. Have your own new memories with him, like I do with Mariette. I can promise you this, a name means nothing. They gave me mine by chance. I took someone else's name, by chance. And Cornflower died along with Benoît Notre-Dame one Sunday in January, at Bingo Crépuscule. If you find a Jean Desrochelles somewhere one day, I'll be happier than you can ever imagine. Write and tell me so. Remember an address that belongs only to That Man. I live near Bernay, in Seine-et-Marne. I live at the End of the World.

Lieutenant-General Byng
at Twilight

That Sunday evening, on the last day of August, in bed in her room at home on the Rue La Fontaine, Mathilde tells her father the whole story and allows him to open the mahogany box. He is still reading when she falls asleep. She dreams of her cats getting into mischief. Bénédicte is shouting.

In the morning, her father brings her a telegram from Germain Pire, from Saintes.

> *Have drawn blank, as you hoped. Stop. Received your message through my brother. Stop. Going to Melun. Stop. Soon mimosas will bloom for me. Stop.*

The next day, Tuesday, September 2, 1924, at around three in the afternoon, another telegram arrives from the little man in the white spats, more clever and spirited than a ferret.

> *He is alive. Stop. Stay there, Matti, vital you stay there. Stop. I am coming. Stop.*

The telegram is from Milly-la-Forêt, fifty kilometres from Paris.

Mathilde is in the morning room, along with her father, her mother, Sylvain, and someone else whom she has forgotten today, when she writes these lines. Perhaps it's Papa's chauffeur, Jacquou, whom she insists on calling Speedy, like the chauffeur from her childhood. Perhaps it's silly old Clémence; perhaps it's a dark shadow over her dreams. The telegram falls from her hands. Sylvain picks it up from the rug and gives it back to her. Her eyes are so full of tears she can no longer see Sylvain, or anybody.

"Shit," she says, "I feel like such a fool."

Then she's in her father's arms. Soon afterwards, she's in her room. And now she opens her mahogany box to toss in the telegram and closes the lid, she thinks, for the last time.

She is mistaken. Time passes, as That Man said, and life is strong enough to carry us on its back.

In July of 1928, almost four years later, a letter will arrive from Canada, written by a trapper and sometime poet from Lake Saint-John, to tell her how he buried five soldiers at Bingo Crépuscule.

In September of 1948, when another twenty years have passed, and even another war, Mathilde will receive still one more letter to place in her mahogany box, accompanied by an object that only just fits inside. The letter is from Lefty, at the Cabaret Rouge.

Madame,

I've seen Justa Bit More again, and he convinced me to send you this, which I found in a lady's attic and which would have been a fine addition to my museum. I well remember our encounter. I hope this bit of wood will please you. Yours,

Hyacinthe Deprez

At the bottom of the letter, Célestin Poux – who turns up now and again, who married, had a daughter named Mathilde, divorced, and is still on the move – has made an effort and written in his best hand:

Didn't need to become an orphan after all.

The object Lefty has sent to Mathilde is the wooden sign from Bingo. Despite painting and repainting, it's still faded, still battered, and the only letters legible on one side are BY and PUS, which Mathilde thinks is just perfect. On the other side, in yellowed oils, is the work of an anonymous, obscure soldier in what is called the Great War, probably to make people think there are also some minor ones around. The picture shows, as Mathilde once imagined, a British officer gazing into the distance. His riding boots are polished to a fare-thee-well, and he holds a swagger stick in the hands crossed behind his back. It is dusk, because off to the right, across the sea, the sun is setting the horizon ablaze. A grey horse nibbles a bit of grass in the foreground. At the water's edge, a palm tree provides a decorative touch. There is also a bizarre construction of some sort on the extreme left, a dome or minaret. At the bottom of the painting, in delicate letters, carefully written in what may be Indian ink, one can read: *Lieutenant-Général Byng au Crépuscule. 1916.*

In short, it is a yellow, red, and black picture probably

painted by a Canadian soldier, since the title is in French. It's almost half a metre wide and requires a bit of pushing before it will fit into the mahogany box.

That September, in 1948, Mathilde consults the Larousse Encyclopedia at the public library in Hossegor.

Julian Hedworth George Byng led the Canadian Army Corps at the capture of Vimy Ridge in 1917. He also executed the first large-scale tank attack at Cambrai in 1918, thereby winning a decisive victory. He was appointed Governor-General of Canada after the war. And finally he served as Commissioner of the Metropolitan Police at Scotland Yard before being promoted to the rank of field marshal and enjoying a well-earned retirement.

Lucky old General Byng, thinks Mathilde, adding the story of his exploits to the box, here you are involved in spite of yourself in another strange affair. Like a certain famously foul-mouthed gentleman, Mathilde now collects postage stamps and carefully arranges them in albums. She has two vignettes issued in 1936 for the inauguration of the monument at Vimy, dedicated to the memory of the Canadian soldiers who died in the war. One stamp is reddish-brown, the other blue. Looking at them, she hopes that the soldier who painted the picture was not among the fallen commemorated by two towers reaching up into the sky. Unfortunately, the dead were legion.

A few years later still, another general – a French one this time, also promoted to field marshal – contributes his testimony, in his own way, to the mahogany box. Early in January 1965, Mathilde receives a letter from Hélène, Elodie Gordes's daughter, who became a friend, along with her brothers and sisters, as did Baptistin Notre-Dame and the two daughters of Six-Sous. Hélène, who teaches in a lycée, sends her a copy of page 79 in a book published by Plon the preceding autumn, *Secret Diaries of the Great War*, by Field Marshal Fayolle. The last paragraph of the entry dated January 25, 1915, reads as follows:

> Meeting at Aubigny. Of the forty soldiers in a neighbouring unit who shot themselves in the hand, Pétain wanted to shoot twenty-five. Today, he backs down. He orders them bound and tossed over the top of the trenches closest to the enemy. This is to be done under cover of night. He didn't say if they'll be left to starve to death. Character, energy! Where does character end and ferocious savagery begin! . . .

From that day onward, Mathilde shares the marked preference once displayed by three gossiping veterans who almost bored her to tears one lunchtime long ago at the Cabaret Rouge. It's just too bad if, in honouring Marie-Emile Fayolle in her turn, she contradicts her customary dislike of the military. There must always be one exception to prove the rule.

Germain Pire
(The rest of the heading is crossed out.)
Tuesday night, September 2, 1924

My dear Matti,

I'll have this letter delivered to you shortly, as soon as day breaks. What I must tell you cannot be said on the telephone, and I also want you to have time to think things over. It's a sorry tale, doubtless the most insane story I've ever heard in all my career, but I'm pushing sixty years old, I've suffered a loss that has much grieved me – and still does, for when you saw me so despondent in 1922, I had recently lost the one person I loved the most in the whole world, my younger brother, Charles – and I'm no longer ashamed to cry. I'm no longer astounded by the acts of madness to which we may be driven by the misery of love.

I've just returned from Milly-la-Forêt. I saw your fiancé, Manech, who is now Jean Desrochelles, and the woman who calls herself his mother, Juliette, who lives in constant fear of you. Jean Desrochelles's amnesia – his inability to remember anything that happened before the snowy morning when a comrade, someone who restores my faith in my fellow man, carried him to safety on his back – is total, absolute. He even had to learn how to speak again. The psychiatrists who have followed his case since 1917 are not optimistic, but they are in a position to know that there are as many amnesias as there are amnesiacs, so who can say what will happen? Juliette Desrochelles owned a small bookshop in Saintes, but she had to move away in 1918, because her appalling deception would quickly have been exposed. She and her "son" now live in Noisy-sur-Ecole, on the outskirts of Milly-la-Forêt. He is in excellent physical health, a young man who is twenty-nine years old, according to his birth certificate, and twenty-six in reality, tall and thin, with brown hair, and blue or grey eyes that startled and disturbed me, as they do everyone who meets him, because although his eyes are intelligent, attractive, and even merry at times, their depths reveal a soul in torment, stripped naked, a soul crying out for help.

I dare say that despite its insane folly, Juliette Desrochelles's sad story is implacably simple, like all things we know in our hearts cannot be otherwise. She bore her only son at the age of forty. Her husband died during her pregnancy, of a heart attack brought on in the bookshop by his fury at a publisher who had sent him copies of a novel in which the heroine's name, by some witchcraft at the printing plant, had been systematically omitted. I leave you free to imagine that the novel was Stendhal's *The Red and the Black*, and the heroine Mathilde de la Mole, for the devil who stole away my brother is everywhere.

So this widow raises her son alone. He is clever, affectionate, docile, whereas she is possessive and unyielding. He is a good student, and after he passes the *baccalauréat* examination at the age of seventeen, he goes to work in the bookshop with her. Three years later, in 1915, the war takes him away. He comes home on leave in November of 1916. She will never see him again.

In late January of 1917, when she hasn't received a letter from him in several weeks, she cannot sleep at night, and by day she haunts the offices of people unable to give her any information. Then a soldier on leave comes to see her even before going home to his own family, staying on the train beyond his stop at Tours, going on to Saintes, and he brings her terrible news. It is Corporal Urbain Chardolot. He has held in his arms the body of Jean Desrochelles, lying dead in front of a trench in the Somme, and he gives her, among other things, her son's last letter, written before the fighting that would kill him. In this letter Jean speaks of his revulsion for the war. What he does not mention, and what Urbain Chardolot cannot hide from the wretched woman, is the fate of five soldiers with self-inflicted wounds who were bound and thrown out in front of a German trench. He stays all day with her, unwilling to leave her alone in her grief. She weeps, questions him, weeps some more. Finally, the corporal admits that through an exchange of identification discs, the youngest of the condemned men has taken on the identity of Jean Desrochelles; that he himself did not say anything about this because he is too sickened and embittered by the war; and that anyway, as the woman now says herself, "Since there's no way to bring Jeannot back, at least let his death save someone else."

My child, I'm sure you can imagine what happened when Juliette Desrochelles was summoned in April to a military hospital in Châteaudun to identify her son. A nursing sister led her into a large room where the patients were separated by white curtains and left her sitting next to a bed where someone who was not her Jean was sleeping. And when he awoke, opened his eyes, and smiled up at her, asking her who she was, she had been watching him sleep and growing to love him for a good hour at least, and besides, he was a reason for her to go on living. She placed a gentle hand on his cheek for the first time and answered, "Your mama."

Of course, Matti, you will rebel against an action that deprived you of hope, let another mother die of sorrow, and drove a father into the lake at Hossegor. Think this over carefully. As the government so often tells us (to avoid explaining things they cannot understand), that's the way of the world. But in this case, I can explain things to you. At best, if you refuse to go along, if you swoop down on this woman with the law on your side, Manech – who is happy and confident, who has trusted and grown attached to her over the past seven years – will spend the rest of his days in an insane asylum. It will also kill Juliette Desrochelles, and despite her deception, or even her selfishness, she does not deserve this. She gave up everything to devote herself to him, she sold her property, left Saintes, her family, and friends she may no longer see for fear of being unmasked. She lives in a little house with a pretty garden near Milly-la-Forêt, where I will take you this afternoon, when you have read this letter. Think about this very carefully, Matti. I know how stubborn you are. Let go of the years, the pain, the rancour, everything. Let life heal your wounds. You see, your engagement has lasted so long already, it can last a little longer.

I enclose the few words Juliette Desrochelles wanted to write to you. You will recognize the handwriting. You were right: she came across your advertisement on a page of newspaper used to wrap a head of lettuce, and in the frantic and naïve hope of discouraging you, she wrote that anonymous letter, which she mailed from Melun to cover her trail.

I know, Matti, that no one and nothing can stop you and never will, as long as you live. Still, to convince you, if that's necessary, I'm going to tell you something strange and very beautiful. At Cambo-les-Bains, in 1918, where Manech was in convalescence and where Juliette Desrochelles came to live in a boarding-house to be near him, he took up painting. I've seen his pictures, in the little house where I'll be taking you this afternoon. All I can tell you about them is that they are completely abstract, explosions of colour, but they are marvellous, they shout out all the things you see deep in his eyes, things as terrible and stormy as a tempest at sea.

You're going to meet a tough rival, Matti. Although I

remain, as you know, your most devoted, faithful, and loving admirer.

Think it over carefully. I'll be with you soon.

Germain Pire

What Juliette Desrochelles has written to Mathilde, in the same handwriting, with the same concision, and on the same pale pink stationery as the letter from Melun, is just exactly what is needed to reduce her once again to tears.

Don't take him away from me, I beg of you, don't take him away from me. It would kill us both.

At noon, when Mathieu Donnay returns home for lunch, Mathilde gives him Germain Pire's letter to read, along with the accompanying note. All he says, like Fancy Mouth in that front-line trench so long ago, is "Shit, what a life!"

She asks him if, given these new developments, he would be against her going to live somewhere near Milly-la-Forêt. She asks him if he would find her a house for rent or for sale there, and someone to look after her, preferably someone cheerful, because Sylvain will have to stay at Hossegor, as it would be inhuman to separate Bénédicte from such a handsome man.

Her father's reply is just what she expected: he knows her – or her heart, at least – better than anyone, and he knows perfectly well that if she has that heart set on an idea, and if someone else doesn't like it, that someone else is simply out of luck.

That afternoon, for what Mathilde will later refer to as the Milly Expedition, sun and sky and all nature are with her. Very femininely, she has tried to look her best. She's wearing lipstick for the occasion. Her eyebrows are shaped, her teeth sparkling, but she doesn't use any mascara, because she knows what a mess tears will make of that. She's in the Delage with Sylvain and her "scooter", which takes up quite a bit of room. Papa and Germain Pire are following in another car, with Speedy at the wheel.

On the town square of Milly-la-Forêt is a large wooden covered market dating from the time of Joan of Arc, or perhaps even her grandmother. Mathilde has Sylvain stop the car. When her father comes to the car window, she tells him that she wants to go on alone to Juliette Desrochelles's house, that she sees a lovely inn on that pretty main square, that he should book a room there for her and Sylvain, and that she also spies, across the square, an estate agent's office, so it would save time if he went over to take a look. She grips her father's hand hard. He says, "Be good," the way he used to do, not so long ago, when she was little.

Not far away, in a village called Noisy-sur-Ecole, she finds the house on a hill, surrounded by trees. It is built of grey stone, with a roof of flat tiles. It has a small garden in front, and a larger one at the back. There are lots of flowers.

When Mathilde is in the house, seated in her "scooter", after they've finished with all the tears and supplications and foolishness, she asks Juliette Desrochelles, her future mother-in-law, to push her out to the back garden, where Manech is painting, and to leave her alone with him for a moment. He has been told of her visit, told that a young lady he has deeply loved is coming to see him. He asked what her name was and thought it pretty.

When Juliette Desrochelles and Sylvain return to the house, Mathilde is about twenty paces from Manech. His hair is black, quite curly. He seems taller than she remembers. He's standing before a canvas, beneath the projecting roof of a shed. It's a good thing she decided not to wear any mascara.

She tries to move towards him, but the path is covered with gravel, which slows her down. Then he turns his head and sees her. He puts down his brush and comes closer, and the closer he comes, the closer he comes, the happier she is she didn't put on any mascara, she doesn't want to cry but she can't help it, she can hardly see him through the welling tears. She quickly wipes her eyes. She looks at him. He's standing two steps away. She could stretch out her hand, he'd come even closer, she could touch him. He's the same, thinner, the most beautiful man in the world, with the eyes Germain Pire described to her, of a very pale blue, almost grey, quiet and gentle, with something struggling in their depths, a child, a soul in agony.

His voice hasn't changed. The first thing she hears him say . . . it's terrible . . . he asks her, "You can't walk?"

She shakes her head.

He sighs, goes back to his painting. She pushes the wheels, moves towards the shed. He looks over at her again, he smiles.

"You want to see what I'm doing?"

She nods her head.

"I'll show you in a little bit," he says. "But not right now, it's not finished."

So while she waits, she sits up straight in her "scooter", she crosses her hands in her lap, she looks at him.

Yes, she looks at him, she looks at him, life is long and can still carry a great deal more on its back.

She looks at him.

Monday Morning

The soldiers from Newfoundland arrived at no-man's-land in front of the trench called Byng's Man at ten o'clock, when a pale sun was finally breaking through the overcast sky and all the cannons, for a moment, had fallen silent.

It had snowed while they tramped through the trenches. Their coats were soaked, and they were cold. As he laboured through the snow, each man dragged along with him the frosty cloud of his breath, and his troubles, and his fears, and the memories of the loved ones he might never see again.

There were ten of them in all, led by a sergeant who was a good fellow, a trapper in frozen wastes even more vast and silent than these, in a far-off country where he battled with only bears and wolves.

While three of them climbed down into Bingo, which had been heavily damaged by shells, three others set off on a reconnaissance of the German trench. Those who were left explored no-man's-land, where they found the scattered bodies of five French soldiers.

The first man they saw was kneeling in a hole, with his

eyes open, and beneath the light covering of snow clinging to him, he seemed like a statue at prayer. Another soldier, very young, the only one who was not wounded in the hand, the only one who still wore his regimental number and his insignia on his collar, had fallen over backwards, his chest torn apart by a piece of shrapnel, an expression of deliverance on his face.

The sergeant was outraged by the barbarity of the enemy soldiers, who had robbed the poor dead men of everything, taking home souvenirs to show off in front of their Fräuleins. He told those with him that every man who dies with his shoes on deserves a decent burial, that they couldn't bury every soldier who fell on the field of battle, but that they were going to bury these men here because the one on his knees was begging them to, and that if they didn't, it would surely bring them bad luck.

So they went to this trouble, those soldiers from Newfoundland, on one cold morning among so many others in the war. Their patrol leader was Richard Bonnaventure, who had explored the Frozen North and hunted with the Eskimos, like the man he pitied, although he had no way of knowing this.

They gathered the bodies and laid them down together in a shell crater, they read the names on their identification tags, and the sergeant wrote them down, one by one, in his notebook.

And then they found a tarp in the enemy trench, good solid canvas, and they laid it over the dead men, and they unfolded the shafts of their shovels, and all together, they filled in the hole, quickly, for the cannons had come to life again, to the east and west, like a long drumroll calling them back to the war.

Before they marched off, Dick Bonnaventure had one of

his men empty the contents of a red tobacco tin into his pocket and hand over the box. He shoved it three-quarters of the way into the earth, after enclosing within a message addressed to whoever should find the grave, a page torn from his note-book on which he had written in pencil, as best he could, resting the paper on his knee:

> *Here lie*
> *five French soldiers,*
> *who died with their shoes on,*
> *chasing the wind,*

the name of the place,

> *where the roses fade,*

and a date,

> *a long time ago.*

HOSSEGOR, 1989
NOISY-SUR-ECOLE, 1991